KNIFE
EDGE

An utterly addictive Northern Irish crime thriller

KERRY BUCHANAN

Harvey & Birch Book 1

JOFFE
BOOKS

Joffe Books, London
www.joffebooks.com

First published in Great Britain in 2021

COVER ART BY NEBOJŠA ZORIĆ

ISBN: 978-1-78931-752-7

To my family

AUTHOR'S NOTE

Here are a few Northern Irish colloquialisms that appear in this book.

Across the water: Mainland UK (GB)
Bake: Mouth
Banjaxed: Broken, often beyond repair
Banter: Friendly chatting, teasing, joking, laughter
Boggin': Filthy
Bold: Bad
'Bout ye?: common greeting
Carryout: Takeaway food; also, alcohol bought from the offie (*see below*)
Catch yerself on: Sort yourself out
Craic: Banter, fun and games
Culchie: Countrified person not up to city ways
Dander: Walk
Eejit: Idiot
Faffin': Messing around
Fry: Specifically, "Ulster fry": sausages, bacon, fried eggs, black pudding, white pudding, soda bread, tatie bread (*see below*), sometimes baked beans, often a fried tomato
Geg: A laugh, e.g. *He's a quare geg, so he is*

Gurn: Complain, e.g. *Quit yer gurning*
Hoak: Rummage
Hotpress: Small room with hot water tank in it, known as an airing cupboard in England
Ma: Mother
Messages: Shopping
Minger: Ugly or unattractive person
Mucker: Mate or pal
Offie: Off-licence
Peelers: Police; also called *Guardee* if from the Republic of Ireland
Scundered: Embarrassed
So it is: Random phrase often heard following a statement, e.g. *It's raining, so it is*
Tae: Tea
Tatie bread: Potato bread
Wee: Small; used to describe pretty much anything, small or not, e.g. *In the name of the wee man*
Wick: Stupid or useless
Youse: lot; also *yous'uns*

PROLOGUE

Leeds

It was always the eyes that told him when they were ready.

Her eyes followed his every move, wide with terror, as he ran his thumb along the length of the blade. There was still fight left in this one. He needed to wait for that moment of resignation, that pivotal point when his prey realized that this was not a film, and that no detective was going to crash through the door at the last second to save her.

The transition point when nightmare turned into reality.

Acceptance.

Inevitability.

Death.

It was harder, with just one. They faded too fast, and stopped fighting too easily. There had to be a way to make this last longer, because only in that moment, with the joy of the kill before him, could he find true peace.

Afterwards, joy turned to ashes in his mouth, leaving him dry and unfulfilled. The longer he could keep this anticipation building, the greater his pleasure. There had to be more.

Maybe if he let them escape? Cat and mouse. He would need to think on that.

He kneeled in the blood pooled beneath the woman, and drew the knife down one more time, with a surgeon's precision. A crimson ribbon followed the tip of the blade, widening and spilling sluggishly across her perfect skin. She was so weak from terror and blood loss that she barely pulled away. Good.

CHAPTER 1

Northern Ireland, one year later

A chill creeped into Nic's bones, despite the heat of the spring day. Her will to fight had seeped away with the blood that dripped on to the carpet. She wanted to just close her eyes and sleep. She shook herself, breathing hard and blinking. If she slept now, she'd surely never wake again.

Focus on the pain. Hard plastic zip-ties dug into her wrists, pulling her arms back and down behind her to a ring set into the wall of the room, just above floor level. Its cold metal was hard and unyielding — at least it had been, when she'd been able to feel with her poor hands. She'd lost sensation in them again, despite her efforts to shift herself around, changing position as much as she was able, sitting on the floor.

A twig snapped outside, loud as a gunshot in the still evening air. Nic's pulse, already quickened by blood loss, took off like a sprinter. She strained towards the broken windowpane, leaning against her bonds, but there was nothing to see in the mottled sunlight except thick, dusty cobwebs and grimy lace curtains. Then a figure flitted past the window, his shadow momentarily darkening the small room.

He couldn't be back already . . . it was too soon.

A door grated open. She could hear him pacing the floor in the next room. He often spent time in there, before he came into her and Colm. Building the suspense. Making them sweat. Nic would never again smell freshly brewed coffee without imagining the heavy, metallic taste of blood overlaying it.

His feet scuffed against the lino. Her breath came in short gasps through the gag. He was right there, at the door.

Then Colm moaned.

Goosebumps ran across her skin. Colm had been still for so long she'd convinced herself he was dead. A little worm of shame curled up inside her: she'd been planning her escape, planning to leave him there. But if he was still alive? She hardened her jaw, trying to force herself not to care: if the opportunity arose, she'd still go. To hell with Colm.

The door opened, wafting in the scent of rich, dark espresso. Nic's stomach roiled. She kept her eyes fixed on the pink-patterned Wilton carpet that looked just like the carpet in her granny's house. If she didn't see his face, couldn't identify him, maybe he'd let her go.

His battered trainers came into her field of vision, the same green, slimy streak along one side. The bottoms of his jeans still bore yesterday's bloodstains, darkened to almost black. He stopped in front of her. She swallowed. Why had he stopped? Despite herself, she glanced up.

A black Iron Maiden T-shirt, fading to grey, strained over his slight paunch. Nic let out a breath she hadn't realized she'd been holding: he still wore the mask. It was the only ray of hope in this nightmare, that mask. If he hadn't let her see his face, maybe he wasn't planning to kill her.

He reached for the keys that jangled on an elastic cord attached to his belt and unlocked the cabinet on the wall. Unhurried, calm.

Bile rose in Nic's throat. *Breathe.*

Light filtered through tattered lace curtains, casting shadows like etched patterns on the bright steel knives hanging inside the cabinet. His long fingers danced across the blades, like a pianist playing a macabre keyboard.

Nic's heart gave a painful thump as he lifted the boning knife from the rack. She bum-shuffled sideways, thighs slipping in the pools of blood. Her naked shoulders slapped against the rough plaster of the wall, skin smarting where yesterday's cuts still oozed. She tugged at the steel ring, more out of habit than in hope of escape, but the angle was all wrong, and she could get no force into it. A small sound, like falling sand. Plaster? Had the ring moved, or was it her imagination?

With methodical slowness, her captor ran his thumb along the blade of the knife. It was just for show, just to prolong the suspense: all his knives were sharp, so sharp you didn't feel the initial cut — not until the hot gush of blood.

The only place he hadn't sliced yet was the centre of her belly, the soft, white part that never saw the sun. He took two steps towards her, then paused. Nic sucked her stomach in. This was not a time for breathing.

Then he spun, light on his feet for such a big man, and plunged the knife downwards. Dark blood sprayed in an arc across the far wall. The smell of coffee mingled with the stench of punctured guts. Colm screamed. The man's arm rose and fell, rose and fell, again and again, coating the ceiling each time with a fresh splatter of blood.

Keening like a wild animal, Nic threw her full weight forward against the ring in the wall, the tendons in her shoulders popping with the strain. Something gave way with a gritty sound, showering her wrists with dirt and old plaster. In one clumsy movement, she scrambled to her feet, pulling the ring with her. Her legs buckled, throwing her sideways into the door frame, but she staggered away and reeled into the next room, followed by an intermittent sucking noise as the knife continued to rise and fall. Colm's screams had subsided into groans by the time she'd run through the other room and out of the cottage, teeth clenched, plunging towards an uncertain freedom.

All was green and moist in the evening light. A mossy track wound its way between low-branched trees, almost invisible in the dappled shadow. She urged herself onwards, whimpering behind the gag as life returned to her limbs. Spots danced in front of her eyes and she shook her head to drive them away, but her steps faltered as she weakened. Blood loss had taken its toll on her body, and the initial rush of adrenaline was fading.

She searched for cover as she ran. On one side of the track, trees grew thick against a drystone wall draped with brambles. On the other side was a steep bank covered in wild garlic and marsh marigold.

A roar came from behind her, back at the cottage.

Nic froze. She tried to swallow but her dry tongue was swollen in her mouth.

No! He was coming for her! Faster—

She tripped on something hidden in the long grass, her numb feet betraying her. Arms bound and useless, she tumbled down the bank, nostrils filled with the scent of crushed garlic. When she stopped rolling, nodding ferns closed over her like a blanket, warm and comforting. A buzzing sound filled her head, and green faded to black.

* * *

Nic opened her eyes to cold darkness. A dull, throbbing ache behind her eyes swamped coherent thought until the memories returned with a rush like a train through a tunnel.

She tried to sit up, swallowing a cry as the zip-ties bit into the tender skin of her wrists. With dogged persistence, she scrambled on to her knees, and from there to her feet, leaning for support against a tree as she forced back the darkness lingering at the edges of her vision. This was no time to faint.

Colm. Dear, sweet Jesus, Colm.

Silence surrounded her like a thick felt curtain, broken only by her own harsh breath and the soft rustling of leaves as she took her first unsteady step. Undergrowth caught at her legs, threatening to bring her down, and thorns sank into her feet and lower legs.

Nic shivered as a breeze caressed her skin, pinpointing the wounds that covered her body. She made herself focus on facts. Hypothermia and blood loss, those were her immediate problems. *Don't think about the madman hunting you in the night.* She needed to keep moving, or she might never live to see the dawn. She pushed blindly on, branches whipping her unprotected face. *Don't think about Colm's last, gurgling moan.*

Keep on moving. Keep on moving.

Nic repeated it over and over in her head like a mantra. She fell heavily, bruising shoulder and hip, but somehow managed to get back up again, and then again, and again. The clouds thinned. Starlight revealed a metal foot-gate, held closed by a loop of string. She used her lips to nudge the string over the top of the post, working around the cloth gag that stretched the corners of her mouth wide and made her want to retch. At last the gate swung open on rusty hinges, squealing into the night. She caught her breath and froze, listening, but there was no shout of discovery, no crashing pursuit. Not yet.

Another bank lay beyond the gate. Once again, she tumbled down it, snapping last year's dead dock stems as she fell. This time she could barely stand, but ahead of her was open space with sky above, coaxing her forward.

A sliver of moon turned the world to shades of grey, enough light to make her way through dew-soaked grass towards a gap that stood pale in a dark hedge. She stumbled as she stubbed her toes on boulders that jutted up from the ground in the gateway, but pushed onwards, repeating the chant.

One of the shadows moved and a twig snapped. Hot urine burned the abused flesh of her inner thighs, the final shame. Then warm breath bathed her face, smelling of sweet, crushed grass.

Oh, a horse. She closed her eyes for a moment, over-whelmed by relief.

A second horse moved out of the shadows, short and fat. It gave a gusty sigh and walked off through the gap in the hedge. With nothing else to guide her, Nic followed it. At the top of a long slope, it stopped, and she walked into the soft coat of its bottom.

Lucky you don't kick, she thought. Then the pony dropped its head down and splashed noisily. Nic groped her way past the animal and dropped to her knees as it moved away. A large plastic bucket was tucked away near the hedge. She'd never have found it if not for the pony. Nic shoved her face into the bucket, letting water soak into the rotten cloth that gagged her, then sucking until she had enough to swallow. The water was slimy with bits of vegetation floating in it, but still the most delicious drink she'd ever tasted.

Revived in body and spirit, she got back to her feet and trudged on, leaving the horses behind. Where there was a water bucket, there had to be people, surely?

Lights flashed, but she couldn't decide if they were real or imaginary. Her mother's voice called her name, close enough to touch, but when Nic turned there was no one there, not even the lights. She was alone. Even the horses had disappeared.

Nic stumbled onwards until she splashed through thick, gloopy mud and half fell into another gate, its metal cold against her naked skin. The iron bolt that held the gate closed was almost her undoing. The weight of the gate made it impossible to shift with teeth or chin or even elbow. She needed two hands: one to lift the gate and one to draw the bolt, but her hands were still bound behind her back. In the end, she turned her back to it and managed to work the bolt free with her numb fingers, grunting with the effort.

"Nic!" her father's voice called.

"I'm coming, Daddy. Wait for me!" she sobbed as she dragged herself through the gap, following the phantom voices. *Keep on moving . . .*

She was on a farm track with a raised middle strip where grass grew. Another light hovered high in the trees, but this one didn't fade when she looked at it. A security light, on a wall above a white farm gate. Beyond the gate was a yard and a house with cars parked outside. There'd be people in there, sleeping at this hour. She pushed at the gate, wasting too much time and energy before she noticed the padlock. *Shit!*

The sky was getting lighter, paling towards dawn, and here she was, out in the open, no better off than when she'd run. She dared not shout out to try to raise the people in the house. Who knew how far away her captor — Colm's murderer — was? *Don't think about Colm.*

A car approached. Headlights lit up a tarmacked road not twenty yards away as the vehicle flashed past. She ran the distance, hobbling over the gravel at the side of the road, and stood in the middle of the lane, watching red tail lights disappear into the distance. Which way should she go? Left, or right?

She spun, seeking a clue. Was the sky brighter to the left? It had an orange glow, not just the sunrise. There must be street lights that way, and civilization. She set off in a stumbling run, squandering the last of her strength. Her feet were numb to the loose gravel. They barely felt anything at all now.

Another engine roared in the distance, passing by at speed. A main road? She panted, each breath louder in her ears than the one before. *So close. So close to help. Just keep going. Keep on moving. Don't think about Colm.*

It was a wide road with a pale hard shoulder. She lurched out into the middle, where hatched white lines marked the centre. Not a car to be seen in either direction. A faint smell of oil assaulted her nostrils, tantalizing and ephemeral, but there was no traffic now.

Nic collapsed, thumping down on to the hard tarmac, and gave herself up to despair. She had no idea how long she lay there, the road surface cold and rough against her cheek, before something big passed her in a buffet of wind and noise, peppering her with dirt. She couldn't find it in herself to care whether it stopped or ran her down.

Air brakes hissed, and a door slammed. Boots slapped on the wet surface as someone ran towards her.

"Are you all right, love?" a man with a Geordie accent asked. "Here now. Let's see you, pet. Oh, fucking hell!"

Arms came around her, warm against her chilled skin, and she was lifted bodily, head lolling. She tried to speak, but couldn't tell if she'd made any sound. The rumble of a big diesel engine drowned out everything: all sound, and all thought.

A blur of flashing lights and voices followed, pestering, coaxing, soothing. Finally, someone cut the zip-ties, and her wrists fell apart. A scream ripped out of her as her shoulders moved, pain flaring through spine and arms.

More voices. A tinfoil blanket that stuck to her raw wounds. Faces loomed and receded: white blobs with gashes for mouths that bled questions she couldn't answer.

Then she was in an ambulance, rocking from side to side as white light dazzled her. A siren wailed. Someone was stabbing her again, a needle in her arm. She fought, fists flying, and tried to push herself free, but firm hands held her. Liquid ice flooded her veins.

She fell back, limp against stiff, white pillowcases that rustled, and she was at peace.

CHAPTER 2

Nic hovered up near the ceiling. Below her lay a woman with white skin barred with red stripes. The woman thrashed and moaned, her dark hair a wild tangle. Nurses struggled to dress her wounds, the bandages unrolling on to the floor in cascades. Why didn't the silly bint stay still and let them help her? Another nurse came into the room and adjusted the drip that ran clear fluid into the woman's thin arm. The woman sagged. Her hands flopped on to the clean sheets, leaving a trail of blood on the virgin white. Nic watched, detached, and the woman's haunted eyes watched her back. Something moved there, in the depths of her pupils. Some fiery demon. Nic drifted towards her for a closer look, but the eyes sucked her in, swallowing her in their flames.

Her skin burned and flared with a pain that belonged to someone else. Nic tried to pull back, away from the woman's pain, but she was held prisoner again, this time in a crippled body. All around her, hushed voices spoke, and even the gentle clinking of instruments was muted.

"You can have five minutes with her, but she's sedated and she's still on morphine, so don't expect much sense yet."

Morphine? Lucky cow, whoever she was. Nic would give her right arm for some morphine.

"Can you tell me, was she raped?" asked a coldly clinical voice.

"No evidence of penetration, but what she *has* been through . . ." The voices faded away.

A shadow appeared next to the bed. She narrowed her eyes against the bright lights. An Indian man, dark in both features and expression. She didn't want him there. The lines of weariness around his eyes told her she'd have to come back to the real world, and she wasn't ready for that yet. Perhaps she never would be. *Don't think about Colm.*

His voice was dry as his skin. "Nicola Gordon?" He took her silence as assent. "My name's Detective Inspector Ram. I'm in charge of the investigation into your abduction. Can you tell me what you remember?"

No. She couldn't.

He had a Yorkshire accent, something she'd only heard on TV before now. All hard vowels and sharpness, but with a slight lilt. She looked away, towards the white blind that covered the window. If she ignored him, perhaps he'd go away.

But the memories came anyway. They'd been making a night of it in Belfast, a whole group of them in Katy's Bar, deep inside the Limelight nightclub. Exams were on the horizon, but it had been Hannah's birthday, and they'd all gone out. Nic hated nightclubs, but Colm had said he'd go if she did, and he was just as bad as her about parties.

She regretted it the moment they made it past the bouncers. A wall of sound drowned out all thought and killed any chance of conversation. Hannah and Lucy went off to the bar without a glance behind, but Nic froze. The familiar panic rose up like a tidal wave, threatening to swamp her, until Colm took her hand in a warm grip.

"Come on," he bawled in her ear. "There's some seats at the far side, further from the music."

Hannah bought a round: some sweet, sticky cider in a bottle for Nic and a pint of Guinness for Colm. Nic sipped from the bottle, not wanting to offend Hannah, but it tasted like vomit. Or maybe that was just the bile that burned her throat.

That was all she remembered, until she'd woken up in the cottage, naked and shivering, bound and gagged.

Nic dragged herself back to the present. The detective had disappeared. In his place sat her mother, trying to smile through eyes that swam with tears. A fat lump formed in Nic's throat, making it hard to breathe. Her chest heaved once, twice. All the fear, and shame, and despair poured out of her in a long, choking wail.

A long time later, her mother let her go. She'd hardly been holding her anyway, afraid, Nic supposed, of hurting her. The arms that lay on the covers were swathed in bandages, and the skin across her back pulled when she moved. She wondered how many stitches she had, and then the shame rolled her up like one of Colm's joints.

"Are you able to answer any questions yet?" her mother asked gently. The cop must have put her up to it. "Colm is still missing."

Nic gasped again, and shook her head. She couldn't say it. Couldn't put it into words. But Colm had parents too. They deserved to know.

She calmed her breathing by force of will, and nodded, avoiding her mother's eye. "I'll try."

This time, the detective seemed a little more alert. He sat up straighter by the bed, and he had a woman with him, also of South Asian heritage. She stood by the door, notebook and pen held loosely by her side.

"I'm told you're a little better," he began. "Would you mind answering a few questions?"

"Colm's dead." She blurted it out, far too loud in the quiet, white room. "He's dead and I'm not, and I don't know why."

"Yes, we thought he might be," Ram said. His matter-of-factness took her breath away, and eroded some more of her walls. "You should know that we found the place where you were held, but there was no sign of your friend. We found blood, which we have sent for DNA profiling."

When reduced to science, the facts were easier to assimilate. Less personal. Not really Colm, just his blood, his DNA. Blood and DNA couldn't whisper in the dark.

"He always wore a mask," she said, then swallowed. "The man who—"

The uniformed officer raised her notepad and scribbled.

"He wore old trainers, and jeans that were soaked in blood, and an Iron Maiden T-shirt. And a mask." Lists were all right. She could manage a list.

"Could you see his eyes?"

Nic shook her head, blocking the memory, but her tongue answered anyway. "Vivid green. Hard. No expression."

"Skin? Any tattoos or marks that you saw?"

"Nothing. Pale skin. White. Lined and dry, like a smoker." When had she noticed that? "Tall, I think. Not sure. Baggy around the middle, like middle-aged spread. Unhealthy."

"If I sent an artist in, do you think you could help us get a picture of him?"

She thought of Colm's parents. "Maybe. I couldn't see much of him."

Ram looked uncomfortable. "Can you tell me what happened after you left Limelight?"

Nic twisted the bed sheet in her hands, squeezing the pain away. "Hannah bought me a drink." Blood seeped through the dressing on her arm. She watched, fascinated, as the bright red liquid spread along the fibres first, a mesh of colour that filled in as the material soaked.

"What happened next?" Ram asked. Something about his tone made her think he'd had to repeat the question, maybe more than once.

Focus, Nic.

"I woke up at night, in the cottage. I didn't know it was a cottage then. It was too dark to see. My hands were tied behind me, and it was hard to breathe." It had been the smell

14

of damp and mould that brought her back to reality. That's when she'd realized she was naked.

"Was Colm tied up, too?"

"Yes."

"How well could you see him?"

"Not well. He was turned away most of the time." He probably hadn't wanted her to see. Their attacker had already made a start on him before she woke up that first time, and the little she'd been able to see of his face had been covered in blood. "I could hear him, though." Moaning.

"Anything else in the room?"

"My clothes were folded in a pile near my feet, and Colm's the same. There was a wardrobe, with the door missing. A fireplace with Christmas cards on the mantelpiece." And a framed Bible verse on the wall above, faded and marked with damp spots, but still readable. "*Blessed are the pure in heart, for they shall see God.*"

It had been no comfort to Nic, and Colm wouldn't have been able see it from where he was tied. Maybe if she'd believed in God, Colm would still be alive.

"What happened then?" Ram prompted her.

Her breathing quickened, pulse roaring in her ears. "That's when he started cutting me."

* * *

Jilly, the artist, was far too cheerful for her job, and not much older than Nic. She had an infectious smile, and a habit of sticking a spare pencil behind her ear. Her short, spiky hair stood up in unruly pink strands where she ran her fingers through it as she concentrated.

"What was the mask like? Any pattern?"

"No. Plain grey. A scarf. Triangular."

"The sort of grey from being washed too many times with black socks, or actual grey?"

"Actual grey, I think. Cotton, like an old-fashioned cloth hanky, but bigger."

15

The pencil moved across the page, shading in the cloth. With the angle Jilly held the page, Nic could see very little of the drawing.

"And the hair was greying? Grey all over, or just at the temples, like this?" She turned the page towards Nic. "Would you like to have a stab at an age for him?"

She was oblivious to the effect of her word choice, sketching away while Nic tried to bring her breathing back under control. Just when she thought she was coping, something else would hit her and she'd be right back at square one.

"No, there wasn't enough of him that I could see." But she really didn't know. "He had a paunch, though — middle-aged spread, you know?"

The door opened. Nic's father stuck his head around, saw the artist, and withdrew with an apologetic grin. Nic relaxed. Dad was nearly as bad with new people as she was. All the family had visited her over the past few days. Her mum was still emotional, but trying to hide it. Ma was the sort who might have gone after the kidnapper herself, and to hell with the law, but right now she said she just wanted to spend as much time as she was allowed with Nic. Cian, her little brother, had said her bandages were cool, and that she'd lost weight, but Hazel, her younger sister, had been silent and withdrawn.

Hazel's grief ran deeper, a silent seam of poison welling up from her own past when she'd been a witness to the death of an elderly man in a robbery that had gone wrong. Hazel would have found it harder to deal with Nic's abduction than anyone else.

Dad was just Dad, making comments about the various bits of apparatus she was plugged into, and turning everything into a joke. Once Jilly had gone, he creeped back in with mock gravity, lifted the chart from the end of her bed, and pretended to read it, his eyebrows climbing higher by the second.

"Do you have any idea how much morphine they've given you? If we could only find a way to get it back out, I could go into business on the streets, selling the stuff."

Dad jokes were never funny, but she laughed anyway, out of habit.

"Ma had to take Granny to a hospital appointment at the Lagan Valley, or she'd have been here. You know what Granny's like. She'd be flirting with the doctors and telling off the nurses, left to herself."

True, but Nic found it hard to think of mundane, homey things like her granny's quirky personality. She tried to keep the smile on her face, but the muscles were weak, and her expression sagged back into apathy.

"The big doctor says there'll be very little scarring where it shows," Dad said.

What about where it doesn't show? What about inside?

"Any news?" she asked. She kept telling herself that Colm might have lived. Maybe he'd escaped too, when their captor was hunting for Nic. But the sound of the knife was always there in her dreams, and the stench of his guts. No one could recover from that.

Dad shook his head. "They've had tracker dogs out, and there've been house-to-house searches, but nothing yet."

He must have noticed Nic's frown — why hadn't Inspector Ram told her any of this?

"It was on the news," he said. "They're asking for information about a grey van too. It was spotted on the CCTV near Limelight around the time the police think you were both taken."

Why couldn't she remember?

After Dad left, the policewoman who'd been with Inspector Ram appeared. She sat next to Nic's bed, in the seat her dad had just vacated. It was probably still warm from his bum.

"Hi, Nic. I'm Detective Sergeant Asha Harvey. I'm afraid I've a few more questions, but first I thought I should answer some of yours. I'm sure you've loads."

This was a change from Ram's world-weary style. Yes, she was full of questions, all right, but where to start? "Can you fill me in on what you've found so far? Maybe it'll trigger my memory."

Asha Harvey flicked back a few pages in the notebook. "I don't know everything, you understand. I'm just one cog in the machine, and most of what I tell you will have to be in total confidence. Are you okay with that?"

Nic nodded, mouth dry. She was still young enough, at twenty, to be flattered.

"We had the dogs out before the rain came on. They followed your trail from the place where you were found, on the main Belfast–Newcastle road. They took us straight to the cottage where you were held, but the perpetrator had already cleared out."

Nic swallowed, but she'd known they'd have to talk about the cottage. She could deal with that.

"Did you find the knives?"

Asha flicked to the back of her notebook and scribbled. "No, but the doctors tell us that a variety of weapons were used on you. Can you describe any of the knives, do you think?"

Oh yes. "He had a locked cabinet on the wall, like a medicine cabinet. The knives were all arranged in that, each one clipped in, in order of size."

"How many?"

"Six," Nic said, without hesitation. "One for each day he held us. They looked like the sort of kitchen knives you'd get in a wooden block, but they were really sharp." If Asha had made the slightest comforting noise, or shown sympathy in her expression at this point, Nic didn't think she could have gone on, but the detective sergeant kept scribbling away in her book.

"Yes? Describe as many as you can."

Nic shut away the emotion, closing her eyes to help her memory. "The smallest was like a paring knife, for peeling veg. Next one up was broader and a bit longer, maybe for chopping carrots." Easy to list them, as though they belonged in someone else's memory — maybe something she'd read about in a book, or seen in a catalogue.

She hesitated when she got to the last one.

"I think we both knew that when he got the big knife out, it'd be the end for us. Or for one of us, anyway."

"Were you able to talk to Colm, then? The perpetrator wasn't in with you the whole time?"

"No. He wasn't always there, but we couldn't talk anyway. We were both gagged. I only heard him grunt or moan."

Six days they'd been there, one for each knife.

"When he came back, he always stayed in the other room for a while, stringing it out." Her stomach turned at the memory. "He made coffee, and brought it in to drink while he . . ." She searched for a word. "While he worked on us."

"We'll come back to that part later," Asha said. "Can you describe the cabinet for me? The one the knives were in?"

Nic shrugged. "Sure, you'll have seen it, won't you?"

Asha shook her head. "He'd cleared everything out by the time we got there. There were holes in the wall, suggesting something had been fixed there, but no cabinet."

"Oh." What had she seen in the kitchen when she ran? "He took the coffee machine too, then? The big, fancy silver one in the other room."

"Yes. There was very little to show he'd ever been there apart from the—" Asha stopped.

"The blood. Yes, Inspector Ram told me about that." As if she needed telling. Nic wondered if he'd left it on purpose, Colm's murderer, or if he just hadn't had time to clear up completely. How many hours had he wasted hunting for her, while she lay unconscious and unaware at the foot of the bank?

She licked her lips. "Dad said something about a van? On the news?"

Asha flipped back a page. "Yes. There was a grey van, a Ford Transit, seen entering the area around the time you went missing. It was caught on CCTV, both entering and leaving, but we couldn't pull an image of the driver. We think the same van was picked up on the Ravenhill Road a bit later, so it was heading south towards Newcastle, but so far we've no evidence of it going any further." She looked apologetic. "There's a lot of CCTV footage to go through, I'm afraid."

"I wish I could remember more."

"Not your fault. Your consultant said she thinks from your symptoms that you were given GHB. You might have heard it called—"

"GHB. Yes. They told us about date rape drugs at the freshers' talk."

CHAPTER 3

"Why won't you just come home? It's not—"

Ma had probably been going to say "not safe", but stopped herself. Nic wanted to go home after the hospital, but Colm's murderer was still out there. And Colm's body, somewhere. Her parents' home in Lisburn felt too far away, and Belfast was where Asha Harvey was based, her link to the investigation.

"I'll be fine, Ma. Hannah and Breige are staying on in the house until after the exams, so I'll have company. I promise not to go anywhere on my own—"

"You weren't on your own last time," Ma said through thin lips. "You were surrounded by friends."

"Yes. Friends who'll probably never drink again after what happened to Colm and me." Hannah had been distraught, sobbing and clinging to Nic when she'd visited her in the hospital. It had been refreshing to be doing the comforting instead of being the comfortee. For the first few minutes.

A knock on the door came as a relief. Her mother could be very persuasive, and Nic just wanted to get out. She had her bags packed and fresh outdoor clothes on. Most of the stitches were out, except a few in some of the deeper wounds.

They were just waiting for Pharmacy to send over the antibiotics she needed to keep taking.

"Come in," Ma said, trying to act as though she hadn't been close to tears a moment ago.

It wasn't Pharmacy, but Asha. DS Harvey, as Nic had to remember to call her when there were others around. Even Ma. Especially Ma.

"Hi, Nic. How's it going?"

"Champing at the bit," Nic said, grateful that Asha spoke to her as if she was a normal person, not an invalid. "Just waiting for my drugs. Don't tell the cops!"

"Good to see you feeling a bit better. Inspector Ram sent me to drive you home, if that's all right?" She turned to Ma with a raised eyebrow and a professional smile. "We'll be keeping an eye on Nic for a while. Nothing intrusive, just a drive-by occasionally, and I'll probably have more questions for her as the case progresses."

Ma's face was warring between indignation, as though she couldn't be trusted to drive her own daughter, and relief that the police were going to be watching out for her.

"I wish you'd help me talk her into coming home instead of back into her student digs. She's still far from recovered, and her exams have been waived, so there's no point in her even being in Belfast at all."

Asha nodded sympathetically. "You might be right, but maybe Nic knows what will help most with her recovery."

The words were firm, belying her non-confrontational body language, and Ma clearly didn't know how to handle someone like this. She tightened her lips, and Nic thought for a moment she might keep fighting, but then she caved.

"All right. I'd better head on then." She bent down to give Nic a tight hug. "Take care, love." Then she left without a backward glance. *Hiding tears*, Nic thought. *Typical Ma.*

"Are you trained in hostage negotiation?" she asked.

Asha grinned. "As a matter of fact, I am. How could you tell?"

22

"I've never seen Ma rolled up so neatly before. It was masterful."

The door opened again to admit the nurse, her face tired after a night on duty. "Here are your tablets, Nic. And a letter for your GP. You'll need to come back to Outpatients for dressing changes for a week or two, until your practice nurse can take it on."

She thrust the blue plastic bag at Nic, already moving back towards the door.

With the frequent shift changes, this nurse was little more than a stranger to Nic, but she made herself speak up anyway. "Thanks. And please say thank you to all the other nurses and doctors for looking after me so well."

The nurse gave a brittle smile and left.

"Well?" Asha got up. "Shall we go?"

Nic had been practising walking up and down the corridors, trying to walk straight to hide the discomfort of thick dressings. Still, she was exhausted by the time they reached the exit.

Nothing had prepared her for the effect of being outside. As the automatic doors hissed apart, traffic fumes and stale fag smoke filled her lungs. She stopped on the threshold, suddenly overwhelmed by the open space in front of her. Instead of crowding her, Asha stayed back out of the way and let her take her time. So many people. Movement everywhere, and noise. Her eyes darted from side to side, seeking anything out of the ordinary, anything dangerous, but no one was interested in her. People walked past, heads down, hoods and umbrellas raised against the steady drizzle, not one person glancing her way.

As her pulse came back down to normal and her fists unclenched, a wave of weakness washed over her. Would it always be like this? She took a deep breath and stepped out into the hurrying crowd.

"Car's just here," Asha said quietly.

It was waiting near the entrance. Nic folded herself into the front seat, relaxing only when the passenger door closed with a dull thud. The windows had a slight tint that gave her the illusion of anonymity.

Asha dropped into the driver's seat. Nic was glad of Asha's quiet presence instead of her mother fussing, making sure her seat belt was fastened and asking her if she was okay. She zoned out during the short drive, hardly registering the traffic and pedestrians as they threaded their way past the Balls of the Falls, up Tates and through Stranmillis. Asha pulled up right outside Nic's house, where there was never usually a parking space at this time of day. The car had barely stopped when the front door opened and Hannah erupted on to the pavement. She flung the car door wide and hugged Nic, crying into her hair.

"Welcome home!"

"Let me out!" Nic said, but she didn't mind this from Hannah. It was just her way, the drama classes leaking into her real life. "Hannah, meet Detective Sergeant Harvey."

"We've met," Hannah said, colour rising to her cheeks. "Hi again, Detective."

Oh great. Hannah fancied Asha. Just what Nic needed. Asha smiled, a professional courtesy that didn't extend as far as her eyes.

"Hello again, Hannah. Thought of anything else that might help us?"

A flash of hope passed across Hannah's face, then she shook her head regretfully. "Sorry. Nothing more. I still don't know how on earth he got both Colm and Nic past us and out of the club."

"It's all right. Maybe the two of you will trigger a memory in each other now Nic's back. Don't sweat it, girls."

The car drove off to the twitching of curtains from the house over the road, one of the few in this little one-way street that didn't have students living in it.

"She is *so* hot! And the uniform! And that hair." Hannah pulled at her own ginger curls as they went into the living room. "It's so unfair that Asian women have such glorious hair. Bet she never has to use straighteners."

"Hannah, calm down. You cannot start stalking a police officer, especially not one working on Colm's murder."

Hannah's face fell. "Oh God. I'm so sorry. Is there anything new?"

Nic ran her fingers over the worn back of the velvet-covered sofa. "Nothing they're telling me about, anyway." The room smelled of Hannah's light, floral perfume. Last night's curry hung in the air, rising from the fabric as she sat down, and seeping from Hannah's skin where their arms touched. Nic's own skin was clammy with the warmth of the room. "Did you lot really not see anything suspicious, that night in Limelight?"

"No, but I was tanked before we went. We all were, except you and Colm. I don't think I'd have noticed if someone had come in wielding a sword and shouting."

"Do you remember buying me a drink?"

"Yeah. A fruit cider, wasn't it?"

"Maybe. I know it tasted rotten and made me feel sick. The police think someone spiked it. They must have done Colm's too."

Hannah was unusually serious, her dark eyes steady. "Yes, but how did he get the two of you out of the club?"

"I don't know." She'd been turning it over and over in her mind, chasing down that elusive memory that had to be buried somewhere, deep in her subconscious. "We need to find out. Want to go to Limelight tonight?"

"Are you serious? I never want to see that place again." Hannah shuddered, but that was just the drama classes too. "What would we get out of it, anyway?"

"I wondered if seeing it again, and sitting in the same seat, might shake something loose."

"Don't you think we should ask the peelers if it's okay? We might be breaking some rule or other. You know. Contaminating a crime scene."

Nic just looked at her. "Contaminating a crime scene? It's been, what? Two weeks since we went there? More? That place is as contaminated as it could be, with or without a crime scene. Just do me one favour, will you?"

Hannah was caught up in the excitement. "Anything."

"No pres, this time. I want you stone-cold sober."

She thought she might have overstepped the bounds of friendship for a moment, as Hannah's face crumpled. "No. I don't drink at all now. I'm too afraid to."

CHAPTER 4

They passed the bouncers on the door of Limelight and made their way through to Katy's Bar. Even on a weeknight, it was busy. On her last visit, Nic had balked at the entrance until Colm tugged on her hand and persuaded her deeper into the heaving crowds. But today, the fact that they were here with a purpose calmed her anxiety.

Stick-thin girls with heavy, painted-on eyebrows danced in small groups, arms above their heads as the music took hold of them. There'd be gin or vodka in the water bottles they carried in their handbags, Nic knew. Everyone did that, to avoid the sky-high bar prices. Sometimes they even got them in past the bouncers at the door too.

"You were sitting over there," Hannah shouted over the music. She pointed to a high table with dark wooden stools, tucked in a corner.

A couple sat there this evening, both staring into their drinks, either no chemistry between them or so used to each other they didn't feel the need to make an effort. What had she and Colm looked like? Friends or lovers?

"I thought you didn't remember where we sat?"

"I didn't until now. Come on. The table next to that one is free."

Two lads had just got up and left, heading towards the Rock Garden for a smoke probably. Nic followed Hannah to the table and perched herself on the high stool. Nothing. Still no memory at all past sipping that drink.

She reached into her jeans pocket and drew out a twenty. "Will you go and buy us drinks? Get me the same as you did last time."

Hannah's face creased with indecision. Nic had made her promise not to leave her alone for a moment, but now she was asking her friend to do just that. "It's all right. I'll be able to see you at the bar, and you can see me too."

Hannah nodded. As her friend shoved her way through the crowds, Nic made sure her hair hung loose around her face, hiding the sutures. For some reason, he'd mostly left her face alone, only cutting close to the hairline, as though he wanted no evidence to show. She didn't know how she felt about that. It meant that if she wore long sleeves, she could go out in public like this without drawing horrified stares, but it also made her wonder if those who recognized her picture from the news saw her as a fraud.

By force of habit she reached for the necklace she'd always worn. Fiddling with it, rotating the shells and beads, used to help her deal with her anxiety. She missed it now, and wondered for the first time why her tormentor had taken it. She'd been wearing it that night, of that she was certain. She always wore it, especially when she was doing something that would stress her out.

If she had it now, it would help to hide some of the scars on her neck and around her collarbone.

Nic closed her eyes, letting the thump of music invade her bones. A cold draught stirred the hair on the back of her neck, and the stench of stale urine drifted in with it. The smell brought with it a flashback, of reeling through a door arm in arm with Colm. They were both giggling, staggering so much that they bounced off walls. The music had been muffled when the door closed behind them, but another sound had taken its place. Traffic. Tyres on wet tarmac—

"One fruit cider, as ordered. Here's your change."

Nic opened her eyes and the memory slid away. Hannah took a long gulp of her own drink, but it looked like an orange juice. Nic turned to see where the draught had come from. A door opened into the toilets, hence the stale urine, but there had to be something else, another door. She got up, pushing her way between drinkers and dancers. The door slammed open as she approached it, to let a group of lads through. One of them made eye contact. Her heart rate picked up, sweat breaking out under her armpits as she flinched away from his gaze.

Beyond the door was a bare corridor with doors to men's, women's and disabled toilets, and another into the rest of the club. Nothing else. No door to the outside. She shook her head, disappointed. It had been a false memory, then. Hannah was at her shoulder, her face crumpled with worry.

"You got problems?"

Nic shook her head, confused. Yes, she had problems. Her friend was dead, and the body still hadn't been found. Hannah knew that.

"That was some sprint for the loo!"

"Oh! No, no problems. I just thought I remembered something. Did you notice if I went to the loo that night?"

"Nic. You could've danced naked on the bar, and I wouldn't have noticed. Lucy was there, remember?"

Yes, and Hannah had been chasing after Lucy all year, trying to decide which way she swung. Nic hadn't had the heart to tell her that Lucy had a steady boyfriend at home in Wales. Besides, knowing Hannah, it probably wouldn't have deterred her.

The fella she'd passed in the doorway was dancing, showing off. His mates clapped and cheered him on as he did a few steps of the moonwalk. Then he glanced her way and caught her eye. A smile lit his face, and he winked.

"Nic! I think you've scored!" Hannah yelled.

Nic turned her back on the dance floor, annoyed that he'd seen her looking. Without thinking, she took a swig from the bottle Hannah had put in front of her. The sickly-sweet taste hit her tongue, and she almost boked. She forced herself to swallow the mouthful — the alternative was spitting it out over the table — but then she pushed the rest away, nauseous.

Her wounds burned, the stitches catching on her clothing, and the heat was beginning to get to her. The loud music, shouted voices, crowds thickening as more people flooded in, all seemed to hem her in, trapping her.

"This was a mistake," she said. "I've got to get out of here."

She didn't think she'd shouted, but maybe Hannah could lip-read, because next thing Nic was being guided firmly across the floor towards the exit. She was jostled and bumped. Someone tried to grab her, and she yelped as a hand gripped her arm where one of the worst of the wounds was seeping through its dressings. Hannah slapped at the offending hand and kept moving.

Bouncers in dark clothes flashed past in a blur, then they were on the street, surrounded by smokers in huddles around the door. She took a lungful of cold air, laced with tobacco and the pungent, burnt-palm-tree aroma of weed. Soft rain settled on her face, and the hiss of cars passing brought her heart rate back down. She forced herself to breathe steadily. *In, one, out, two, in, three, out, four* . . .

"You okay?" Hannah's eyes were troubled. "We shouldn't have come."

"Would you like me to call a taxi?" someone said.

Nic nodded. The walk home stretched out in front of her like a marathon.

Voices hummed in the background, a fractured audio kaleidoscope.

". . . pretty sure that's her. Must be wearing heavy make-up . . ."

". . . the papers exaggerated. She looks fine to me . . ."

"Yes. From Limelight, please. Three passengers."

"Thank you," Hannah said, "but it'll only be two passengers."

Nic tried to concentrate, but her mind was whirling. Maybe it was the second-hand weed on top of her painkillers. Who was ordering the taxi?

"Colm?" That was always his role. The get-us-all-home-safe man.

A stranger came up close, bending to speak in Hannah's ear. It was the guy from Katy's Bar, the one who'd been watching her. All her alarm bells sounded. She backed away.

"It's okay. We'll walk home. The fresh air'll sort me out. Thanks for taking the trouble."

He shook his head. "It's no trouble. I'd rather see you both safe home."

He didn't crowd her, staying back out of her personal space. His face was neutral, kind, but not intense. The sort of face you might trust, if you had any trust left in you.

"It's all right," Hannah said. "He's a friend." But he wasn't. Nic knew all Hannah's friends.

The smokers' conversation had dried up as they leaned closer to listen in. Everyone was looking at them. Nic breathed through her mouth, panting. No way was she getting in a taxi with a stranger.

He backed down first. "It's okay. I'll let you two go on."

But his eyes were tight with concern. Concern for her, a stranger? Or worry that she might remember him?

A car pulled up across the road and sounded its horn. It was unmarked, no taxi sign on the roof, but Hannah set off anyway and Nic followed, not wanting to be left with the too-helpful man. They dodged between cars and on to the opposite pavement.

"Taxi to Stranmillis for three people, name of Burns?" the driver said through his open passenger window.

"That's me," Hannah said, and opened the back door to get in.

Nic grasped her wrist. "Just a minute. Which company are you from?"

The guy looked taken aback, but he answered promptly enough. "Greenline Cars, Private Hire, love. Here's my ID."

He held up a credit card-sized piece of plastic with his photo on it, and a Belfast City Council logo.

"Okay," Nic said, but she took her phone out of her back pocket and snapped a photo of him, clicked share and messaged it to herself. She smiled at the startled driver. "Now I'll get in."

"What was all that about?" Hannah whispered as the Skoda pulled away from the kerb. "It's a bloody taxi!"

Nic closed her lips, watching the driver in his rear-view mirror. He kept glancing back at her. She kept her phone in her hand, warm against her clammy skin, but the journey was as uneventful as any taxi ride through Belfast at night. It wasn't until the car stopped right outside their house that it occurred to her to wonder how the bloke at Limelight had known what address to give to the taxi firm.

* * *

After a restless night, wrapping herself up in the quilt, then throwing it off as her skin burned, Nic woke with the mother of all hangovers, so unfair after only one sip of cider. A shower and pot of tea cleared her mind a little, and a plate of hot, buttery toast chased away the remnants of nausea. She sat on the battered couch in the front room and worked her way through the coincidences until she came to her own conclusions.

She pulled the dog-eared calling card from her jeans back pocket and tapped the number in. Asha answered on the second ring, and didn't sound at all surprised to get such an early call.

"Yes. He's one of ours."

Nic stirred the maple syrup and cream that she'd been craving while she was on hospital rations into her porridge. There were black patches on her arm bandages where the cuts had bled last night, and she'd probably need to get the dressings changed a day earlier than planned. That prospect brought an internal groan. It wasn't just the waiting around in Casualty that she dreaded, but the pain as the supposedly non-stick dressings were pulled away from her wounds.

"When were you going to tell me you were having me watched?"

"I did say we'd be keeping an eye on you, remember? I promised your mum, apart from anything else. Oh, and that wasn't really a taxi either. Your instincts were correct there too."

When had she become so important that the PSNI were prepared to waste manpower on her like this? Was there a real threat that Colm's murderer might return and finish her off? She pushed her porridge away, no longer hungry.

"The taxi was my ex-partner, Dave. He owed me a favour, and I knew he'd be in the area."

"So, who was the man in the club?"

"Oh, he was official. That was Detective Constable Birch. It was me he phoned, not Dave. Apparently, you took a dislike to him."

Nic couldn't think of a reply. "Tell him sorry," she said after a moment. "It wasn't personal, just I'm a bit wary of strangers at the moment."

"Don't worry about it. He has a hide like a rhinoceros."

Nic wondered if Detective Constable Birch was listening to the other end of the conversation.

"Will you be home later, Nic? I'd like to ask a few more questions."

"Yes. I'm going nowhere today." Too bloody exhausted. The bandages could wait.

"Good. I'll bring traybakes."

Asha was as good as her word. She turned up on foot, bearing two paper cups from the Clements coffee shop on Stranmillis Road, and two huge portions of millionaire's shortbread.

Nic focused on the paper cups, straining for the aroma of coffee, but there was nothing. She relieved Asha of the traybakes and stepped back to let her in.

"What's in the cups?" she asked, trying to keep her voice light.

"Hot chocolate with cream and marshmallows," Asha said. "You didn't think I'd bring you coffee, did you? Have you any idea what that stuff does to your insides? Turns them into tar."

Nic grinned, embarrassed to have been caught out in her suspicions.

Hannah still hadn't surfaced, so Nic brought Asha into the small, shared front room, and closed the door behind them for privacy. As soon as Hannah made her usual knees-together run for the loo, the creaking floorboards above would alert them. Meanwhile, this was the warmest place in the house.

"Any news?" she asked, while Asha took the plastic lid off her cup and licked the cream off it.

"Nothing new. We have some leads, but I can't share them with you, I'm afraid. The press is giving us a hard time, and the local politicians are making noises about police incompetence, but there's nothing to be gained by telling any of them what we know." She looked at Nic over the top of her cup, steady brown eyes assessing her. "I think you've been wise to refuse to give a statement. They're like vultures."

"You know I will, if it'll help."

"Yes, I know."

She wrapped her hands around the cup, letting the heat seep into her cold fingers. "I was wondering—"

"Yes?"

"Do you think I could go back to the cottage?" she blurted out.

Asha spilled some hot chocolate on her hand and swore before licking it off.

"I know. Stupid idea, right? Last place I should want to go. But I need to see it again, I think, just like Limelight. I need to see if it kick-starts my memory."

Asha put her cup down on the coffee table and sat back. "Do you know why I'm really here?"

Nic shook her head with a sinking feeling.

"Inspector Ram wanted me to persuade you to go back to the cottage. I told him it was needlessly cruel, but he said it might be the best thing for you." She gave Nic a crooked grin. "I'd written him off as a bit of a robot, only interested in his crime statistics, but maybe he's more of a people person than I gave him credit for."

"So, I can go?"

Would it still smell the same? The sharp, metallic tang of blood, and fresh coffee? She took a sip of the drink, scalding her tongue. Why did she really want to go back? Did she think she'd find something the police had missed? Seriously?

"Yes. Whenever you're ready." Asha took a deep breath. "Are you sure about this? Would you like your mum or Hannah with you?"

"No! Definitely not. I don't think I could face that. You'll be there with me, right?"

"That I will. I'll give Aaron a call — he's parked up the road. Do you mind if he drives us? That's DC Birch, by the way. The interfering busybody from last night."

Oh, flip. "Yes. It'll give me the chance to apologize."

"No need. He was actually singing your praises. Taking Dave's photo was clever. And he said you sent it to someone as well?"

Nic shrugged. "Yeah. To myself, but he didn't need to know that."

While Asha was phoning, Nic climbed the stairs to wake Hannah and tell her where she was going.

"Asha's taking you? Can I come?" Hannah slurred, emerging from deep under her quilt with her hair looking like a hedgehog.

"No, sorry. We're going right now, and you're not even showered, never mind dressed. I'm sure there'll be plenty of opportunities to get to know her better."

"No fair. I think you're keeping her for yourself."

"Maybe." She dodged out of the door, slamming it behind her. Something hit the back of it with a soft thump. "And now you've lost your slipper!" she called as she began the painful journey back down the stairs.

DC Birch was in plain clothes, too. He drove an unremarkable grey VW Golf, far from new, and had somehow squeezed it into an almost non-existent space only a couple of doors up from Nic's house. She slipped into the back, behind the driver. A pair of laughing eyes met her gaze in the rear-view mirror. "Hello again. Sorry if I freaked you out last night."

"It's okay. Sorry I was so rude."

"Never apologize for being on your guard." His eyes were serious now. "Good move with the phone, by the way."

Nic ducked her head and shuffled across the back seat to sit behind Asha, away from those observant eyes.

DC Birch drove efficiently, moving effortlessly through the remains of the rush hour traffic. Across the river, along the embankment. There were rowers out on the Lagan, and a solitary sculler, slipping through the water like a knife through—

Nic looked the other way, at the red-and-white apartments that towered on the left, their tiered balconies facing a patch of green, the closest some of their occupants would come to the countryside. Then they were round the bend and away from the river.

Asha and DC Birch chatted in low voices, like old friends more than work colleagues. Nic zoned them out. Buildings flashed past: old 1950s bungalows on one side and a row of shops and restaurants on the other as they climbed away from the city. Was this the same route her kidnapper had taken? Suddenly the car felt claustrophobic. She loosened her seat belt, holding it away from her healing chest.

The atmosphere in the car was stifling, and now the vehicle was accelerating, speeding past a slow lorry. She couldn't get enough air. She punched the button for the electric windows, but nothing happened. The back ones must be locked. She rested her forehead against the cool glass, but her breath misted it.

The engine note changed. Down through the gears as it slowed, then lurched off the road. Nic wiped the glass. They were stopping at a garage forecourt. Relief swamped her. She could get out and breathe.

"I need a coke," Birch said in explanation. "Want anything from the shop?"

Nic tried to open the door, but it was locked. Her chest was tight. She hadn't enough air to speak. Birch looked over his shoulder. His eyes widened.

"Asha, let Nic out. Now."

Asha was out of the front seat and had the back door open in a heartbeat. Nic fumbled to release her seat belt, half scrambling, half falling out of the car. Asha took her hands for support, but let go as soon as Nic was on her feet.

She filled her lungs with cold air, gulping it down. Gradually, the nausea subsided, and her chest stopped heaving, but she was left with a pain behind her eyes, and an ache in her jaw. Her cheeks chilled as tears dried in the brisk wind that blew across the car park. "Sorry."

Asha had one arm draped across the car roof, shielding Nic from the curious children in the next car. "What for? You're doing amazing, you know. Don't be so hard on yourself."

Aaron had disappeared. Nic appreciated his tact — or maybe he just *really* needed that coke. Either way, she was glad he hadn't hung around to drown her in concern. Asha seemed to know to stay back and give her space.

With the worst of it over, Nic realized her mouth was dry, the taste of blood in her throat where she must have bitten her tongue. She was plucking up the courage to go into the shop when Aaron reappeared with a bulging plastic bag.

"Got snacks and drinks for us all," he said. "Don't know about you, but I'm starving."

Asha pulled a face. "What do you think this is? A day trip to the beach? We're what? Five miles outside Belfast, and you already need a picnic?" She took the bag off him and poked around inside. "Ooh, prawn cocktail. My favourite!"

With that cryptic comment, she sank back into the passenger seat and started to dig out crisps and cans. Aaron winked at Nic over the top of the car roof. "She's all bark and no bite. I'm not afraid of her."

"Aaron! You didn't get me coke, did you? You know I can't stand that muck."

His face fell. "Well maybe a little bit afraid of her. Only sometimes, though." He stuck his head in through the driver's side window. "I'll go back in. What do you want instead?"

Nic wasn't really listening. A grey van had just pulled in off the main road, and now it sat in the forecourt near a fuel pump. The filler cap was on the wrong side for that pump, and it wasn't as though the garage was busy. Plenty of free pumps. No one got out, but the sun reflecting on the window prevented her seeing the driver.

"Aaron?" she asked. "If you're going back in the shop, could you try to get a look at the driver of that van?"

His head snapped up, but he looked at her, not the van. "Behind me? Asha, can you run the plates?"

Nic read out the number, and Asha tapped away at her mobile phone. Aaron set off towards the shop, not seeming to glance at the van, but before he'd made it halfway across the forecourt, it reversed and shot off around the back of the car wash. He didn't change pace, but continued as though he'd never been interested until the van was out of sight. Then he jogged back to the car.

"Single driver, I think, but I couldn't see much. Any luck with the plates?"

Asha was talking rapidly to someone on her phone. "Thanks, Jamesey." She ended the call. "False plates. That number is registered to a Fiat Panda that was written off in an RTA two years ago."

The ground tipped under Nic. She leaned against the car for support, fists clenched. He'd been right there, watching her. Following her.

CHAPTER 5

"Maybe we should take you back home," Asha said.

"No. Not home." Had he followed them all the way from the little terrace in Stranmillis, or had he spotted her in the traffic? She'd had her face pressed up to the window, after all. She swallowed, more from reflex than need, since her mouth was dry. "We'll go on, if you're okay with that? After all, if he's seen me here, he probably knows where we're going, doesn't he, so he'll have no need to follow us." She was talking too fast, trying to convince herself.

"He didn't follow us from Belfast," Aaron said. He had his head down, fiddling with his phone. "I was keeping an eye out the whole way, and I would have noticed a grey van behind us. It might have been sheer bad luck, or maybe good luck." He made a satisfied noise. "I got Ken to check the traffic cams. The van turned in from the city-bound carriageway, so he definitely wasn't following us. He must have genuinely come in for fuel, then spotted you standing by the car. I'll ask the garage here to check their forecourt CCTV, in case they got a shot of the driver."

A weight lifted from Nic's chest. But what was he doing out here, on this road? The one that led eventually to the cottage.

"Different plates to the one we were looking for," Asha said. "Either he changed the plates, or we have the wrong criminal. This one might just be a petty car thief." But there was no conviction in her voice.

"Are you sure you're up for the cottage?" Aaron asked. He passed Nic a can of generic lemonade across the car roof.

She popped the top and took a long swig, hiccupping at the bubbles. "Yes. I think I'd rather get it over with, if you don't mind."

"Your wish is my command. Please enter the flying carpet, keeping hands clear of the sides."

Nic surprised herself by choking out a laugh at the corny joke. He grinned back at her like a schoolboy, far too young to be a detective.

Asha snorted. "Don't encourage him. You get to walk away, but I have to work with this apology for a clown. Every single day."

Nic got back into the car with a lighter heart. "Do you mind unlocking the windows? I'd like a bit of fresh air."

"See?" Asha said. "I told you that deodorant was too overpowering."

"You've got to be kidding," Aaron retorted as the car slid out into the traffic on the main road. "All the girls love Lynx. Haven't you seen the TV ads?" When they were up to the speed of the traffic, he glanced at Nic again in the mirror. "Tell her, Nic. It's irresistible, isn't it?"

"Yeah. Irresistible," she said, joining in the banter. "To an actual lynx, maybe."

Asha laughed, and for a brief moment, Nic was happy. She belonged. She was safe, not trapped, and these people would keep her that way. This optimistic mood lasted until the car slowed with its right indicator flashing. She recognized the hard shoulder at the side of the road, and the hatched area in the centre where she'd fallen to her knees, exhausted, cold and bleeding. She clutched her hands together in her lap, making the half-healed wounds sting and embracing the grounding effect of the pain.

This must have been the lane she'd staggered down. It was steep and narrow. She remembered how dark it had been that night, before the moon had broken through the clouds. A muscle twitched spasmodically in her thigh, a tiny patch of denim jumping. Then the car slowed even more and turned up a farm track, so narrow that branches from the trees scratched the doors, and the passenger-side mirror flicked in. They bumped along the track for a while, then Aaron stopped the car.

"This is as far I can go. We'll have to walk the rest."

They all got out, quiet now in the shady green of the lane. Nic moved round the car door and closed up with Asha until their arms touched, and that contact steadied her enough to be able to nod in answer to Asha's raised eyebrow.

"I'm okay," she said, as much to reassure herself as the two police officers. No one had actually asked her, anyway.

The track wound on past a couple of gates into fields. At one, a pair of horses stood with tails swishing lazily in the spring sunshine. Were these the two she'd walked into that night? In that case, that metal gate must have been the one she'd struggled with.

Asha led the way to the left, away from the horses, ducking under a line of blue-and-white police tape tied to the trees. The track had pretty much disappeared now. Low boughs arched over their heads, and a mossy trail underfoot silenced their steps.

The cottage loomed at them from the shadows, its walls the same green as the woodland it nestled in. Moss and algae had overrun the walls, and ivy trailed across the roof, but the front door was free of growth, crossed over with vibrant red-and-white police tape. As she got closer, Nic saw that someone had clipped the ivy away from around it, to allow the door to open. Was that his work, or the crime scene investigators'? If his, then he must have had this place prepared in advance. Did that make it better, or worse?

Asha reached out and pushed the door open. Nic tensed at the sound it made as it grated across the lino. If she closed her eyes, she could be back there, her arms dragged behind her, lacerated skin burning. But she didn't close her eyes. She went to step forward, but Asha stopped her.

"Aaron?" Asha said, her voice hollow in the silence. "Take a look at this."

Aaron touched her shoulder and she stepped back. Whatever was in there, Asha didn't want her to see it, and that meant Nic didn't really want to see it either. She turned her back on the cottage, letting her eyes rest on the shades of green that bathed the clearing. Somewhere high above, a lark sang her chirruping song, and closer in a robin hopped from twig to twig, his head cocked to one side as though listening to the quiet voices in the cottage.

A foot scraped on the worn lino, sending a shiver along the skin of her back.

"Nic, I think you should see this," Aaron said gently. "Asha disagrees, but I think you're strong enough, and you'll need to know sometime anyway. Don't go inside, though. We'll need to get CSI out again to check for traces." He said the last part to Asha in a more natural voice.

Asha stood back from the door to let Nic see inside. On the back wall, where the coffee machine had stood on a shelf when she last glimpsed this room, someone had scrawled a message in dark red paint.

The race is not yet run.

She couldn't tear her eyes away from it. Where was the fear she should feel at a threat clearly meant for her? Instead, a bubble of laughter forced its way from her throat, loud in the quiet woodland.

Aaron moved her gently away, but she kept her eyes on the wall until she was far enough back that the cottage door blocked her view. Asha broke off from the phone call she'd been making and turned troubled eyes on to Nic.

"Are you okay? It's probably just local lads up to no good, daring each other."

Nic shook her head. The laughter ebbed away, leaving her drained and shaky. "No, I'm fine. Much better, actually.

He's just lowered himself to the level of a bad TV crime series. It makes him more human, somehow. Less scary."

Asha continued to search Nic's face, then she gave a tight smile. "Good. That's good." The mobile in her hand gave an indignant squawk and she put it back to her ear. "Sorry, sir. I was checking Nic was okay. Yes, sir. We'll stay put."

The voice on the other end seemed to calm down, and now Nic thought she could pick out the sing-song tones of Inspector Ram.

Asha ended the call, and suddenly the woodland grew quiet. The robin had disappeared, the lark was long gone, and not a leaf stirred. Nic hardly dared to breathe, lest she disturbed the silence, then Asha spoke in her ear.

"Are you okay if we wait here for the forensics team? I can get a coat from the car if you're chilly."

She shook her head. She *was* cold, but Asha couldn't know that. The bandages would cover any goose pimples, and there wasn't enough light to see if she might be pale, but Nic knew she didn't want the three of them to split up. She'd watched enough *Scooby Doo* when she was growing up to know that they were safer together.

As though he'd read her thoughts, Aaron took his own jacket off and handed it to her. It was made of coarse wool and smelled of aftershave with a faint trace of tobacco, something warm and mellow. She wrapped it around her shoulders, letting the residual warmth from his body soak into her. "Thanks."

"Don't mention it." He grinned. "No, really, don't mention it. The lads at the station'll think I'm going soft in my old age."

The forensics team took for ever to turn up. Eventually a blackbird gave his stuttering alarm call, and shortly after, a couple of figures appeared at the outer tape, carrying metal cases. Nic expected them to don the paper suits you saw on TV, but they came in their ordinary clothes.

"Morning," the one in front said. She was a petite redhead with a pale complexion. "Hope you lot haven't trampled our lovely crime scene with your big boots." She had a slightly guttural Eastern European accent that made her seem exotic for Belfast.

"Better than the fag ash you leave behind everywhere you go!"

"She never smokes on duty, and you know it," said the second newcomer in a voice that could pickle gherkins. "Where's this supposed message then?"

Nic instinctively disliked the older man. His hair could do with a wash, and one greasy lock was carefully trained like an ornamental pear tree, espaliered across a white concrete wall. He was running to thickness around his middle, but his wardrobe hadn't caught up with his spread, so a hint of hairy belly peeked coyly out between the buttons where his shirt front gaped. She realized she was staring, and turned away, hoping her revulsion hadn't shown on her face.

"In here," Asha said, gesturing to the cottage. "We haven't been in, just looked through the door." She was extra cool and professional, and Nic thought Asha probably shared her distaste.

The redhead ducked her head as if to apologize for her colleague, but as she followed him through the door, she slanted her eyes at Asha and winked.

Nic tried to see what they were doing through the open door, but the older man blocked her view. Deliberately, she thought.

Asha touched her arm with gentle fingertips. "We could go now, if you like. Or would you prefer to wait until they've finished and then go inside?"

"How long will they be?"

"Hopefully not too long," came a voice from inside. "Provided I can keep Marley's eyes off my titties and on the job."

An indignant mumble was all Nic heard of the reply, but Aaron, who was closer, burst out laughing. "In your dreams, Marley. Jana's not interested." He turned away and muttered. "Not in men, anyway. Isn't that right, Asha?"

Asha didn't miss a beat. "In her dreams," she said with a straight face. "A redhead? Never."

"Heard that! I'll wear you down yet, Miss ice-cold Asha, just you see."

Nic found herself grinning along with them, enjoying the banter, until she remembered where they were. The smile froze on her face. As if it sensed her mood, a cloud crossed the sun, turning the clearing into a place of darkness and shadows.

"You'll be glad to hear it's just paint," Jana called in her clear, high voice. "Negative for both Sangur and Kastle–Meyer tests."

"Whatever that means," Aaron said. "You okay?" This to Nic.

She realized she'd been clutching her forearms so tightly she'd set the wounds bleeding again. The sleeve of her cream sweater was blooming with a red stain where her fingernails dug in. She unclenched her fingers, unable to meet Aaron's eye. "I'm fine. Just a bit chilly."

The truth was, the darkened clearing seemed to be filled with watching eyes. Adrenaline was flooding her veins, telling her to run, to get away from this scene of death. It was too like the place she remembered from the night she escaped, except there was something missing now. What was it?

She turned slowly, trying to remember which way she'd run. To the right, surely? Yes. The drystone wall had been on the right, and the slope to her left, where she'd fallen. Which had quite probably saved her life, in retrospect. She retraced her steps, zoning out the drone of voices from behind her where the forensics folks were discussing their findings with the detectives.

There. She'd hardly registered it last time, but there'd been something beyond that wall, hadn't there? A large, shadowy shape, about the size of a transit van. What was there now? The grass was short-cropped, littered with rabbit droppings and shaded by the trees. She leaned against the rough lichened stones and looked over. The other side was a sheep-grazed field with clumps of gorse growing around the edges and outcrops of rock in slabs of grey, showing how thin the topsoil was.

"Remembered something?"

Asha moved like a cat. Nic hadn't heard her approach until she spoke, but she didn't jump. There was something safe about Asha.

"I think there might have been something parked here that night, just over the wall, but I can't see any tracks."

"You think, or you definitely remember?"

Nic closed her eyes, trying to bring back the feelings from that awful time. She'd been frantic with fear, expecting at any moment to be grabbed and hauled back into the cottage, but she'd been hunting for an escape route. She'd seen the wall, mostly covered with brambles except for here, but the shadow had deterred her.

That was it. There'd been a red light flashing on and off at head height. A tiny light, but bright in the gloom under the trees.

"I'm certain, and it had an alarm."

Asha made a small sound of disbelief.

Nic was relieved to be able to remember something so substantial. "There was a tiny red light flashing, like the one in Ma's Jeep."

Asha's face cleared. "Great. Good work, Nic."

The two scientists were finished. Aaron stood talking to the man, Marley, while Jana packed away the little tubes and plastic bags they'd collected, then they both set off back along the mossy track, still bickering quietly.

CHAPTER 6

The interior was dark and dank, even gloomier than she remembered. Her eyes had adjusted to the dim light during her captivity. Now, coming in from the bright morning, even shadowed as it was by trees, Nic could barely see into the corners of the first room.

She moved quickly through, averting her eyes from the message scrawled on the wall. It probably *was* just local kids, not her kidnapper. He wouldn't be stupid enough to return here, surely? The creak of the connecting door was as familiar as her own pulse bounding in her ears.

She stepped through, on to the threadbare pink carpet with its crusty bloodstains over by the wall, where she'd been tied. Pale pink plaster lay in lumps where she'd ripped the ring out of the wall, and a dark patch on the peeling wallpaper showed where her back had rested. All her muscles contracted at the sight, sending ice picks of pain across her wounded skin.

"This is where you were?" Asha asked, her voice muted.

"Yes. Right there."

"Where was Colm?" Aaron asked.

"Over there, beyond the bed frame." She pointed. "It was too dark to see him clearly, over in that corner. I heard him, though."

Asha and Aaron stepped around the big, old-fashioned bed that had been turned on its side. It divided the room neatly into two private cubicles, keeping the two captives isolated from each other.

Nic forced herself to follow the two detectives. The place where Colm had died looked just like her own little corner of hell, except that his ring was still attached to the wall. The same bloodstains darkened the carpet, scuffed where his feet had scrabbled to push away from his killer in his final moments. The sound of the knife hitting home would haunt her nightmares for years to come.

"Do you remember anything else?" Asha asked.

Nic shook her head. "Nothing new, sorry."

"Which way did he come from?" Aaron asked. "Did you hear him passing this window on his way in, or not?"

"Only the last time he came. I saw his shadow pass the window, but all the other times he just appeared. The first thing we knew was the outer door opening, usually."

"I wonder why he did it differently that time. I might have a poke around that side of the cottage." He drifted outside, passing the window as a faint break in the filtered sunlight.

Nic closed her eyes, breathing in the smell of mildew and rotten carpet. The scent of blood had faded, thank God, and that of coffee, but there was something else missing too. What was it?

Aftershave. Not the same as Aaron's, but something sharp and tangy that had caught the back of the throat.

"What have you remembered?" Asha asked softly.

"I don't know if it's important or not, but there was a clean smell in here, like aftershave or shaving gel. Maybe deodorant. I didn't think Colm wore anything like that, so maybe it was his killer?"

She opened her eyes to see Asha smiling warmly at her, and felt a glow of joy begin deep inside.

* * *

48

The drive back to Belfast was easier. She was finally doing something useful, so useful that Aaron was driving them back to the station on the Lisburn Road. Apparently, Inspector Ram wanted to speak to her again.

The inspector looked less worn out this time, as though he'd had a good night's sleep since Nic last saw him. His brown eyes watched her steadily as she followed Asha into his office. The room had a temporary feel, as though he was camping out in Belfast.

"I'm sorry for the state of the room," he said, by way of explanation. "I'm on secondment here for the duration of this case, so I'm still finding my way about the place. I'm usually based in Leeds, West Yorkshire Police. It's good to see you looking so well, Miss Gordon. The last time I saw you, you were in a great deal of pain."

Nic swallowed. The pain was still there, but it had become a part of her, an extension of her other senses. She'd learned to deal with it, that was all. "I'll live," she said, then cursed silently. "I mean—"

He smiled, which made him seem a decade younger, then his face sagged back into its natural serious expression. "I understand you've been through a trying morning, and I'm afraid I'm about to add to your sorrows."

Beside her, Asha's head snapped up. "What is it, sir?"

He twisted his mouth in an expression of distaste. "A body has been found."

The floor tilted, the checked lino stretched and shifted, then the world steadied itself again and Nic remembered to take a deep breath. Someone pushed a chair up behind her knees and she sagged back into it. Asha was searching her face, a crease between her brows.

"A bit abrupt, sir, if you don't mind me saying. I know I said she's tough, but there are limits."

"Is it him? Where did you find him?" Nic asked, disgusted to find herself near breathless. "Have his parents been told yet?"

"The body is of a young male around Colm's age. He was found in a landfill site near Lisburn." Ram sat down behind his desk and steepled his fingers. "Did you ever meet Colm's family?"

No, she hadn't, but then he'd been from somewhere way down south so she wouldn't have. "Aren't they here?"

"We've been unable to trace any family for the young man," Ram said. "Did he ever mention anyone?"

"No, not really. He said they didn't have much money, so they couldn't get over here to visit him."

"Did he study physics too?"

She almost laughed. "No, Colm didn't have much of a head for science — he said so himself. He was supposed to be studying psychology, but he wasn't really going to his lectures. He got claustrophobic in crowds."

"Hmm."

Ram didn't seem surprised, but then Nic supposed he must be getting information about Colm from his other friends too. Hers would only be confirmation of facts.

As if he'd been reading her mind, the inspector fixed her with a flat look. "There's no record of him being enrolled at the university. We've also been unable to find anyone else who knew him as well as you did. It's possible he had no other friends."

No. Everyone knew Colm. She caught herself — knowing him was different to being friends with him. "Hannah—" she began.

Asha shook her head. "Hannah said she only ever saw him in your company, Nic. She'd no idea where he lived or what he studied, if anything. All your other friends said much the same. They tolerated him because of you, but none of them really knew him at all."

The air in the cramped office was filled with dust and the faint traces of stale tobacco smoke that must have soaked into the chair fabric in the days before the smoking ban. She fought down the claustrophobia and made herself breathe regularly. *Two in through the nose, hold for four, six slowly out through the mouth.* Gradually, the panic receded and she could think clearly again.

"Tell me the rest, the bit you're keeping back."

Asha flinched. "There's nothing—"

Ram shook his head, a half-smile quirking the corners of his mouth. "You are a perceptive young woman, Miss Gordon."

"Sir!"

"It's all right, Sergeant. Miss Gordon will be better off knowing the facts. She is strong, this one."

Asha subsided. "Yes, sir." But a crease between her brows spoke of a troubled mind.

Nic wanted to reach out and touch her, to reassure her, but she restrained herself. Ram was right: it was not knowing, being kept in the dark, that terrified her. If they told her the rest, however awful, maybe she'd have a better idea of where the danger was coming from.

"Tell me," she said simply.

Ram settled back in his chair. "Colm was a ghost, a fiction. No record of him anywhere."

Nic tightened her lips to stop herself from protesting, and the inspector gave a short nod of approval.

"I have a team trying to identify the body from dental records as we speak, but it might take some time. If we even find a match."

Nic reassessed her memories. Colm had been charming, vulnerable, almost. They'd had a lot in common. He'd talked of his social anxiety, and his fear of crowds, but perhaps it had been a show of false empathy to gain her trust. "What was he? A confidence trickster?"

"We may never know," Ram said. "Perhaps he was just lonely."

Yes. That was the impression she'd had on that first day. Too shy to seek company but yearning for companionship. It was why she'd let him come close to her: confident people made her wary, but he'd been more afraid even than her. Who was he? Really?

"I met him in the library. Thought he was a first year." She'd gone to her usual seat in the ground-floor café of the McClay Library, to one of the high-up stools where she could eat her sandwich with little risk of being disturbed, but there was already someone sitting there. In the very seat she always used. All elbows and knees. "He was quiet, you know? Harmless, and a bit afraid."

She must have made an exasperated sound as she sat in the next seat along and fished out her lunch, because he'd looked at her like a rabbit caught in headlights. She'd dragged the morning's lecture notes out of her bag to read through while she ate. It probably wouldn't help her exam results, but it acted as a shield against casual conversation. Usually.

"Who made the first move?"

"Him. I think he asked me something. About the cafeteria."

"Did you ever go to his digs?" Asha asked. "See where he lived?"

She shook her head. "No. He'd just turn up there every lunchtime. He was always there before me, so I didn't even see which way he came. He didn't have a mobile, either. He said he'd dropped it in a puddle and hadn't got around to replacing it." She smiled. "I think it was just an excuse. I doubt if he could have afforded a new phone."

"What about his personal hygiene?" Ram asked. "His clothes?"

"He always wore faded jeans and a black hoodie. A leather jacket on cold days, a bit big for him."

Asha was scribbling in her notebook again. "Was it a real leather jacket, or a cheap fake?"

"A fake, I think. The seams were fraying like fabric. And the hoodie was a bit greasy, you know? It was faded too, around the neck, where his beard rubbed it." Tiredness washed over her, draining her mind. "He really didn't deserve to die, did he?"

"No, he didn't." The resolve in Ram's voice surprised her. He raised his eyes to her face. "I don't want you to think that we will scale down this operation just because he doesn't have friends or family to miss him."

"You're wrong," Nic said. "He did have one friend, and I do miss him. But you're really no further on, are you?"

"We're trying to trace the van," Asha said. "They're still going over CCTV footage, especially from this morning."

Only this morning? It felt like days since she'd seen the grey van in the petrol station.

"He's clever, this man. He always covers his tracks well," Ram said slowly.

Nic let out a breath. "He's done this before? Is that why you're in Belfast?"

Ram nodded. "He has. More than once, I'm afraid. He has a distinctive MO."

"MO?"

"Modus operandi," Asha offered. "The particular way he does things."

The abyss opened again. "What is his MO?"

Ram answered her. "His first attempt, that we know of, was on a nineteen-year-old medical student in Leeds. She was estranged from her family at the time, and he befriended her, pretending to be in a similar situation. She trusted him. Then he drugged her and abducted her — tortured her. Luckily, she was stronger than he expected. She fought him, and she got away. He didn't give up, though. He followed her, just letting her glimpse him in the distance, frightening her. Thankfully, she had the sense to return to her family and seek help. They reported the events to the police. Once he saw she was safe, he gave up the chase."

"But he tried again, with a homeless man this time," Asha continued, when it seemed Ram had lost track of his thoughts. "And he was successful. The body was found in a commercial wheelie bin, thankfully before it got as far as the landfill site. The knife wounds were quite distinctive, and matched those on the young woman who escaped."

Nic wondered about the woman who'd got away. Was she coping? Did nightmares stalk her sleep? "How is the first woman? The one who escaped?"

But Ram was in full flow. "His next victim was another homeless man," he said. "This time he changed his method and took another victim, a woman, a day later. We found both bodies in the place where he'd killed them. He'd made himself a den in a derelict mill near the River Aire. We got lucky, in a way. The mill was zoned for redevelopment, and one of the planners stumbled across the bodies. Otherwise, it could have been months before we found them. That was when the national newspapers took an interest, and the tabloids gave him a nickname: 'The Slasher'. I suppose they hadn't much to choose from, since the name 'Ripper' was already taken." His mouth twisted with distaste.

"That was a year ago," Asha said. "Then nothing, until last month."

The door opened and Aaron reversed in, carrying a tray with steaming, mismatched mugs of tea on it, and a plate of plain digestives. "Lisburn Road's best cuisine," he said, putting it down on the corner of Ram's desk, and pushing a pile of paperwork perilously close to the opposite edge. "Thought you'd need it by now."

Nic made herself relax her clenched fists. The first sip of tea burned her mouth, but the pain was a welcome distraction.

Aaron took a Manila envelope out of his pocket and put it in front of Ram. "Preliminary lab report, sir."

Ram slid a single folded sheet of paper out and flicked it open, scanning the lines of printed text. "No surprises there, then. Any news of missing persons?"

"Rutledge thinks he has a lead, sir. One of the Shaftesbury Square girls said there's a lad used to hang out with them, but no one's seen him in a couple of weeks. Matches our fella's description."

"Get Jilly to do a sketch, would you?"

"Already doing it, sir." Aaron glanced at Nic. "Need me to do anything else?"

Ram shook his head. "Just keep looking. I'd like to ID this body as soon as possible."

"Yes, sir." He disappeared, leaving the room feeling very quiet, and somehow much bigger.

"I think it's time I took Nic home, sir," Asha said.

"No! I'm fine. I'd like to see the sketch, to see if it's Colm or not."

Ram considered for a moment. "All right. You can stay here for now. There's a canteen upstairs if you're hungry, or there's a sandwich shop just down the road."

Nic stood up, leaving her half-drunk tea on the tray. "Thank you, Inspector. I'll not be a nuisance."

Asha came out with her, a puzzled crease between her brows. "That was the first sign of humanity I've seen from the old bugger. You must be a good influence on him."

"Oh, he's human, all right."

Nic and Asha both jumped. The voice had come from behind them, deep and rough as a Shankill pavement. Nic turned to see an elderly black woman in uniform, so stout the buttons strained to fasten over her belly. Her unlined face made a striking contrast against her silver hair.

"Didn't see you there, sarge," Asha said.

"No, I don't suppose you did." There was a warmth in her eyes, at odds with her harsh tone.

How did such a heavy woman move so quietly? There'd been no one in the corridor when they came out of Ram's office, and they hadn't exactly been walking slowly.

"I don't suppose you bothered to look up the previous cases, either, Detective Sergeant Harvey. If you had, you'd know why Inspector Ram is so determined to catch this man before he kills again. Why he came all the way over to cold, wet Belfast, and why he is more human than most of the other losers in this sorry station."

Asha moved uncomfortably, but answered with respect in her voice. "I did, of course. What did I miss?"

The older officer tapped her nose. "The first victim, Meera Patel. Find out a bit more about her, and you'll find out all you need to know about Inspector Ram. Then tell me he's not human. And you, girl," she said to Nic. "You're a brave one." She turned and walked back down the corridor, swinging her hips with every stride. Nic was pretty certain it was done for effect, and couldn't help smiling.

"Well," Asha said. "I guess I'd better do some digging through the files. Want to get lunch first, or keep me company?"

"I'm not hungry," Nic lied. Her stomach growled indignantly. "But maybe we could get a sandwich and eat while we work?"

"While *I* work, you mean. Data protection. You can't see the files, I'm afraid."

Nic expected cardboard boxes of paper files, but Asha used a computer terminal in a busy open office, tapping away and humming under her breath.

A short while later, Nic was bored. She'd counted the tiles on the ceiling and worked out a rough estimate of the surface area, and then the volume of the room. She'd even counted the little holes in the polystyrene tiles that made a pattern and was busily working out how many there were in total on the ceiling by the time Aaron reappeared, ushering a girl out of a side room.

She looked about fifteen under her heavy make-up, the sort that wasn't intended to be viewed under unforgiving fluorescent lighting, and she clutched her handbag to her belly as though it was her lifeline. The artist Nic had already met, Jilly, emerged from the room a few minutes later and dropped a page of A4 on to Asha's desk.

"Aaron thought you'd want to see this before I give it to Inspector Ram." She grinned at Nic, who grinned back.

Asha took a long look at the drawing before pushing it across to Nic. She lifted it carefully by the edges as though leaving fingerprints wasn't an option. A young face looked up at her from the page, eyes haunted, face thin with a straggly beard that extended mostly down his scrawny neck and barely touched his cheeks. It was similar to Colm, but the expression in the eyes was too solemn, almost as if he'd given up on life, or thought life had given up on him.

"Well?"

"It's very like him, but I couldn't be sure. The Colm I knew was more animated, you know? And I think his face was fatter, although the beard is the same, and the eyebrows, and he wore his hair exactly like this." Perhaps she didn't want it to be Colm, because that would just confirm that he was dead.

"It's not an exact science," Jilly said reassuringly. "The mental picture we hold of someone is always tinged by the way we interact with them." She perched on the corner of the desk. "There was an interesting piece of research done by—"

"Thanks, Jilly," Asha interrupted her. "You've done a great job. I think Inspector Campbell was wanting you to do a sketch for him as soon as you're finished here."

Jilly gave Nic a rueful grin and stood up again. "Okay. I know when I'm not wanted."

"No, you don't," Aaron said from behind her. "If you did, you'd be away by now."

She stuck her tongue out at him and disappeared through the door with a swing of her hips. Aaron watched her go with an expression like a hungry dog, then disappeared back towards Ram's office with the sketch in his hand.

Asha returned to her work with a groan. "I'd have sworn there was nothing new to learn here," she muttered, "but if Lonnie says I've missed something, then I have."

"Who is she?" Nic asked. She had no fear of being over-heard. The noise level in there was deafening, nearly as over-whelming as the nightclub.

"Sergeant Jacob. She was the first woman of colour to join the old RUC. I gather she's taken a lot of flak over the years. Name-calling, racial slurs, nasty practical jokes, but she's one tough woman. You don't mess with Sergeant Jacob." Asha shook her head. "If there's anything she doesn't know about policing in Belfast, it's not worth knowing." She frowned at the screen. "Oh!"

"Oh, what?" Nic asked, trying to see around the edge of the monitor, even though she knew she shouldn't.

"I've found it. The first victim, Meera Patel. Patel is her stepfather's name." She read a bit more. "She changed her name at fourteen, but before that, she was Meera Ram. She's his daughter."

CHAPTER 7

He took time over the act of sharpening his knives, making certain there were no nicks in his beautiful blades. This simple act settled him, the sound of rasp on metal, and took his imagination flying into the future, when he'd have all his players where he wanted them.

His little mice were running free, and his plans were coming together beautifully. Coming to Belfast had been a smart move. No one was looking for him here, and the students around the university were just delicious. When he'd picked Nic out of the crowd, it had taken him a while to decide that she was the one. He needed someone like the Indian woman, someone with a bit of fight in her, but with a lot to lose too. Nic wasn't a loner, not exactly, but she was quiet, introspective, studious.

There was something about her. The way she tucked her hair behind her ear when she was reading. That touch-me-not expression she had when people approached her, especially men. She had an inner strength, he was sure of it.

And so he'd followed her, found out as much as he could about her. Where she lived, who her friends were, her family. Then, he'd prepared his sites, fine-tuned his strategy.

So far, everything was going to plan. Disposing of the body had been harder than he expected. Last time, he'd just left them to be found, but that didn't fit in at all with his plans for Nic. No, indeed.

Loosening the ring that held her had been tricky. She'd slept so fitfully, it had taken all his skill to do it without waking her. The man had seen, but there was nothing he could do about it. He could hardly warn her, gagged as he was.

There had been a bad moment when she tumbled down that bank, then lay motionless for so long. He'd had to check she was still alive, hadn't broken that pretty neck of hers, but she'd just knocked herself out.

He frowned, remembering the way she'd left the hospital in the company of the female detective. He hoped she wasn't going to have a police escort all the time, or he'd have to alter his plans. Not that he wasn't prepared to — flexibility was the key to survival, but he preferred it when things went his way from the beginning.

Nic was special. She deserved to have a very special experience, the full range of emotions, and he had some wonderful ideas how to achieve that.

Take the message on the cottage wall. Yes, it had been a risk to go back, but it had felt like the right thing to do. Vague enough to keep her guessing, with an undercurrent of threat. That should make her sweat.

And then he'd seen her on the petrol station forecourt. The shock of seeing her so close, the frisson of risk if she saw him, had almost counterbalanced his fury. Going to the cottage so soon after she'd been released from hospital had been a ballsy move by the bitch. He just wished he'd been able to see her face when she saw his little message.

He moved to the next knife.

CHAPTER 8

The student house was quiet after Nic said goodbye to Asha and Aaron, who'd driven her home. Hannah and Breige were both out, but there was a note on the kitchen table in Hannah's scrawl.

Gone to get takeaways for tonight and something to eat. Back by 5.

Nic looked at the clock. It was nearly 6 p.m. already. She opened the fridge door, scanning the empty shelves. Seriously? If she didn't shop every week, the other two would surely starve. They must have been living off takeaways for the couple of weeks since she'd been taken. She sighed and closed the door again. She wasn't really hungry, not after the cheesy chips at the police station, but her body clock told her it was time to eat again. There was a box of chocolates up in her room. One of the leftovers from well-wishers when she was in hospital. Lindt, her favourite.

She dragged herself up the narrow stairs to her room at the back of the house, fishing for the bunch of keys. They all locked their rooms whenever they left the house out of habit. Breige's parents, their landlords, insisted for security reasons. That way, if someone broke into the house it would make it difficult to access all the rooms, and they'd make a quare noise, breaking down these thick Victorian doors.

So when her eyes settled on the chest of drawers at the foot of her bed, her heart fluttered like a trapped bird, then settled into a loud, fast beat. The photos of her family always sat at a forty-five-degree angle to the edges, victims of her exacting neatness. Not only had they moved, but the one of her and Hazel, taken in Donegal last summer, was missing.

Her eyes swept the room, looking for other clues, for evidence that an intruder might still be there, but the room was as immaculate as always. Except for the bed. There was a dent in the centre of the quilt, just where someone might have stood if they'd climbed in through the window.

Nic backed out on to the landing, locking the door behind her with a shaking hand. She tapped in the number Asha had given her and waited for it to connect.

Asha answered on the second ring. "What's up? Missing me already?"

The words wouldn't come. Nic's tongue was thick in her mouth, refusing to obey. She could only moan.

"Stay right there. We're on our way."

She was sitting at the bottom of the stairs when the Golf screeched up outside, a blue flashing light turning the half-glassed door into a kaleidoscope of colour. She stumbled to the door and turned the lock.

Asha crashed through with a face like granite, Aaron barely a step behind her. "What happened?"

Nic worked moisture into her mouth. "Someone's been in my room."

"Stay here," Aaron said. "I'll check."

"You'll need this." Nic handed him her bunch of keys. "It's locked."

Asha and Aaron exchanged a look, then Asha put an arm gently across Nic's shoulders, and steered her into the sitting room. She switched on the living flame electric heater, and the room immediately began to warm up. Nic shivered, despite the clinging dressings on her arms and legs.

"Tell me," Asha said, sitting down beside her on the sofa.

"I always keep my photos lined up to the millimetre." She shrugged away her embarrassment. "But they'd been moved."

"Could one of your housemates have been in there? Or your landlord?"

"No. We don't have keys to each other's rooms, and the landlady is Breige's mum. She always texts the day before if she needs to visit us for any reason. Besides, there's one missing."

Aaron stuck his head around the door. "I've called Forensics. They're on their way." He grinned down at Nic. "How're you doing? Want another of my delicious cups of tea?"

She managed a weak smile, but shook her head. "No thanks. I prefer my tea to taste like tea. Yours tastes like tar."

They froze as footsteps sounded on the path, approaching the front door. The lock turned. Then Hannah's voice. "Detective Birch? What's going on? Is Nic okay?"

Aaron closed the door as he replied, so Nic didn't catch what he said, but both Hannah and Breige sounded anxious, their voices high and tight. A few minutes later, the tap ran and cups clattered from the kitchen. Nic met Asha's eyes. The detective was biting her lower lip, eyes dancing. "He's found new victims for his tea, by the sound of it." Then her face turned serious again. "You said a photo was missing?"

"Yes. It was one I had of Hazel and me in Donegal. She hates having her picture taken, so it was about the only one I have of her." She swallowed. "Had."

"Hold on," Asha said. "I'll be back in a moment."

The room was so quiet, Nic could hear the rapid ticking of her watch. Suddenly, she couldn't bear the silence anymore. She stood up, the cheap sofa creaking as her weight left it, and opened the door. Asha was standing outside the front door, but she'd left it open a crack. Her back was to Nic, so couldn't see her, otherwise she'd probably have been more careful about what she said.

"Yes. At least two men, and quickly, please. I want to make sure the family is safe. Have them insist on seeing everyone, in case there is a ransom situation." She shrugged her shoulders, an impatient gesture wasted on whoever was at the other end. "I know it's not his MO, but he's never stolen a photograph of a family member before either." Her lips tightened. "Call it a hunch, if you like, but—"

Nic must have made a sudden move that caught Asha's eye, because she spun around and their eyes locked.

"Just do it, okay?"

She ended the call without taking her eyes off Nic, but she didn't come straight back inside. Aaron broke the spell. He spoke from just behind Nic.

"Are you sure about that tea? Your friends think it's great." Over his shoulder, Nic watched Breige pour hers down the sink, pulling a face.

"No thanks," she said automatically. Funny how manners were so deeply ingrained in her that they still mattered, even when the world was falling apart.

The draught as the door opened made her shiver again. She walked back into the small sitting room like a sleepwalker, her body numb while her thoughts battered at the inside of her skull.

Asha followed her, but neither of them sat. They watched each other like wary strangers, until Asha took a deep breath. "It's probably nothing, but I'd rather not take chances."

"A hunch, you said. What was the hunch? Do you really think he might target my family?"

Asha's face was troubled. "Truly? I don't know, but this is a deviation from his usual pattern, and any deviation worries me. I'd just rather be safe, so I've sent two uniforms over to your home to make sure everyone is okay. If Inspector Ram will give me clearance, I'd like to put a watch on them too, but funding being what it is . . ."

Tension leaked out of Nic, leaving her drained again. She sank back on to the sofa. "I think I should go home. If you and Aaron are keeping an eye on me anyway, we might as well pool resources and take the rest of my family under the umbrella."

Asha raised an eyebrow. "Are you sure? It'd definitely be easier to keep track of you all if you were in one place, at least at night."

"I'll get packed," she said, heavily. It was exactly what she didn't want. Her mother would be tearful, Dad would hide his worry under jokes, Cian would barely notice, and Hazel? What would Hazel think? "Will they tell Hazel about the photo?"

"No. She's not quite eighteen yet, is she? I was going to speak to your parents this evening, put them on their guard."

"Would you let me speak to her? Hazel has . . . problems. PTSD from something that happened when she was at school. She was caught up in an armed robbery where a man was killed, and she sometimes has trouble dealing with the memories, but she trusts me."

"All right. But you won't be able to pack your stuff until SOCO have checked the room."

The door bumped open as someone shouldered their way through, and Jana's loud voice sounded, clear and penetrating.

"I knew Asha wouldn't be able to wait to see me again!"

"Jana!" Aaron said from the kitchen. "My favourite boffin."

There was a crunch as Jana put her kit down on the tiles in the front hall, and a buzz of to-and-fro banter, then the creak of floorboards as she climbed the narrow stairs to the first floor. Nic leaned her head back and closed her eyes, trying to block out the sounds of movement from her bedroom. Her arms throbbed and her legs itched under her jeans. Every little hurt shuffled itself forward, vying for her attention. If she let it, her mind took her straight back to that dank room, to the strain in her shoulders from having her wrists secured behind her, to the zip-ties digging into her flesh, to each individual, careful cut he inflicted on her. He'd watched her face while he cut her, green eyes hard as marble over the top of the mask. She'd wondered if he was waiting for a certain reaction, and if he'd stop hurting her if she gave him it, but no matter what she did, he still came back again and again with one of those knives.

She'd tried to be brave at the beginning, fighting down the screams, and telling herself they'd find her soon. Any moment now, the cops would come crashing in and arrest him, or her mother would appear from nowhere and knock him unconscious, but it never happened, and by the time the first cut had sent its tendrils of thick blood trickling down her arm, she was screaming and thrashing, trying to kick him, to throw him off her.

"All done," Jana said, peering around the door. "Not a trace of a print except Nic's. This guy is good."

"Thank you, Jana," Asha said. "Can Nic go up there to pack her stuff now?"

"Yes. All clear." The little redhead gave Nic a grin that dimpled her cheeks. "Hi there, Nic."

"You're leaving?" Hannah asked as Nic emerged into the hallway. Breige stood behind her, back to the sink at the end of the little galley kitchen. Her face held hope, and for the first time, Nic realized her two friends must have been just as frightened as her by the intruder.

"For a wee while, anyway. I think I'll go home for a few days, maybe. Leave you two in peace."

Hannah's expression wavered between relief and guilt. "Probably do you good, a change of scene."

"Yeah." She trudged up the stairs, aware of Asha following behind. Aaron was already in her room, examining the window frame.

"Jana thinks he got in here. Did you leave your window open?"

"I always sleep with it open a crack, but I usually close it when I leave the room." She bit her lip. "But I do forget sometimes. I never thought anyone could get in that way. It's so high up."

Aaron looked out into their tiny back yard and the communal alleyway behind that ran the length of the terrace. It could be accessed from both ends, for taking wheelie bins out, and gates opened off it into each house's rear space. Their house had a small kitchen extension with a flat roof, but it was set off to one side from her window.

"We think he used the wheelie bin to get on to the flat roof, then jumped across the space to catch your windowsill."

Nic eyed it dubiously. "He'd have to be pretty athletic, and the man who cut me was running to fat around the middle, seriously unfit. And how did he get over the back wall in the first place?" Breige's mum had made sure they had a good, stout lock on the back gate, and the wall was over six feet high.

"Neighbour's wheelie bin," Aaron said. "He moved it back afterwards, but there's a dent in the lid where I think he pushed off to scale the wall."

"Will you be okay on your own in here while you pack?" Asha asked, and Aaron's head snapped up. He mustn't have heard their conversation from up here.

"Yeah."

When they'd left the room, Nic opened the top drawer and looked at the neatly folded pants and bras. Had he rifled through here? Had he pawed at these? A wave of nausea drove her to close the drawer. She couldn't bear to wear anything in this room again, not after he'd been in here. In the end, she just took her laptop bag, tucking her iPad into the front pocket. She had plenty of spare clothes at home, and if she ordered some more online, they'd arrive before she ran out of undies with a bit of luck.

She was about to leave her room when her mobile phone rang, muffled, from the bottom of her bag. Confused, she dropped it on the bed and began to hunt through the pockets for it. She must have slipped it in there by accident.

Her hand closed on the vibrating rectangle of plastic just as the ringing stopped. She lifted it out, and looked at it in horror. This wasn't her phone. Hers was an iPhone. This was a brick phone, some cheap make she'd never heard of, yet it had been her own ringtone. It vibrated again and chirped to announce the arrival of a text.

Fingers shaking, she pressed the button and the screen lit up. There was one missed call showing, and a little envelope in the corner of the screen. It took her a moment to work out how to open the text without a touchscreen.

I'm watching you, it said. *And your pretty little sister.*

She dropped it as though it had scalded her, but it bounced harmlessly on the bed. She looked out of the window, searching for anything out of place, any shadow that could hide a voyeur, but there was nothing.

"Asha!" she shouted.

Another text came through. *Tell no one or your sister is mine.*

Was he inside her head?

Feet thudded up the stairs and Asha and Aaron appeared at her door. "What's up?"

Nic dropped the phone into the bag, back where she'd found it, and pasted a smile on her face. "Sorry if I startled you. It was just to let you know I'm ready." She shrugged the bag on to one shoulder. Just knowing that phone was in there made it feel double its usual weight. She slipped past the two detectives and headed down the stairs.

"Bye, Hannah! Bye, Breige!" she called. "See you soon. Good luck with the exams."

CHAPTER 9

The rush-hour traffic had built up, with impatient drivers trying to cut each other up at the roundabout by Stranmillis College. Aaron drove in concentrated silence, and Asha didn't seem chatty either. The sense of urgency from commuters racing home infected Nic. The little car couldn't go fast enough for her, and her pulse sounded off in her ears like a timer counting down, but to what she couldn't say.

The sense of urgency built as they crawled past the House of Sport and on to the Upper Malone Road. They were past the golf club and into open countryside before the car got out of second gear, and by then Nic felt as though she would explode at any moment.

When Asha's phone rang, Nic jumped.

"Detective Harvey."

The voice at the other end sounded urgent, matching the atmosphere in the car. There was another sound in the background, but it took Nic a moment to identify it. It was a woman crying hysterically.

"Lights," Asha snapped at Aaron. He flicked a switch on the dash and the car shot forward. In front of them, the Nissan Micra that had been travelling at a sedate forty miles an hour swerved and pulled over on to the edge of the road.

Aaron twitched the wheel and flashed past with a roar that belied the look of the car from the outside. Hedges and bushes flashed past, but the noise from the engine drowned out any chance Nic had of hearing the conversation Asha was having. She realized she was digging her nails into her palm again, and made herself stop.

Traffic moved out of their way, and they shot through the railway bridge at Lambeg in the face of an oncoming truck with millimetres to spare. Aaron chose the main roads rather than the warren of residential streets to get to Nic's house, relying on his blue lights to clear a route for him. It worked. They pulled up in the cul-de-sac in a ridiculously short space of time, but not soon enough for Nic.

Two patrol cars were parked on their neighbour's precious grass strip along the pavement. There'd be hell to pay later, Nic thought irrelevantly. Mr Cane would be sending the bill to the PSNI for damage to his property.

As soon as the car was stopped, Nic hauled on the door handle. Damn it all to hell! That child lock again. Asha turned around, apology in her anxious look.

"Sorry, Nic. Please will you stay in the car with Aaron while I find out what's going on?"

"No! Let me out! This is my family—"

Too late. Asha slammed the door behind her, hopped over the low garden wall and disappeared into the house. Nic's house.

"Aaron. Let me out. Please."

His eyes regarded her through the rear-view mirror, and there was sympathy there, but he shook his head. "Sorry, Nic. More than my life's worth. If Asha says to stay here, then she has a good reason for it."

Nic pressed her face to the cool glass, trying to see what was going on inside her house. The front door was closed now. Next door, the elderly couple who had moved in only last year hovered on their driveway, watching Nic with confused faces. The man (she still didn't know what they were called, but Ma would) took his wife's hand and squeezed it.

After an eternity, Asha came out. As she opened the car door, a wailing like a distant siren sounded, cut off when Asha slammed the door closed behind her with a dull *thunk*. She turned around to look at Nic between the headrests. "There's no easy way to tell you this, Nic."

But Nic knew without needing to be told. "He's got Hazel, hasn't he?"

Asha nodded, her face still and professional. "She'd walked out to Tesco for your mum. When the patrol got here, she'd only just left, but they hadn't passed her on their way in. One of them stayed here, and the other one retraced her steps. They put an announcement over the tannoy in Tesco, but she didn't come forward."

Hope flared painfully in Nic's chest. "But she wouldn't. She can never understand the announcements in those places. They're just noise to her."

Asha sighed. "Yes, that's what your mum said, so the officer got the supermarket to show him their CCTV footage. She never got as far as the shop at all. We're trying to work out where she disappeared, but the likeliest is that he was waiting for her."

"That empty house," Nic breathed. There was a rental house near the end of the street, but it hadn't had a tenant in months. The front garden was lined with thick evergreens, the perfect place to hide, and Hazel would have walked right past it on her way to the shop.

"Yes, we think so. We have CSI looking for tyre tracks now, but you know he leaves very little evidence usually."

Now was the time to tell them about the mobile phone. But she couldn't. Not now he had Hazel. The open door tugged at her. She needed to be wrapped in Dad's arms, to see Cian's lopsided smile, and to see her mother being strong as always. "Can I go inside? Please?"

Asha got out and opened the door for her. Nic snagged her backpack and flew across the front garden, up the steps to the bungalow. Then she stopped dead. The wailing she'd heard was much louder now. The ululating cries turned her abused skin to ice under the bandages. That was her mother's voice, twisted almost beyond recognition by grief. Nic swallowed. She'd never seen her mother lose control. Never.

With a shaking hand, she pushed the glass front door open, glad of the cool against her palm. It grounded her, made it possible to take another step on to the doormat. It felt like years since she'd seen the worn carpet and the telephone table.

You're procrastinating, she told herself. *Get in there. Help them.*

She pushed herself down the hallway, fingers trailing along the radiator. A female uniformed officer pushed herself away from the wall, where she'd been leaning.

"You must be Nic. They'll be glad to see you." She gestured into the kitchen. "Everyone's through there."

Nic moved like a sleepwalker through the kitchen and down the step on to the grey-tiled floor of the sunroom. Light flooded this room, and a patio nestled just outside, hemmed in by a low wall and rockery. Her father sat in a wicker armchair, his face drained. Cian was curled up on a beanbag, holding Pumpkin, the fat ginger cat, tight to his chest. Unusually, the cat wasn't objecting, though her expression was mildly traumatized.

Ma stood, quiet now, staring out into the garden. She had her back half turned to Nic, but the unforgiving sunshine turned the tears on her cheek silver, and a convulsive sob shook her shoulders.

"Ma?"

She still didn't turn. Dad tried to get up, but seemed to lack the strength. He sagged back into the seat again. "It's hit Ma hard," he said. "She was the same when—" He stopped.

"When I was taken."

He nodded.

"How do we know it's the same man?" Cian asked. "Maybe she just got talking to a friend. She'll be home in a while, wondering what all the fuss is about."

Deep in her backpack, the treacherous phone vibrated. Her hand twitched, but she caught herself. She couldn't

71

check it here, not with everyone watching. Instead, she went over to her ma and put her free arm around her waist, giving her a squeeze, but Ma was as rigid as a mannequin.

"I'll dump this in my room and come back," she said, hefting the backpack. It was all she could think of to get away. Even then, Cian stared at her, frowning. She turned and virtually ran along the corridor to her room then lifted the backpack on to her bed. A glance out of the window showed no one in the back garden, but her window was right by the back door to the garage, so someone could appear at any moment.

She unzipped the neck of the bag and felt inside for the phone, but didn't pull it into view. Sitting next to the bag, with her back to the window, she peered into the darkness, trying to read the tiny, monochrome screen. The latest text was just one word long.

Swapsies?

It was what she used to say to Hazel when they were children, and Nic still used it sometimes, for a laugh, but just among the family. It had started when they were tiny, with Hazel two years the younger. Sitting at the kitchen table, with an iced bun each from the shops. Nic had licked all the icing off hers, while Hazel just stared at the one she held in her tiny hands.

"Swapsies?" Nic had said, and held out the sticky, slobbered remains.

"Swapsies," Hazel agreed, and passed across her own pristine cake.

Their dad had told the story so many times over the years that Nic felt as though she actually remembered it.

A spark of anger flared inside her, burning her throat. How dare he? How dare he use that word? If he harmed one hair on Hazel's head—

"Nic?" Ma called from just outside the door. "I'm sorry. Will you come and join us?"

"Just a minute, Ma. I'm changing my top. The bandages have leaked again."

It was true too. And it gave her the excuse of drawing the curtains for total privacy. She hit reply to the text and typed: *If you hurt her, I will hunt you down.* Then she deleted it and tried again.

When and where? If you hurt her, deal's off.

Then she deleted the last sentence and hit send before she lost her nerve. She stuffed the phone into the back pocket of her jeans, quickly slipped a clean T-shirt over her head, and opened the curtains again.

* * *

Asha and Aaron had joined the family in the sunroom and Ma was busy making tea and coffee in the kitchen. Nic hadn't offered to help. Being busy was Ma's coping mechanism.

"Any news?" she asked Asha.

"We're waiting for the boffins to come and set up recording equipment on the phones."

"Again," Cian said under his breath, but loud enough to hear. It was no wonder he was struggling to cope. At fifteen, he was neither boy nor man, and he still hadn't quite grown into his big hands and feet. Nic wished she could still sit him on her knee and comfort him as she had when he was tiny.

Commotion at the front door heralded Ram's arrival. Asha got up and left the room, closing the door behind her. Everyone strained to hear what was said, but they spoke too quietly.

The door opened to let in two officers in plain clothes who didn't look much older than Cian. They grinned, ducking heads to avoid eye contact, and started fixing a box to the phone line where it came into the house, in the study that opened out of the sunroom.

"They tap the phone so they can record any calls, and hopefully trace them," Ma said. She was holding two cups of coffee in each hand. Nic didn't need to see into them to know what they held: the smell caught at the back of her throat and almost made her gag.

Ma's face sagged. "Oh, I'm sorry. I forgot!" She threw the contents down the sink and switched the tap on to wash the liquid away, but it was too late. Nic was back in that room again, her senses filled with the cloying scent of blood, sticky under her when she shifted position.

"Nic!" Aaron said. "You're safe."

With a huge effort, Nic dragged herself back to the present. "Sorry." She met her ma's haggard eyes. "Sorry, Ma."

Ma's face softened. "Don't be sorry, love. Go and sit down and I'll put the kettle back on."

Nic perched on the edge of one of the dining chairs. Cian was closest, his head level with her knees. She was probably the only one who heard him mutter, "Can't even drink coffee now."

She ignored him.

"There," one of the boffins said. "That should do it." He straightened up and looked around, as if a little surprised to see so many people in the room. "Well. We'd better be off, then."

When the two of them had gone, Ram came in with Asha to join Nic at the table. *It's like them and us*, Nic thought. *Family on one side of the room, police on the other, and me sat between the two, as though I can't decide which camp I belong to.*

Ram sipped his tea as though it was foul-tasting medicine. "For the sake of your missing daughter, whatever we discuss here today should be considered confidential. Do you all agree to this?"

Nic and Dad nodded, Ma said, "Of course," and Cian shrugged. When Ram's gaze sharpened on him, he assented reluctantly.

"Yeah. Not as if I'd be putting it out on social media."

Ram went on. "Good. Just to bring you up to date," he said. "We have found evidence of a vehicle parked on the driveway of number six. It left tyre tracks in the moss and leaf mould, and those tracks match the ones we found in the field behind the cottage earlier today."

"So it *is* him," Ma breathed.

"I'm not ready to confirm that yet, but signs are suggestive, yes. This information will not be released to the press."

Nic tried to concentrate on his words, to remember what she was supposed to know and what she wasn't. She couldn't show that she already knew he had Hazel, before the police confirmed it. In her back pocket, the filthy phone stayed still and silent.

"We have officers combing the area, and doing door to door in case anyone saw anything, but as you know, the driveway to number six is secluded. Still. He must have driven to the house and away again, so anything will be useful. We are also studying CCTV from all the streets leading away from here."

Yes, but if he'd gone out past Friends' School there'd be no cameras, Nic thought. He could be through the rabbit warren of housing developments and away before anyone knew, and no surveillance to show which way he'd gone.

"He must have another hiding place." Nic hadn't realized she'd spoken aloud until all the faces turned to her. She flushed. "Well, he can't use the cottage again, can he? He must have somewhere else."

"I agree," Ram said. "It is that which we need to locate. I would also like very much to know why he has taken Hazel, and not tried to take Nic again, as the message in the cottage suggested he might."

"What message?" Ma and Dad spoke almost at the same time.

Ram frowned. Either because he hadn't meant to give away that piece of information, or because he felt the family ought to have been told about it earlier. Nic thought probably the latter, since he seemed too well in control of himself to give away anything he didn't mean to.

Asha filled them in. "He's been back to the cottage and painted a warning on the wall. It said, 'The race is not yet run'. We took it to mean he was still coming for Nic."

Ma's face had gone very still. "If he still wants Nic, what better way than to take her sister, to force her to hand herself over?" She looked at Nic. "I do hope you won't be so stupid, Nic?"

"Of course not! Do you think I'd go back to him willingly? To let him finish what he'd started? I'm more use to Hazel here, helping the police with every little detail I can remember." Her voice was steady and calm, no hint of the turmoil raging inside her. Partway through her speech, the blasted mobile vibrated again.

"Nic has been of immense use to us," Ram said. "Her insights will help us find her sister, I'm sure."

No pressure then, Nic thought.

CHAPTER 10

It was ages before Nic could sneak a look at the phone. She sat on the loo, finding it hard to focus on the words as she scrolled through the message. It was directions to somewhere, but they didn't make sense. There was no starting place given.

Right at the T-junction, right again, half a mile then right again up a track. 400 paces then left. No rush. I'll be waiting.

She tried to imagine it as setting off from home, but that didn't work. Definitely not from the house in Belfast, either. Where was this place?

It came to her with a sickening thump of her heart. The cottage. It had to be.

She got the iPhone out and loaded Google Maps, satellite view. Yes. There was the T-junction, and the next turn, and then he must mean a farm track that ran straight as a motorway up into the hills, ending at a group of buildings. He must be holding Hazel in one of those barns. As the crow flies, it was probably only a few hundred yards from the cottage. What was his obsession with that area?

A little voice inside urged her to tell Ram, or at least Asha. Asha would help her, wouldn't she? It made sense to at least leave a note saying where she'd gone, so they could track her. After. Even if it was only to find her body, Ma and

Dad would want to know what had happened to her. Because this was going to be a one-way trip. The cold feeling in her gut told her that.

But how was she going to get away?

The opportunity came sooner than she expected. Ram sent everyone away, and after a few encouraging words with Ma, he left himself in Aaron's Golf. Asha hesitated at the door. She took Nic's hand in her own and squeezed it, and Nic surprised herself by not pulling away.

"Take care, won't you? Phone me if you think of anything that might help, or if you see anything suspicious."

"I will," Nic said through numb lips.

"We're leaving Constable Green here. He'll be outside in the car until someone relieves him."

"Okay. Thanks."

Asha raised her eyebrows. "What for? Letting him take Hazel?" she said bitterly.

"For being a friend."

Asha gave a tremulous smile and then left, her eyes suspiciously shiny in the light from the hallway. It was a revelation to Nic to discover that she wasn't the only one carrying guilt for Hazel's abduction.

Sleep refused to come that night. Nic lay awake, staring at the ceiling, making shapes from the patterns of light creeping in around her curtains. It was so quiet here compared to Belfast. No drunks reeling home, crashing into bins and singing out of tune. No taxis revving their engines. No constant drone of traffic in the distance. She might as well be back in the cottage for all the noise, until a helicopter passed overhead.

For a moment, she wondered if it was police surveillance, then common sense took over. It'd be on its way into Thiepval Barracks, just up the road. There had been a time, when Nic was a child, when dozens of the big Chinooks had flown in droves across the skies. Each one had a vehicle suspended underneath it in a net, like in the action films. They'd found out later that it was the result of a power war between two high-up officers in the barracks. One had refused entry to the other's vehicles, so he simply flew them in over his rival's head.

Even that memory did little to relieve the growing sense of dread that sat like a lead weight on Nic's chest.

Eventually, she gave up on sleep and got up, not really sure of what she was planning. She threw on jeans and a cotton jumper and snagged her leather jacket from the wardrobe. Real leather, not like poor Colm's. Finally, she stuffed her hair inside a beanie hat and slipped her feet into a pair of worn trainers she should really have thrown out months ago.

She went outside to ask the constable in the car if he wanted a hot drink, but when she looked in, he was deep asleep. The window was down an inch, and she could hear his snores, gently rising and falling. This opened up possibilities. *Swapsies?* A plan began to form.

Nic ran lightly back to the house and took the key to Ma's Jeep from the hook just inside the front door. It was parked down the street, presumably because there'd been no room yesterday, with all the police vehicles, to get it any closer.

She held her breath as she passed the car again, but the policeman was still sound asleep. The Jeep's indicators flashed briefly as she unlocked it and she slid into the driver's seat, glad of the cool leather.

The old car started at the first turn of the key, letting out its usual deep diesel roar and probably a puff of black smoke from the exhaust. Biting her lip, she stared in the rear-view mirror, but there was no movement from the police car. She adjusted the seat position, and fastened her seat belt, smiling bitterly as she did it. Being pulled over for driving without a seat belt would be the least of her worries. Driving without insurance, taking a car without the owner's permission, driving while under the influence of prescription painkillers, and worst of all, betrayal of a promise to a friend.

Sorry, Asha, she thought as she put the lever into drive and let the car roll forwards. *Hazel has to come first, and only I can do this.*

She'd forgotten how powerful the big Jeep was. Her foot never left the brake pedal, hovering and touching at every slight bend in the road. Her knuckles gripped the wheel, tightening spasmodically every time car headlights approached from in front or behind. It took for ever to negotiate the traffic lights and roundabouts before she was past the motorway and heading out into the countryside.

About a mile down the road towards Ballynahinch, Nic had to pull over and get her iPhone out for directions. By then, she was fairly certain no one was following her, and she had the road to herself. She checked the other phone, handling it as though it might bite, but there was nothing new.

Now she was committed to a course of action, the anxiety sloughed away, leaving her a little high at the prospect of confronting her abductor. Even if she had to die to do it, she needed to see his face, to hear his voice, to ask him why.

As she pulled back on to the road, a flash of something behind her caught her eye in the mirror, but it must have been a reflection because when she turned around to stare at it, there was only shadow.

She missed the junction in the dark and had to turn the big Jeep in a gateway. Thank God it was so quiet. No sign of any other cars on the road. Just as she managed to pull out on to the road again, bumping up on to the far verge, the dazzling beam of headlights gave her the lie. Another Jeep trundled past slowly, forgetting to dip his headlights. It left her half-blind, and she almost missed the turning a second time. If she hadn't been travelling so slowly, she might have, but she swung the wheel just in time, gunning the engine, and frightening herself at the sudden surge of power.

Hedges encroached on the lane, making a dark tunnel of the country road. Blind bends came out of nowhere, and a steady drizzle began. As Nic searched for the windscreen wiper switch, the old Jeep surprised her by turning them on automatically, rubber squealing as the wipers dragged themselves across the glass.

From this direction, she'd be passing the farm track, but she had no idea how to find it in the dark. If she kept going, though, and came at it from the direction he'd given her, he'd surely know it was her. Why warn him?

She stopped again, not bothering to pull into the side of the road. Her phone lit up, showing her current position and the little pin she'd dropped on the barn. It was still a couple of miles ahead. She bit her lip, thinking furiously. When she'd set off, she'd had no plan, expecting to be caught and stopped at any moment, but now she had to decide what to do.

Her life was not important, but Hazel's was. If some carelessness on Nic's part caused her sister harm, there'd be no point in her even being here. She needed a weapon, something to give her an edge.

There'd be a tyre lever in the boot, surely? Ma would never drive a car without the means to change a wheel. She switched the engine off and slipped out. The floor of the boot lifted, and there was the spare wheel, but no sign of a jack or tyre lever. Shit. Where else could it be? She looked in the back seat and felt under the front seats. In desperation, she tilted the backseat cushions forward, and there was the tyre lever, with the hydraulic jack. It was a good, long, heavy-duty affair. Nice and weighty in her hand. She put the seat back down and checked the distance on her phone. One point eight miles. Maybe this was close enough, if she pulled the Jeep off the road and out of sight. She could walk that in half an hour, and it was still hours to dawn.

Wishing she'd chosen a warmer jacket, Nic set off at a brisk walk, arms swinging. She hefted the tyre lever a few times, taking practice swings with it. Maybe it would be useless against his knives, but the cold metal in her hand gave her confidence. She was doing something positive. Taking the initiative. Using the element of surprise.

Yes, but he knows you're coming, the small voice in her head whispered. *It's a trap for you, not for him.* She swallowed the foul taste in her mouth and carried on, head held high.

On foot, there was no missing the farm track, even in the dark. It was framed by high hedges, dark and menacing, and she didn't want to use the torch on her phone — it'd be visible from miles away. Nic hesitated at the end: once she set off down there, she'd be trapped. No way out. Maybe there was another way. She'd passed a field gate a short way back.

It was chained shut, but she climbed over it with very little noise, just a slight clanking as the chain rattled against the gatepost. It seemed loud in her ears, but probably wouldn't have been audible twenty feet away. She landed in thick grass on an uneven surface, turning her ankle. Pain shot through the joint, and she clung to the cold metal gate with her free hand until the agony subsided to a dull ache. She didn't think she'd yelped, but couldn't be sure.

The hedge loomed above her as she made her cautious way, checking the ground each time before she transferred her weight. It was a tiring and slow progression, and she jumped at every sound, but after what felt like hours, the hedge turned a corner. She couldn't tell if this was the cluster of buildings the map had shown, or if her field had ended and there was further to go. All sense of time and distance was distorted by adrenaline and the throbbing of her ankle.

Beyond the hedge, something moved with a swishing sound as the hawthorn was pushed aside. Nic's heart thudded painfully, then settled into a fast, pounding beat that thumped in her ears like a steam engine. He was here, almost close enough to touch!

Then a soft snuffling and the suction of hooves in mud, followed by a distinctive farmy smell and a soft lowing sound, reassured her. Cattle. Thank God.

Nic made her way along this hedge, looking for another gate or a thin bit of hedge she might be able to push through. She'd gone a good way from the corner before she found an opening, slimy with cowpats and smelling of slurry in the damp night. Ahead of her, by the faint starlight from a gap in the clouds, she saw the buildings. Not too far away, and if she set off at a diagonal across this field, she'd come at them from a totally unexpected direction.

The cattle followed her, their feet thumping the ground. She wanted to shine her iPhone torch to see what they were, in case they were bulls, but she couldn't risk it. Instead, she kept her pace steady, holding the tyre lever in front of her in case of obstacles, but this field seemed quite level. When she stopped, close to the buildings, warm breath touched the back of her thighs, and she put her hand out in reflex. It was a calf, less than half her height. There were maybe half a dozen crowded close to her, their coats damp and curly after the drizzle. One licked her hand with a slimy tongue, and she almost squeaked, pushing the woolly head away from her.

A post-and-rail fence stood between her and the buildings. She slipped between the rails, squeezed into the narrow gap of rough ground, one hand on the wall for balance in the dark. Because it was pitch black now.

Always darkest before dawn, she told herself. Both literally and figuratively in this case, since the building and the clouds blocked out even the starlight. The constant drizzle had sapped away her strength, soaking her jeans and the bandages underneath until they were like lead weights on her limbs. Her hair had escaped from under the hat and hung lank and damp against her neck, trickling water down inside her jacket.

Why am I even here? I should have told Asha.

But she *was* here, and there was no going back now. Only forward. Hazel might be just beyond that wall, maybe bleeding. That thought straightened her shoulders, and she shuffled as quietly as she could towards the end of the barn furthest from the farm track. She stumbled over an invisible obstacle on the ground, clattering the tyre lever against the corrugated iron wall as she saved herself from falling. It rang out with a dull clang that sounded deafening in the night. On the other side of the fence the little herd of calves still shadowed her, their feet making soft swishing noises in the long grass.

At last, she reached the end and peered around the corner. There was little to see, but she stared into the darkness, willing her eyes to adjust. When nothing had moved for several minutes, she began the slow, heart-hammering journey around to the yard she'd seen on Google Maps.

The smell of slurry was stronger here, blotting out any other scent. The wall on her right disappeared, leaving a yawning, black chasm. Nic paused, afraid to move across it, but there was no sound from within. She took a deep breath, inhaling oil and spilled diesel. This must be a tractor shed.

She moved across the open door as quickly as she could over the rutted ground, feet sliding on cow muck. The building she wanted was the next one along from this. It was where his directions were sending her, and she could almost feel it drawing her closer. Hazel must be in there. She must. Nic hefted the tyre lever again, changing her grip so it would have more weight if she swung it.

There had to be a door at this end of the shed, opening into the yard. She felt her way along the front, letting her trailing fingers show her the way. There. A door. And a padlock, fastened. Her belly twisted in frustration, before her brain processed the swinging hasp. The padlock was locked, but the latch wasn't across.

Nic knew she couldn't rush this bit. She explored the surface of the door, looking to see if it was hinged or sliding, and which way it opened. When she was certain she knew, she braced herself, left hand on the leading edge and body weight back, ready to heave. Her right hand held the tyre lever above her head, poised to bring it down on the kidnapper's head if he was fool enough to be there, waiting for her.

The door slid silently open on well-greased runners. Air stirred, laden with dust that nearly made Nic sneeze. It smelled of long-dried grass and soil. There was another scent overlying it though, one she'd recognize anywhere. Aftershave, sharp in the cold night air.

Nic dodged inside, listening for movement, but all she could hear was her own pulse, pounding in her ears. She moved towards the back of the barn, both hands gripping her weapon now, taking short, shuffling steps. Her right foot landed in something wet and sticky that made a slight sucking noise when she lifted it, and the heavy, metallic scent of blood rose, clogging her nostrils.

She was too late! He'd killed her. Hazel's body was here somewhere. She fumbled in her pocket for her phone. The screen lit up automatically. It wasn't much, but she turned it around to illuminate the floor in front of her. Darkness spread out from her feet like an oil spill, then the phone went dark. She needed more light.

Nic made herself slow down, swiping the screen this time to activate the torch. The beam of light was blinding after so long in the dark, but she swung it around, lighting up every corner of the small space. She was alone. No murderer. No Hazel, either dead or alive. The blood was sticky, still wet in the centre but clotting at the sides. Embedded in the sticky edges was a thin piece of white plastic. Her heart turned over in her chest. A zip-tie.

So much blood. She was back in the cottage, hearing the knife tearing into Colm's belly, smelling the butchery, hearing his gurgling scream. Now Hazel. Something snapped inside her and she sank to the ground, curling into a foetal ball in the sticky blood.

The silence was shattered as engines roared up the track, headlights splitting the night. Car doors slammed.

"Nic!" Asha's voice was sharp with fear, but Nic barely registered her presence.

Hands turned her over, fingers probing her neck. A light shone in her eyes, and she didn't blink. It was a tunnel, welcoming her, inviting her to follow Hazel. If she strained her ears, she could almost hear her sister, calling her.

CHAPTER 11

"She's alive. Strong pulse."

"Can't see any wounds on her. I don't think this is her blood."

"What's wrong with her? Nic!" Someone shook her and the tunnel exploded into shards of light.

One of the calves lowed, sounding almost human, like a soul in torment. Who let them in? It took a moment for Nic to realize it was her voice, and she was moaning the same words over and over. "No. No. No."

"Nic, it's me, Asha. Wake up!"

"Asha?" Her speech came thick and slow, as if her tongue was too fat for her mouth. "What are you doing here?"

"We followed you."

Nic's thoughts tumbled over one another. The texts, the sleeping police constable, Ma's car so conveniently positioned. She'd failed. She'd brought the police down on Hazel's kidnapper. Was he somewhere close, watching? He could hardly miss the commotion — now she saw that, along with Asha and Aaron, the place was full of uniformed police.

But she'd swear there'd been no movement in here before she'd arrived. He must have only had Hazel here for a short time.

Aaron was wrapping her in tinfoil like a Christmas turkey. Laughter bubbled up from nowhere, hard and loud and unrestrained. "You gonna cook me?"

The detectives exchanged worried looks, and Aaron stepped back, his face twisted with some strong emotion.

"Hey, hey! Give me some room to work here, and take your big, clumpy police boots off of my crime scene."

Stale cigarette smoke washed over Nic as Jana leaned down to her. "Let's get you out of here, girl, so I can look for evidence. That's if these clumsy PC Plods have left me any to work with."

Nic felt rather than heard the mass exodus as embarrassed coppers backed away into the yard. Jana helped her to her feet, disregarding the blood that dripped from her. They lurched out into the night, with Nic blinking in the bright lights. She raised her arm to shield her eyes, and almost hit Jana with the tyre lever that she must have clung to throughout. Someone unpeeled her fingers and took it from her.

There was an ambulance sitting in the yard. Its back door opened and a green-clad paramedic jumped out. She took Nic's other arm and helped her up the steps, lowering her down on to the stretcher-bed against the right-hand wall. The laughter had gone now, leaving her drained of emotion. She shied away from the scene in the barn, and what it meant, and focused on the details around her.

"Hi, Nic. I'm Gail. Just going to take your blood pressure now, so hold nice and still for me. Everything's going to be all right."

No, it isn't. Nothing was going to be all right ever again.

The paramedic fastened a cuff around Nic's upper arm, and she flinched as air filled it, digging into the half-healed wounds under her bandages. The paramedic didn't seem to notice, her eyes on the machine. She clipped a plastic clothes peg-like device on to Nic's finger, illuminating it in red for a second before the jaws closed over her skin. All around them, equipment beeped.

"Can you tell me if any of this blood is yours?" Gail said in that detached, professional voice that must be hammered into everyone medical from their first day of training.

"No. Yes. Probably some of it, but it's okay. The doctors know about the wounds."

Gail's eyebrows shot up. The back door opened briefly and another paramedic put his head inside.

"Bit of background you need to know, Gail." They stood murmuring for a few minutes, but Nic zoned them out completely. She didn't need to hear a catalogue of her injuries again.

Next time her thoughts turned outwards, she was alone in the back of the ambulance. The rear door stood open, but it was so dark out there compared to the brightly lit interior that all she could make out were shadows. Then the ambulance dipped as a dark figure climbed the steps. He straightened up to reveal the serious face of Inspector Ram. He was carrying a plastic bag with something bulky inside it.

"May I?" He gestured to one of the grey seats on the other side of the ambulance. Nic assented and he sat down stiffly, like an old man. "It's not human blood."

With those words, it was as if the sun had come out.

"Jana believes it to be pig's blood, but she'll not know for sure until she gets back to the lab. She said I should tell you that straight away."

"So it's not Hazel's."

"Not Hazel's. So far, we have found no evidence that Hazel has ever been here. We will, of course, keep looking, but it seems this was a set-up. Something to play with your mind, perhaps."

"She's still alive."

Ram's eyes half closed for a moment. "We have no evidence either way, but it's likely, yes. How did he contact you, by the way?"

"He left a mobile phone in my laptop bag when he broke into my room."

Ram nodded.

A suspicion formed in her mind, faint as wisps of mist, but there nonetheless. "You knew!"

"Yes. We are not quite as stupid as the public seem to think. Jana found it, and we've been monitoring it ever since. And a tracker on your mother's car. That was how we got here so fast."

Anger began, a slow burn inside her chest. "And did it help you? Are you any closer to finding him?"

He smiled. "I believe we might be. Jana says you can go home, but she needs your clothes to test. She says to tell you to put them in this bag and tie the top. Here's some spares to keep you warm. Not the most stylish, but it was all we could come up with. Asha says don't worry about the fit: they never fit anyone, apparently."

When he'd gone, she peeled her blood-soaked clothes off and put them in the empty bag. She stuffed the leather jacket in with barely a pang. Clothes could be replaced, but people couldn't. Ram had left her a jumpsuit, so dark green as to be almost black. It had the PSNI logo on the breast pocket.

Asha was right. It hung loose from her shoulders, yet was tight around her bum when she sat down to slide her feet into the boots Ram had provided. They were clearly police boots too. Stiff leather, designed more for protection than comfort, cold to her bare feet. She opened the door with difficulty and descended into the yard, walking like an old woman.

When she appeared inside the ring of light cast by a series of high-powered work lamps, the buzz of conversation halted briefly before stuttering on self-consciously. The officers standing around all cast her one quick look, then found something interesting in the other direction. All except Asha.

She came over with a twisted smile. "Inspector Ram told you it wasn't Hazel's blood, didn't he?"

"Yes. The kidnapper must have set the whole thing up. But why?"

"That's exactly what we're asking ourselves too." She laid gentle fingers on Nic's arm. "Are you up to going back inside?"

89

Was she? "Am I allowed in? Contaminating the scene and all that." A phrase she'd stolen from Hannah.

"According to Jana, the scene was destroyed by 'all the PC Plods galumphing across it'. Her words."

"Yeah. I heard her shouting at you all when she first arrived. She's scary, isn't she?"

Asha grinned at her, but the harsh lighting showed up the lines of strain around her eyes. "Come on. Let's go have a look in case you see something we missed."

Flattered despite herself, even in the knowledge that Asha was clearly intending to cheer her up, Nic followed the detective into the barn. Shed, really. It was no bigger than the tiny single garage at home that they'd never been able to fit a car into. The patch of blood was taped off, but it no longer held any terrors for Nic, now she knew it was of animal origin. She stood in the middle and turned slowly, taking in every detail she'd not been able to see earlier.

The shed wasn't quite as empty as it had felt. There were a few rectangular bales of hay in the corner furthest from the door. Pitchforks were lined up next to them, prongs down, and a stiff yard brush. She kept turning. A quad bike with mud caked on the tyres and splattered across the body, except where someone's legs had shielded the seat as they rode. Some of the mud was darker than the rest. Still wet. As she watched, a lump detached itself from under the wheel arch and fell to the floor with a dull thump.

And that was it, apart from — Nic took two quick strides across the dirt floor. Her hand reached out in reflex, but she stopped just short of the feathery scarf draped in autumn shades of green and brown where it hung from a nail by the door.

"You recognize it?" Asha asked quietly.

"Yes." Her voice came out as a croak, and she cleared her throat. "The last time I saw it, Hazel was wearing it. They're her favourite colours. I bought for her last birthday."

"It couldn't be another similar one?"

"No. If you look at the label, it'll tell you. They're all individually hand-dyed. No two are the same. I bought it at a craft fair."

"Okay. He's left it here as a message, then. Hazel was probably never anywhere near here. Any more messages on that phone he gave you?"

"Shit. I left it in the back pocket of my jeans." She'd taken her own phone out, but forgotten about the brick.

"I'll get it." Asha disappeared into the yard, leaving Nic alone in the shed. She turned around again, making sure she hadn't missed anything else. The pool of blood was irregular now, where she'd fallen down into it, and there were bloody footprints leading in and out of it, all overlaying one another. God only knew what Jana would be able to make of that mess.

She closed her eyes and breathed in, searching for the scent of aftershave she'd smelled when she first got here, but it was gone, replaced by blood and disturbed dust, and the smell of wet mud from the quad. She reopened her eyes and went over to Hazel's scarf, running it through her fingers. That's where the smell had been strongest, by the door. She buried her nose in the soft material and inhaled, but all she could smell was fresh air and the faintest scent of the Radox shower gel Hazel used.

Asha came back with the cheap phone in her hand and a strange expression on her face. "There's a new message." She handed it to Nic.

Fooled you. Dump the bodyguards or the sister dies. It's still you I want.

"What will I do? He must know by now that you've read the texts. He's been one step ahead the whole time."

"Well, for now, we'll get you home. You need to clean up and get some sleep, and we'll talk in the morning. Aaron will drive you."

"What about Ma's Jeep? I can't leave it in the middle of nowhere."

"I found the keys in your jacket pocket. One of us will drive it back for her. Just try to get some rest."

To Nic's surprise, when they emerged from the shed, the first rays of sunrise were lighting the sky to the east. Aaron waved to her from the laneway. "Car's down here, Nic."

They walked side by side in silence. Aaron was unusually quiet, perhaps reading her mood, and exhaustion had creeped over Nic, leaving her too tired to speak. The usual grey Golf was parked at the far end of the lane, reversed in. She climbed into the front seat this time, resting her cheek against the window. She was asleep before Aaron had started the engine, and didn't wake until he shook her shoulder.

"Sorry, Nic. We're here. Your mum and dad'll want to see you're safe, so brace yourself."

He was right, of course. They'd lost her once, and now they'd lost her sister too. They'd be in pieces.

She had to use the door frame to haul herself upright, and straightening was like forcing open a rusty hinge. Aaron took her elbow in a light grip, helping her balance as she stepped painfully up the driveway and into the house.

All the lights were on, despite the fact that the sun was well and truly up by now. With a feeling of déjà vu, she heard the murmur of voices from the sunroom. She dreaded facing them. Last time had been bad enough, but now she was carrying the guilt of deception on her shoulders too. She stumbled to a halt in the hall.

Aaron turned to face her. "You can do this. You're stronger than you think."

Her mouth was too dry to speak, so she shook her head instead.

"They love you. Go on." He gave her a gentle push. She forced her feet forwards.

"Nic, love!" Ma called as soon as she turned the corner.

Arms wrapped around her and she buried her face in Ma's soft chest, breathing in the comforting, familiar smell of wash powder and soap, and the Ted Baker body spray she used.

"Shush, now. It's all right. You're safe now." Ma rocked her gently, as she had when Nic was a child, after she'd skinned her knee.

The familiar words washed over her, releasing all the barriers she'd thrown up since that night when she crouched, naked, on the gravel, waiting to be run over by a passing car in the dark. A sob worked its way from somewhere deep in her belly, growing like a fat helium balloon as it rose through her until she thought she'd burst like a ripe peach. It erupted as a wail, with hot tears sheeting down her cheeks.

She was three years old again, and Ma had the answer to every question. She was safe now. Nothing could hurt her. No one could come near her.

CHAPTER 12

Dad had run her a hot bath with way too much scented stuff in it, so the water was slimy against her skin. It felt good to soak, though, and Nic imagined the filth and contamination of contact with her tormentor sloughing away as she scrubbed with the loofah. She sank back under the surface, and all the sounds of the house faded into clanks and pops as her ears filled with water. Her hair fanned out and floated around her, light and free.

She stayed there until the warmth began to leave the water, and the skin of her fingertips was wrinkled and pale. The heat had sedated her, making it hard to lift herself free from the water's clinging grip, and the cool air raised goosebumps on her skin. Before reaching for the towel, Nic adjusted the shaving mirror on the sink so she could see her body. The wounds were healing and the last of the stitches would be out in a day or two. She should probably have tried to keep them dry, but too late now.

If she let her eyes drift out of focus, the patterns made by his knives looked like the veins in fine Italian marble, like on the altar in church. Her skin was pale enough for marble, but marble didn't feel the cold. She shivered and wrapped herself in the giant towel Ma had left out for her, sealing away the scars.

She twisted her hair up in another towel and brushed her teeth, watching the electric toothbrush as it buzzed across the enamel. She glanced once into the dark eyes, shadowed with pain and grief, then looked away and finished without the mirror.

Plaiting her hair helped her forget. The simple, repetitive action as her fingers wound the damp locks together soothed her, and the ache in her arms as the blood slowly left them kept her mind off other pains. Finally, she put on brushed cotton pyjamas and crawled into bed, pulling the duvet up over her head. The last thing she remembered before sleep dragged her down was Cian sitting on the edge of the bed. He leaned down and whispered in her ear.

"I'm sorry I was so mean earlier. It's not your fault Hazel was taken. I know that now."

Her lips were too tired to move. She might have made a small sound, but couldn't be sure. Darkness creeped in from the edges, despite the sun flooding through the gap in her curtains, and all pain retreated.

When she woke, stretching and yawning, it took a good few minutes before she remembered. Then it all came crashing back.

Nic sat up, shoulders suddenly tense. A muscle twitched in her upper arm, an irritating little tic that made her heart beat faster in response. She ran over the events of the last few days, recalling details she'd forgotten. Memories that had surfaced under the morphine in the hospital, memories she'd supressed, then they were gone again, like mist if you tried to grab it. She let her breath out in a frustrated huff and got up.

Out in the hall, the smell of fresh bread got her nostrils twitching, and her belly rumbled. When had she last eaten? She padded down to the kitchen. No one there, but the green light was flashing on the bread maker, which explained the smell, and there was fresh butter and chocolate spread on the table. She licked her lips. Clothes first, food after.

Back in her room, she found an old pair of jeans in a drawer. She wasn't surprised, after the last few days, to find the waist hanging loose when she fastened them. She dug around until she found a belt and ran it through the loops before pulling a long-sleeved T-shirt on. She'd kept the bandages off after her bath. Light fabric moved across her bare skin for the first time since her ordeal had begun.

"You're up," Ma said, unnecessarily. "Hot chocolate or tea to drink?"

She'd always drunk coffee in the mornings, but by now everyone knew to avoid even mentioning it. Hot chocolate was for invalids, and people who needed cheering up or comforting. It was the drink of surrender.

"Tea, but I'll make it. Thanks, Ma. For everything."

Nothing like food in your belly to revive the flagging spirits. She'd read that somewhere, but never appreciated how true it was. All the fear and guilt from the night before were still there, but she could box them up, sort through them like notes for a physics report, and assess them with a clear head.

First things first: why had he taken Hazel? Was it to hurt her as he'd hurt Nic, or to tempt Nic out into the open so he could finish what he'd started? The messages he'd sent indicated he still wanted her. Did that make Hazel more or less safe than if she was his primary target?

No idea. She filed that question away, because it was too painful to consider just yet.

Why had he abducted Nic and Colm in the first place? What could possibly be his motivation?

Nic padded through to her room and grabbed an A4 lined pad and a biro, pouring herself a second cup of tea on the way back through the kitchen. She began making notes, chewing the end of the pen in between sips.

By the time Asha arrived, looking far too fresh for someone who'd probably had less sleep than Nic, she'd covered three pages of A4 with her thoughts.

"What's all this?" Asha asked as she sat down opposite Nic, with her back to the window, and snagged a clean mug. She poured herself a black tea and spooned in sugar.

"Just trying to get my thoughts in order." Nic pushed the pad over to her. "Why? Why did he take me and Colm in the first place, and why does he want me so badly now that he's prepared to risk being caught by taking Hazel, and setting traps he must have expected to be sprung by you lot?"

"Is that what you think?"

"Yes. I reckon he thought I'd tell you about the phone, and set up the whole thing to taunt you. I didn't, as it happened, but you still found out. I think he'll assume I'm cooperating fully with the police, and have been from the get go."

"Aren't you?"

A blush rose up her neck. "I didn't tell you about the phone, did I?"

Asha smiled. "No, but if it happened again, would you?"

Would she? "Perhaps," she said slowly. "It'd depend if I thought it would endanger Hazel or not."

"Want to know what I think?"

Nic met her eyes and nodded.

"I think Hazel is safest while you are free. He's shown he has no compunction about killing, but he does seem to have this bee in his bonnet about finishing the job with you. I think he needs to keep Hazel alive in order to be sure of getting you."

"I was thinking along those lines too. I wondered if we could use the mobile to demand proof that she's still alive and well." *And if she is*, Nic thought, *I'll gladly exchange my life for hers.*

"That's what Inspector Ram suggested too. A photo of her holding today's newspaper, maybe?"

Nic's mind whirred off like a moth, drawn back to the cottage again. She'd been naked and bleeding. With Hazel's past, and having seen what he'd done to Nic, her sanity could be destroyed before the cutting even started. She wrenched her thoughts back to the problem in hand, forcing herself to think dispassionately.

"I'll get the phone."

"Wait! Nic, where will he send the picture? That thing just about handles texts, but you can't take or receive photos with it."

"Can't he email it or something?"

"I hope he does, because then our tech boys can track down his IP address and we'll have another piece of the puzzle, but I suspect he's too wily for that."

"Can we tell him to print it out and post it?"

"Takes too long, and we don't know if he has access to a printer. I think we'll just have to demand the picture and see what he does. That alone will tell us a good bit about him, anyway."

Nic stared sightlessly out into the garden over Asha's shoulder. When she'd escaped the cottage that night, she never thought she'd be sitting here a couple of weeks down the line, trying to psychoanalyze her abductor. Especially not with Hazel's life at stake. The sense of responsibility overwhelmed her. Her heart rate picked up, and a buzzing began inside her head. This was on her, all of it.

Colm, tortured and killed because he'd gone out for a drink with her. Hazel, already barely holding on to her sanity. Her family, being forced to go through all this again. All her fault.

A slight movement caught her attention, just the other side of the low hedge separating their garden from their elderly neighbours'. There was someone standing there, too tall to be either of the old folk.

A shard of agony pierced her side, and she gasped, half rising to her feet.

"What is it?" Asha was rising too. She spun around to see what Nic was looking at, but in that moment, while her body blocked Nic's view, he'd gone. There was nothing to see, just the striped lawn and the neatly trimmed hedge.

Nic tried to speak, but the words wouldn't come. She just pointed.

Asha was out of the sunroom, through the French doors and up the steps in a heartbeat. She ran across to the hedge and looked over, then ducked down and looked under, where it was thinner near the base, moving along the length of it. She straightened and spoke to someone out of Nic's line of sight, then she turned and walked slowly back to the house, her forehead creased.

"What did you see?" she asked as soon as she was inside.

Nic shook her head, trying to rid herself of the hallucination. "It must have been my mind. I thought I saw Colm. Sorry."

"Could it have been someone a bit like him?"

Nic shuddered. "No. He was even wearing the same clothes: the greasy hoodie and the jacket. Who were you speaking to?"

"Mr McGoran. Your next-door neighbour. He came out when he saw me snooping around, but he said he hadn't seen anyone just before that."

Goosebumps raised on Nic's arms, under the sleeves of her shirt. "I think I must be hallucinating, Asha. I'm sorry."

"He did say he'd been in the room that looked out at the garden, but he'd been bent down laying the fire, with his back to the window. I didn't want to worry him with the thought of intruders, but it's quite possible there could have been someone there. How easy is it to get in and out of his garden?"

"There's a path down the far side of the house. We were up and down it all the time when Cian was a kid, fetching his football back."

Asha nodded slowly. "I think we should probably tell Inspector Ram."

"No! Please don't. He'll think I've lost the plot, and he might not let me in on so much." She was pretty surprised he'd let her in on all the facts of the case he had so far. Nic had little experience of police investigations, and she wasn't exactly a huge fan of detective stories, apart from the odd episode of *Sherlock*, but it did seem odd that she was being allowed so close to the investigation.

"It's not usual, but I don't think the inspector is your run-of-the-mill detective. Besides, it saves money, having you spend so much time in the station. Otherwise, we'd have to have an officer with you all the time, and we're short-staffed enough as it is."

Especially now they had to have an officer with her family full-time as well.

Asha's mobile went off in her pocket. She fished it out and glanced at the screen before answering it. The expression on her face was almost comical. She mouthed something at Nic as she put it to her ear. "Yes, sir?"

Ram, it had to be. Was the man telepathic? She tried to meet Asha's eyes, silently pleading with her not to tell him.

"Yes, sir. I'm at the Gordons' place now. I'll ask her." She put her hand over the mic. "The inspector wants to know, would you be prepared to have a look at the body they found? To see if it was Colm — the man you knew as Colm."

"Okay." Nic swallowed. "I think." She really wanted to stay close to the investigation, so she'd do anything to help. Anything to keep herself in Inspector Ram's good books. She still didn't know how much he'd trust her after she'd tried to keep the brick phone to herself, so maybe this would go some way towards bringing her back into favour.

"She says she will, sir. Will we head down there now?"

As Nic lowered herself into the front seat of the non-descript Ford next to Asha, she couldn't help glancing at the next-door neighbours' front drive. Had there really been someone there? Someone who looked just like Colm? Or had the whole thing been her imagination?

Instead of the Lisburn Road Police Station, where Nic expected to go, Asha drove her to the Royal Victoria Hospital. She queued with everyone else to park in the multi-storey and eventually squeezed the car into a narrow space on the top floor.

"Why didn't you use police privilege, or whatever it's called, and park near the entrance?"

Asha grinned. "Tried that once. Got clamped. Never heard the end of it from the guys. It was all woman driver jokes for weeks."

"The casual sexism of the PSNI we hear about on the news?"

"Nah, just any chance to wind up a detective."

They walked past the cloud of smoke from pyjamaed patients with drip stands in tow, and along the covered walkway.

"This way," Asha said, pointing to a sign: *Mortuary.*

The hospital smell of surgical spirit and disinfectant creeped into her nasal passages, making her nose twitch. What would a mortuary smell like? Death? It was suddenly very real. If this was really Colm, would she even recognize him?

"In here." They were in front of a clean-looking red-brick building with a cream-coloured stripe just above door level. It looked modern, like a new office block. The only clue to a more macabre use was the vented tower, a bit like the tip of a church steeple, that seemed to grow out of the brick paving stones. The double entrance was made of smoked glass, for privacy, Nic supposed. Asha pressed an intercom button next to the inner door.

"Detective Sergeant Asha Harvey with Nicola Gordon to identify a body. I believe Inspector Ram was in touch with you earlier?"

The door buzzed open and they passed through. Nic tried to breathe through her mouth, but she couldn't help tasting the air. It seemed thick, heavy with the smell of corpses. They were met by a cheery, round-cheeked lad, his huge Afro barely restrained by a mesh hood.

"Hi there. We was expecting you earlier," he said in a strong London accent. "Get lost on the way?"

Asha didn't answer, so Nic said, "Queues for the car park were halfway around the hospital."

He grinned. "You didn't park in the VIP spot we keep special for the boys in blue, then?"

Asha flushed. "You mean the one I got clamped in last time?"

"Yeah, that'd be the one."

Nic couldn't help responding to him. "What's that accent doing this side of the water? I've only ever heard it on *EastEnders.*"

"Yeah. That'd be 'cos I'm from the East End, innit?" He dropped into a stronger accent, so thick she could barely follow him. "Followed the Prof over. Promised me a land of milk and honey, but what did I get?"

Nic shrugged.

"Same as everywhere else, 'cept there's not so many like me over here, and people speak funny. Name's Yussuf, by the way."

They followed him into a sterile lab with four tables lined up in the middle of the room, all stainless steel with a separate sink at one end of each table. A wall had a row of steel doors set into it with locking handles. Yussuf went through the room and into another room at the end. This was smaller, with just the one table. On the table, covered by a pale blue sheet, was a shapeless mound.

"You sure you're okay for this?" Asha asked.

Nic gripped the side-seams of her jeans to stop her hands from shaking. "I think so."

Yussuf moved to one end of the table and lifted a corner of the sheet. Before she could see anything, he lowered it again and looked pleadingly at Asha. "This isn't pretty. You sure about this?"

Nettled, Nic pulled the sleeve of her T-shirt up and held it out. The scars wound like angry serpents up her arm. "I know what to expect."

"Okay. Sorry." Yussuf lifted the sheet and folded it back.

This was the first corpse Nic had seen. It didn't look real, more like a waxwork. It couldn't have been Colm she'd seen earlier that day, because here he was, just as she remembered him, down to the straggly neck-beard. Then she leaned down and looked closer, finding it easier than she'd expected to ignore the gaping wounds that disfigured his decomposing face.

"It's not him!"

"Are you sure?" Asha said in a tight voice. "Look again."

"I could look as many times as you want, but it wouldn't change a thing," Nic said, hope giving her confidence. "He's very similar to Colm, but I'm sure it's not him."

"One more thing." Yussuf drew the sheet back a bit more, exposing a raw strip running across the shoulders and chest where the skin seemed to have been peeled away. "I found evidence of a tattoo, including this partial of a talon." He pointed to a splotch of green. "And maybe the hilt of a sword?"

Nic shook her head. "No, I'm sure I never saw anything like that." Relief flooded through her. "What colour are his eyes?" she asked.

Yussuf donned a pair of thin rubber gloves from the box by the sink and gently lifted one of the lids. The eyes were grey.

"See? Colm had brown eyes. It's not him."

CHAPTER 13

Research always pays off, he thought as he drove slowly past the Victorian terrace with the wrought-iron gate and crazy paving. Silhouetted against the half-glazed front door, a slim shape fumbled for her key, juggling a backpack and the bag of shopping she held in her arms.

Right on time. If she followed her usual routine, she'd put the shopping away in the kitchen then go upstairs for a shower to wash the smell of the lab off her skin. He shivered at the thought. There'd be silver scars twining their way up her slim arms by now, like climbing roses. He continued along the street until he found a parking space a good hundred yards or so past the house. From here, he could make his way down the alley at the back, where they left their wheelie bins. He'd researched this meticulously, so he'd be ready when the time was right to catch his little mouse again.

He took a knife to the gap between gate and fence, lifting the latch easily enough. People never learned. They'd be careful for a while, maybe a few weeks, then gradually they became more and more complacent. As time passed, and nothing bad happened, they'd convince themselves it was all over, and soon the precautions would disappear completely.

Not even a padlock. And now he'd managed to lure her father away, he'd have her to himself.

The back of the house was in darkness, but he wasn't worried. Mentally, he followed her through her routine. She'd be turning the corner at the bottom of the stairs about now. A light came on in a window about twelve feet from the ground: the half-landing on the stairs. He moved his gaze to a window on the top floor, just under the eaves. There. A second light came on, and a shadow loomed momentarily at the frosted glass as she lowered the blind for privacy.

Now was his moment. She'd take at least ten minutes in the shower, washing that glorious fall of black hair. Plenty of time for someone as agile as him. And thank the devil for Victorian external plumbing. The downpipe was strong and wide, with plenty of hand- and footholds. Heights had never bothered him.

The sound of running water brought him to a stop. The pipe vibrated as the shower drained just inches from his fingertips. That same water had caressed her skin before it chased in spirals down the plughole. His breathing quickened at the thought. Then his hand slipped: his palms were sweating, and he had to snatch at the sill of the bathroom window to keep his balance.

It was only with difficulty that he brought himself back under control, annoyed at having let himself slide for even a moment like that, but the anticipation for this one had been so long, and the build-up so wonderful, that it was getting harder and harder to restrain himself.

That's how people get caught, he reminded himself. *You can't let your guard down. Time to relax later, once you have her.*

The catch on the old-fashioned sash window gave in to the tip of his knife as he'd known it would. It had given easily the last time, when he'd done his dry run a few weeks earlier. The scentless soap he'd applied to the wooden frame enabled it to slide open soundlessly, and he slipped through the gap, leaving the window open, and avoided the creaking floorboard that had made him jump last time. There was a chimney breast that had once housed a fireplace in the bedroom, but now just jutted out into the room. It left a lovely shadowed alcove with plenty of room for a slim person to hide.

And beautifully timed. The shower shut off. She hummed to herself as she got dried: Ed Sheeran's 'Galway Girl', if he wasn't mistaken. Nice song, and almost apt too, just the wrong side of the border.

The bathroom door creaked open, letting out a pale bar of moonlight from the window spill out on to the patterned carpet, but she didn't switch on the light. Of course, she wouldn't, not with the window bare and open to the outside. Her bare feet padded along the varnished floorboards.

She made an impatient noise as she noticed the open window, and padded across to close it and draw the curtains, bringing her right past his hiding place. He took a deep breath and held it, then drew the wadded cotton from the zip-lock bag that had kept the chloroform fumes from evaporating. In one move, he wrapped one arm around her waist, pinning her left arm to her side, and used his other hand to cover her nose and mouth with the cotton.

They always took in a deep breath to scream, but she didn't. Instead, she brought her free hand up in a fist and punched him, hard, on the bridge of his nose. His eyes watered, and his vision blurred, but he managed to hold on to her, keeping the wad against her face.

She must have realized she couldn't get a good-enough angle to get an effective punch in, so she changed her approach. Nails gouged deep furrows across his hand and forearm and he almost gasped at the sweet shock of it, but held his breath. She didn't, though. Her chest expanded, pushing the wet towel against his restraining arm, and immediately she weakened.

He turned so he could see her eyes. Hatred burned there, but also fear. He smiled, lungs burning with the effort of holding his breath.

Her hand moved again, but there was no force in the attack this time, and a moment later her arm fell limply to her side. He took no chances, keeping the cloth over her face until she took another gasping breath. Her full body weight collapsed against him, and he lowered her down gently, cradling her bare shoulders.

There they were, the scars: snail trails in the faint light from the hallway. He replaced the wadded cotton in the bag and sealed it before standing up and stepping away to take a deep breath of clean air.

He wasn't finished yet, though. The drug wouldn't last long enough for what he needed, so he reached into his jacket pocket and withdrew the syringe, needle already attached, and the tiny bottle he'd filched from the hospital. Hand shaking slightly, he drew up a measured dose, and cleared the air from the barrel. He'd seen them do it so many times as he watched, invisible, from the sidelines.

The big thigh muscle was his target. He pulled the towel up to reveal her shapely leg, and the nest of dark hair at the top of it as she lay sprawled, unconscious. He licked his lips, forcing his mind back to the job in hand, and felt for the magic spot.

The needle went in smoothly, but the anaesthetic must already have been wearing off, because the woman kicked out and moaned, her eyes opening with a glazed look of incomprehension. *Too late*, he thought, and pressed the plunger.

It didn't act as quickly as he'd hoped. She waved her arms like a rag doll. One of them connected with the side of his head, and he reeled sideways, just catching himself before he toppled over. She was trying to push herself to her feet, and her lips worked, but she still wasn't awake enough to form words. Still, the moans were becoming louder, and there was a risk she'd be heard.

He clenched his fist and brought it around in a blow to the side of her jaw that snapped her head back on that slender neck. Her eyes crossed, glazed, and she collapsed back down in an untidy heap.

His breath rasped. His throat felt as raw as if he'd been half strangled. His fringe clung damply to his skin, and the hand that still clutched the syringe shook. This was no good. Everything had been going so well. He glanced at his wrist-watch. Still on time, despite the unexpected fight. He reached into the deep pocket of his jacket, the opposite side to the one that had held the drugs, and pulled out a wisp of soft silk, taking a moment to hold it to his nose. It smelled of her, still, after all this time. He laid the blouse down on the bed as though she'd put it there ready to wear after her shower.

The other item had sunk into a corner of the pocket, giving him a moment of panic, but then his fingers closed on the thin, scooped-out shape, and hauled it out. This he arranged above the neckline of the blouse as though she was planning to wear it around her neck.

The next bit was the tricky part. He couldn't risk being seen with a naked woman over his shoulder, but he'd thought ahead and brought a giant kit bag. The woman was tiny and slim, and the drug would keep her limp enough to pack into the bag. He left the zip open a few inches above her face for air, then hitched the straps over his shoulders, settling the bag against his chest so he could support her with his arms.

The stairs were a risk, as he hadn't had a chance last time to check for loose floorboards, but he trod the edges with care and made it down the two flights without making any noise.

From down the hall, a TV droned on with a news bulletin. He smiled, wondering if his actions in Ireland had made it as far as British television. If they hadn't, they soon would once the news of tonight's success leaked out.

He passed the closed door to the lounge, and entered the dark kitchen at the back of the house. The back door was locked, of course, but it was a Yale lock, designed to keep people out, not in. He closed it quietly behind him and the same with the gate, using his knife to ease the latch both times.

The four-wheel-drive truck he'd bought at the auction all those weeks ago was roomy in the back. He put the woman in, still secure in her bag, and scattered sports kit over the top for the look of it. A net bag of footballs in the back seat completed the picture of a sports coach travelling abroad to train a new team. He settled into the driver's seat and started the engine.

* * *

At Cairnryan, queuing for the 3.45 a.m. ferry, he was unsurprised when the police at the security checkpoint gave the car no more than a cursory glance. This was the time of night when the human body was at its lowest ebb, and the mind would take an easy route if it could.

Vastly daring, he wound his window down and smiled at the grumpy-looking Scotsman who was taking note of his registration number. "Cold night for the season," he said. "Want me to open up the back?"

The bloodshot eyes regarded him sourly over a knitted scarf. "Dinnae bother. I can see you're away to play football."

And as simply as that, he was through the dangerous part and into the queue for the boat. He'd stopped at a lay-by to check the woman and top up her dope juice. She was sleeping like a baby, breathing steadily. Good, strong young woman like that shouldn't have any problems with being sedated for so long, and if she did? Well, she wouldn't have to worry too much longer.

He grinned at himself in his rear-view mirror, then caught a glimpse of a dark shadow just to the right of his eye, where her fist had caught him earlier. He explored the area with fingertips. It was tender and a little swollen, the beginnings of a shiner. Bitch! She'd pay for that later.

CHAPTER 14

"You see what this means?" Nic said. "That could have been Colm I saw earlier!"

Asha looked troubled. "Are you sure? I'm not certain I'd remember someone's eye colour so clearly. I'm not even sure I could tell you Aaron's eye colour, and I've been working with him for years, on and off."

Nic smiled. "Greeny-brown. Yes, I'm sure. Colm had terrible acne on his chin too. I'd forgotten to mention that to the police artist, but some of his spots looked like Mount Vesuvius. I kept expecting them to erupt and spew pus everywhere."

"Ew. Thanks for that image. I get what you're saying. We'll just have to go and see Inspector Ram. Maybe he can shed some light on this. Thanks, Yussuf."

The technician draped the sheet back over the body, the still-unidentified body, with a surprisingly gentle touch for so brash a personality. Nic was moved to wonder who the poor soul was that had been killed. Another victim to add to the murderer's reckoning. What had he done with Colm's body?

On the way back to the car, Nic breathed in the outside air, relishing the exhaust fumes and dust as a welcome change from the stultifying atmosphere of the mortuary. She couldn't stop thinking about the dead man back there, wondering if he had any friends or family missing him. If he'd been on the streets a while, it might take weeks before they identified him. He could have come from anywhere.

"What about that tattoo? Can't you identify him from that?"

"We're working on it," Asha said, sounding distracted. "It's not as easy as it sounds, though. Do you have any idea how many tattoo parlours there are in Belfast alone? And we've no way of knowing if this fellow even came from here originally. Roughly twenty per cent of the homeless people on our streets are from somewhere other than Britain or Ireland. That makes it hard to trace them."

Asha was quiet on the way back to the police station, driving with her usual care, but as though her mind was elsewhere. After they'd parked up through the big gates, Asha brought Nic inside and asked the duty sergeant for a visitor's badge for her.

While they waited for it, the door buzzed open to let a postman in. He dropped a stack of mail on the desk, but kept hold of a parcel, wrapped in battered brown paper and tied up with string. The address was written in a large hand in felt-tip pen.

"Think this one might be a mistake," he said to the duty sergeant. "Unless you have a Chill-on-knee Yack-a-boo working here?"

The sergeant took it off him and weighed it in his hands. "No one here of that name. Maybe we should alert the bomb squad. What do you think, ma'am?"

Asha held her hand out for the parcel and examined it. "Feels like clothes to me. Something cloth, anyway." She read the address, and Nic craned in to see it too.

Schillone Yakabu was written in a neat hand on the paper. The rest of the address looked to be correct for the station in Lisburn Road. "What's the postmark?" They squinted at it. "Does that say $800?"

"There's a flag. Green and black," Asha murmured. Then her face cleared. "It's okay, Sergeant. I think I know who this belongs to. I'll take it up."

Asha led the way upstairs towards Ram's office, but before they got there, she turned aside and knocked on Sergeant Jacob's door. "I wondered if this might be for you, Sergeant. It's addressed to a Schillone Yakabu?"

The elderly officer raised her head, eyes narrowed. "Never heard of her. Hand it over."

Asha handed over the package, a little uncertain. Lonnie snatched it from her and ripped open the packaging. Yards of brightly coloured fabric tumbled out across the desk, patterns of yellow and green and bright red. Nic gasped at the beauty of the stuff.

"I thought you'd never heard of Schillone Yakabu," Asha said dryly.

"I was christened Schillone Yakabu," the sergeant said, "but never heard of any Chill-on-knee Yack-a-boo. Is there any wonder I changed my name?"

Asha laughed. "I'm with you there, Lonnie. My parents did all my anglicizing for me, before I was born. My dad's name was Devendra Hari and my mum's surname was Harvey, so they decided to simplify things and adopt her name for the rest of us." She turned to Nic. "Would you mind waiting in here for a bit? Sergeant Jacob will look after you, won't you, Sergeant?"

Lonnie's eyes crinkled in a smile.

"Yes, indeed. You can come in here and wait for a while."

Nic entered, careful not to tread on the fabric that now spilled across the floor, and looked around for somewhere to sit. Every surface was covered with piles of cardboard folders. She lifted some off a computer chair and balanced them on top of another precarious stack.

The old sergeant glanced at her over a pair of reading glasses, her eyes kind, as her hands worked to gather up the material and fold it into a small bundle.

"I'm sorry to hear about your sister. If anyone can get her back safe for you, it's that man from Leeds. If I were you, I'd put your trust in him."

Nic's guard began to melt away. She glanced at Asha, who nodded approval, then whisked down the corridor towards Ram's office.

Nic had been so buoyed up after realizing the body wasn't Colm, but then Asha's behaviour had thrown her completely. It was as if she'd taken a step back, distancing herself. The only reason Nic could think of was because the detective must think something might happen to Hazel.

She swallowed down the tears that burned behind her eyes, and picked up the stapler from the sergeant's desk, fiddling with it to give her hands something to do. "I'm sorry, Sergeant. Asha had me down at the mortuary to identify a body, but it wasn't Colm — the guy who was abducted with me."

"It wasn't? Who was it, then?"

She was typing now, seemingly intent on the task in hand. The steady rhythm of keys, and the old sergeant's calm voice, instilled confidence, as if nothing Nic said could shock her.

"Asha says they don't know yet. She says it might be hard to identify him if he was living on the streets for a while."

"And Asha's correct, but I think there's something else bothering you, am I right?"

The sergeant's eyes were kind, and looked as though they'd seen so many bad things over the years that nothing could move them to tears anymore. The room was barely bigger than a cupboard, this place where Sergeant Jacob worked her way towards a retirement that surely couldn't be far away. They were alone, and the door to the corridor was closed.

"I thought I saw Colm this morning. He was watching me over the neighbour's hedge in the back garden, but by the time Asha went up to look, he'd gone."

The sergeant nodded encouragement.

"At first, I thought I'd just imagined it, but when I realized the body in the mortuary wasn't him, I thought maybe, just maybe, he might have escaped. Maybe he was trying to

113

reach me. If he did, he'd be terrified of being caught again. I know I am, and I have virtually full-time police protection. He has no one."

"And did he look as you remembered him from before, or was he injured?"

The bottom fell out of Nic's world. How could she have been so stupid? "As he was. He looked exactly as I remembered him. No scars." She took a deep breath, letting all the tension seep out of her with it. "It must have been my subconscious. I really wanted him to have survived, Sergeant. I know he was a fraud, not what he pretended to be, but I liked him."

"There's no wonder, you know. After everything you've been through — everything you're still going through — it's bound to mess with your head. You just stay strong, honey."

A draught on the back of Nic's neck made her turn. Asha stood in the doorway.

"Do you want to come down and tell Inspector Ram your idea about contacting the kidnapper?"

Nic looked at the elderly sergeant.

"Go on," she said. "Trust him to get your sister back for you."

Ram was writing furiously when Nic went in, and he didn't look up, just inclined his head towards one of the chairs on her side of his desk. She took the hint and sat down, tugging her sleeves over the scars. Asha gave her a reassuring look and backed out of the room, closing the door behind her.

When Ram had finished, he put the biro down, and Nic noticed it was an expensive-looking Cross pen, at odds with his slightly shabby appearance.

"Do you have the phone with you?"

Nic pulled it out of her pocket, checking the screen before putting it down on Ram's desk. No new messages. Nothing since last night, not since she'd gone to the barn and been followed by the police.

"Did Asha tell you what we were discussing this morning?" Nic asked.

"She did. I think it's worth a try. In case you're wondering, we have tried to trace the phone that's been sending texts to this one. He's using a webmail to send them, unfortunately. Untraceable." He picked up the phone and turned it over in his hand. "We also tried to find out where this phone was bought from its International Mobile Equipment Identity, but it seems he picked it up second-hand at a Nutts Corner car boot sale. The seller, who we did manage to trace, doesn't remember who bought it, but it was last month, so our lad must have been thinking ahead even then."

"Before he took Colm and me?"

"He bought this on the fifteenth of April, and he didn't take you until the twenty-fifth. Ten days."

Ten days. Had he stalked her, to find out her habits? Or had she been a random choice? No. If she'd been random, why would he have risked taking Colm too? Maybe Colm had been the random choice, the unlucky bonus body. Stinging in the palms of her hands brought her back to herself. She'd been digging her fingernails in again, leaving the same little crescent-moons they always did. At least she hadn't drawn blood this time.

Ram handed the phone back to her. "What would you like to say?"

Nic unlocked it again and opened the last text, selecting reply. She bit her lip and then started typing, hardly even irritated by having to use the number keys to type letters.

I need to know Hazel is unharmed. Prove it to me, and I'll give myself up to you at a time and place of your choosing. No police, just us.

She turned the phone around and showed it to Ram. He read it with an impassive face. "And do you mean it? About no police?"

She swallowed. "I don't think he'll go for it any other way, and he always seems to know when you're involved, doesn't he?"

"You may be right. He certainly wants us to think that, anyway." Ram took a deep breath through his nose. "If you send that text, there will be no going back. You know that, don't you?"

Nic nodded. She hit the send button and waited for the reaction to hit. It didn't. If anything, she felt lighter, less burdened. She was doing something.

A knock at the door broke the tension that had been building in the room.

"Come," Ram said.

"Sir!" Aaron stuck his head around the door. His face lit up when he saw Nic. "Oh, hi, Nic."

"What is it?"

"Sorry, sir. We have a positive ID on the body in the morgue."

"We do? Did the girl ID him?"

Nic was confused for a moment, thinking he meant her, until she remembered the girl she'd seen Aaron escorting from the building yesterday, the one who'd given Jilly the description for the sketch.

"Yes, sir. She says there's no question it's him. She recognized the tattoo, and, er . . ." He glanced at Nic, surprising her by flushing. "And a few other, er, significant features unique enough to make her certain."

"Good. What name did she know him by?"

"That's the thing, sir. She says his name was Carol Albescu and he was Romanian, but when he got here he realized Carol was mostly a girl's name and adopted the name Colm White instead."

Nic couldn't process the words for a moment. She turned them over and over in her mind, trying to pull the meaning from them. Carol Albescu. Colm White. "But it isn't the same person. It can't be."

"What did you say Colm's surname was?" Ram asked gently.

"I didn't know his surname."

"How many Colms do you suppose there are in Belfast?" Ram probed. "A dozen? A hundred? How many of them are aged in their early twenties? With a straggly beard."

Nic shook her head helplessly. "I was so certain it wasn't him."

"But you agree this dead man's face is like Colm's — as far as you are able to tell, with the wounds and decomposition, that is? It is very unusual to meet someone who looks exactly like you, don't you think? And he has been tortured in the same way that you and Colm were tortured."

Nic nodded agreement.

"It's possible he hid the tattoo on purpose. Some people are wary of tattooed men, and he wanted to make friends."

"But his eye colour? I was certain about that!"

"Is it possible that Colm wore contact lenses?" Ram was shuffling through his notes. "He could have worn coloured lenses. I understand they're quite popular."

"I . . ." Nic's certainty had begun to evaporate. "I didn't really notice . . . it's not like I was staring into his eyes all the time. He did wear lenses, though. He sometimes complained about them making his eyes dry. That's how I knew he wore them."

"What about his accent? Did you notice anything odd about that?"

"He said very little, but he did have a slight accent, yes. He said it was a Cork accent, and I believed him. I don't really know what a Cork accent sounds like."

"I think that settles it, then. We might well have our missing person after all. Did the girl say if he had any family, Aaron?"

"No, sir. She said he'd come here on his own. Funnily enough, he did get here via the South, but I don't know if he was ever near Cork. I can ask her?"

"Leave it for now. It seems the unfortunate young man was just another random choice by our killer." Ram regarded Nic over his steepled fingers. "You cannot blame yourself, you know. It's possible you were both just random victims, picked because you were sitting so close to the back door of Limelight, and because you were both alone. I understand the club was packed that night. No one noticed

117

either of you being moved, which was a piece of luck in the kidnapper's favour, and there's no CCTV there, or wasn't on the night."

"The camera in the back hall was out of order. Someone had stuck chewing gum over the lens," Aaron added. "Whoever did it stayed out of sight, so all we got was a blurred, out-of-focus bit of hand. No distinguishing marks. It was done around the time we think he took the pair of you, so it was probably him, but he left no evidence behind, and the club owners removed the gum and chucked it before we got there. Before they knew it could be important."

If it had been a spur-of-the-moment act on the night, did that make her feel better or worse? It was Colm who'd selected that particular table, so at least she didn't have that on her conscience.

"If I'm a random victim, why is he so determined to finish the job? How did he know where to wait for Hazel, the one place on her route where he could safely hide?"

The question had reared up from nowhere, but she realized it had been nagging away at her since Hazel disappeared.

"He's proved before that he is not only good at researching his subjects quickly, but he's also a master of the snatched opportunity." Ram glanced down at the phone, lying silently on his desk. "That's why I think he'll probably take your bait. As to why he wants to finish you off? That I don't know." He took a deep breath that seemed to come from his soul. "I just know he doesn't like to leave unfinished business."

He must mean his daughter. But she had survived, hadn't she?

"Aaron, will you please drive Miss Gordon home? Then you can leave her."

"Sir?" Aaron's brow creased. "What's going on?"

Ram raised his eyebrows, suddenly looking less like a tired man in a worn suit, and more like a senior detective who didn't like his authority being challenged. Aaron coughed and backed down.

"Okay, okay. You ready, Nic?"

Nic slid the brick phone into her back pocket, certain it weighed less than the last time. A thought struck her. "Are you still monitoring this phone?"

Ram smiled. "Yes, we are, but he will know that, and expect it. I'm certain he will find another way to get in touch with you. Good luck, Miss Gordon."

Aaron was silent as they walked the corridors. At the head of the stairs, he stopped. "Wait here a moment, will you? I'll be right back."

He walked briskly back the way they'd come, then turned right into an office. The buzz of voices from inside rose in volume, and then fell again as the door closed behind him. Nic leaned back against the wall and closed her eyes, trying not to think about what lay ahead. The sounds of the busy police station washed over her, and the smell of coffee insinuated itself into her attention. Bad machine coffee, but it still made her stomach churn with anxiety.

Somewhere nearby, two men were chatting with the occasional clink of metal against ceramic as one of them stirred their coffee.

"Who is this Paki inspector then, anyway?"

"Ram, he's called. 'Cept Kernaghan calls him Pram. I'm going to come out with it in front of him, one of these days, I'll bet you!"

"Don't let Harvey hear you. They're thick as thieves, those two."

"Feckin' takeover's what it is. Before you know it, the whole PSNI will be Paki or black, and you and me'll be out on our ears. Surplus to requirements. Faces don't fit."

The other man laughed nervously. "I don't know about that. Lonnie's all right, isn't she?"

"Tip of the iceberg, mate. You mark my words."

Down the corridor, a door opened. Asha stormed out.

"Here, shut the fuck up! It's her."

Asha cast a furious glare at Nic as she shot past her. "Wait there. Don't move a muscle!" And then she marched off down the corridor towards Ram's office. His door slammed, and a few minutes later the sound of raised voices drifted down to her. Voice. Unmistakeably Asha's voice, and she wasn't speaking English, either. Her voice climbed and sank through octaves like a complex piece of music.

One of the coffee-drinkers, a skinny man with thinning red hair cropped close to his skull, stuck his head out from the door to Nic's right. "It's all right. She's gone. That was a close one, though."

As he turned to go back inside, he caught sight of Nic where she leaned against the wall. "Hello there," he said in an overfriendly tone. "Fancy a coffee? We've a pot made in here, and there's biscuits."

Nic shook her head, wondering how someone could be so racist in one breath and then think it was okay to chat up a stranger in the next. Her stomach clenched in revulsion, but before she could think of a suitable reply, a young constable appeared at the other end of the corridor with a sheaf of paperwork clutched to his chest. He stopped at Ram's door and raised his hand to knock, then seemed to think better of it and returned the way he'd come.

"Bit of a barney going on there, I'd say," the friendly racist said. He came all the way out and leaned one shoulder against the wall next to Nic, closer than necessary, so his face was inches from hers. "They can be a bit like that, those Pakis, you know? Never used to be like it in the old days. RUC had no time for them. Too excitable, I reckon."

Nic was saved from having to say anything she might regret by Aaron. He'd walked softly up behind the other man and stood there quietly. Nic's eyes must have darted towards him over the uniformed constable's shoulder, because the other man straightened up and stepped away. When he saw who was behind him, his face twisted into a scornful smile.

Aaron turned to Nic. "Want some fresh air? There's a bad smell around here."

"Oi! Say that to my face, dickhead."

Aaron turned slowly and looked the other man in the eye. "Constable Aiken, the DCI was asking me if I knew where you were just now, so maybe there's someplace else you should be?"

Aiken's face twisted in hatred, but he backed down. He looked at his watch. "Oh, is that the time? I really must be going." He spoke woodenly, through a set jaw. "You coming, Bill?"

The other uniformed copper appeared, the pair of them turning away and walking down the corridor without a glance at Aaron and Nic. Once they were out of earshot, she sagged.

"That was awful! I didn't think that sort of stuff went on anywhere these days. How do they get away with it?"

"It's never really gone away in the force, and it won't while time-servers like those two are still around." He looked tense, more upset now they'd gone than he had while he was facing off against Aiken. "I'll have to report him, of course."

"Does Asha know? Or the inspector?"

"I expect Inspector Ram's got his own ways of dealing with racism. I hear it's even worse in his neck of the woods. Asha?" His lips tightened. "Despite all that bluster, the truth is the bastards are too wary of her to say anything to her face. She's a tough cookie."

"Yes, but she shouldn't have to put up with that. I thought physics was bad with the sort of casual sexism that goes on all the time, but this is truly awful."

"Hmm." Aaron seemed preoccupied with the situation in Ram's office. Nic followed his gaze and looked back towards the office, where Asha had finally fallen silent. "Asha wasn't happy about Inspector Ram's plan."

Nic swallowed, following his lead. "I don't know why. She knew about it beforehand, because we cooked it up together this morning. Anyway, it was more my plan than the inspector's."

"That's not the way she sees it. I don't think she intended you to be staked out as bait, without police backup, like the proverbial sacrificial goat." Aaron was still looking over her head at the entrance to Ram's office.

"I can't see how it could work any other way. He's too wary to fall into a trap, I think." Nic had already come to terms with her own fate. It was as if she'd been living on borrowed time since that night in Limelight, and soon she'd have to face the consequences. If she could limit the damage to just herself, then any sacrifice would be worth it.

She thought of Hazel in the killer's hands. *Please don't let him hurt her. She's been hurt too much already, and she's only seventeen.*

Although Asha's voice had gone quiet, still the door didn't open.

"We'd better make a start," Aaron said.

"She told me not to move from here."

He sighed. "Not that I'm scared of her, you understand, but perhaps we'd better wait for a bit."

The hands on Nic's watch moved around the face until they'd been standing there for more than thirty minutes. "Something's wrong."

Aaron didn't disagree. "Wait here."

Nic rolled her eyes. "No. I'm coming."

His mouth twisted. "God save me from bossy women. Come on, then."

There was no sound from beyond Ram's door. Aaron and Nic exchanged a look, then Nic rapped sharply on the grey-painted wood.

"Come." Ram's voice sounded hoarse, as though he had a bad cold.

The inspector was sitting at his desk, but his whole body language spoke of defeat. Asha had her hip on the corner of the desk, and an arm around his shoulder. Her face was as tortured as Ram's and if Nic hadn't known how tough the detective sergeant was, she might even have thought she had been crying.

CHAPTER 15

Nic froze just inside the door, Aaron a step in front of her. After all the shouting, this was the last thing she'd expected to see.

Ram had a phone in his hand. He seemed to notice it for the first time, and placed it on the desk as if it were as fragile as eggshell.

"What's happened, sir?" Aaron asked. "Ash?"

"The first victim of our kidnapper, the one who escaped? He's just taken her from her home in Leeds. Snatched her without anyone being aware."

"How could he have done that? He was here in Northern Ireland last night, at the shed where we found Hazel's scarf. He couldn't have got all the way over there in that time, could he?"

Aaron started tapping away on his iPhone. "He might have been able to, if he'd planned for it. And we already know he's good at planning."

"How would he travel? Ferry would be too slow, wouldn't it, unless he went to Scotland, and then it's, what, a five-hour drive to Leeds?" Asha pulled Ram's keyboard and mouse across to her and turned the monitor. "I'll do ferries if you do flights, Aaron."

"Ferry's out," Aaron muttered. "But there are a couple of flights he could have taken to Leeds Bradford Airport and then driven from there. What time was she taken?"

"Between five and five thirty today. Her flatmate spoke to her when she got back from work just before five, then she went upstairs for a shower and didn't come down. By the time he went looking for her, she was gone."

"Are we sure it's our man?" Aaron asked. "Maybe she just up and left. People do, sometimes."

"It's him," Ram said heavily. "He left a calling card."

Nic's head shot up. "What did he leave?"

Ram brought his eyes up to meet hers. His were bloodshot and puffy. "He left the blouse she'd been wearing the day he took her the first time, and he left something else too." He took the mouse from Asha and clicked on a minimized file icon at the bottom of the screen. A picture appeared of a pale pink, silky blouse with delicate embroidery on the collar. He clicked the right arrow and Nic gasped.

"That's mine!" It was the necklace she'd been wearing in Limelight, and there was no mistaking it because she'd made it herself from seashells she'd picked up on the beach in Strandhill when her family had holidayed in Sligo years ago. It was unique, right down to the swirly bit of secretion on the queen scallop she'd used as a centrepiece.

"He's pretty determined to tie the two cases together, isn't he, sir?" Aaron said thoughtfully.

"This is definitely personal for him, I think," Asha said, casting a worried look at her boss.

"I'm going for a walk and to make a phone call," Ram said. He stood and shrugged himself into his suit jacket. "Use my office for as long as you need, and try to work out how the hell he got there from here in time. Once we know how he travelled, we might have a chance of identifying him."

He closed the door behind him, leaving a stunned silence.

"What's with him?" Aaron said.

"Meera Patel, the victim, is his daughter," Asha said. She didn't wait for Aaron to respond. "Now let's get on with this before any more harm comes to that poor wee lassie. We've got to find this bastard."

"Okay. What time do we reckon he was at the shed last night?"

"Well, Nic got there at quarter past three in the morning or thereabouts, and he was away by then, but the blood wasn't clotted, so he can't have been gone long — assuming he's working alone, that is. It was cold that night, and that was a lot of blood, but it still can't have been more than a few minutes, surely?"

"I'll ask Jana," Aaron said. "Say an hour from there to the City Airport, that takes us to around four fifteen. I'll check flights from then onwards."

"He must have got the ferry," Asha said. "He'd be worried about being picked up by the security cameras in the airport, surely?"

"Too tight for time."

"He could easily have caught the seven thirty from Belfast to Cairnryan with time to spare. That gets him in at, let's see, just before ten in the morning. If he grabbed the woman at five, that gives him seven hours to drive there, find her and work out how to grab her. It's doable."

"You could be right about the security, but the first flight out to Leeds Bradford is also seven thirty in the morning. Loads of time to catch that. Land at eight thirty and a short drive to Leeds. He'd probably hire a car. Should be able to find records for that. It gives him all day to track Meera Patel down and form a plan."

Nic listened to the exchange, becoming more and more bewildered. "Guys?"

"Check with the car hire companies. Ask for a list of men in the age group who hired a car that day that ties in with the times of flights landing from Belfast. Some of them will dig their heels in and quote data protection at you. Just do what you can. If need be, we'll apply for a warrant."

"Guys!"

They both looked up, surprised, as if they'd forgotten she was there.

"How will you recognize him? As far as I know, there are only three people alive who've actually seen him, and two of them are in his hands right now. I'd struggle to recognize him if I met him in that corridor out there. I've only seen his eyes."

"We can't," Asha said in a small voice, "but we've got to do something to try to work out how he got from here to there. That's how it works. Lots of slog, tracking down leads, however faint and unpromising. Sometimes we get lucky and someone has noticed something unusual, some behaviour that makes them suspicious."

Nic's stomach contracted sharply. "But what about Hazel?"

"We haven't forgotten her," Aaron said quietly. "You'd probably feel better if you could do something to help."

Nic clenched her fists. It was all moving too fast, and in the wrong direction.

"I do understand that there's another life at stake here, and I feel terrible for the inspector but as long as your attention is focused on Leeds, Hazel could be lying somewhere bleeding to death." Nic's voice broke and she turned it into a cough that probably fooled no one. "I'm guessing I'm not allowed to phone car hire companies, but maybe I could do a search for abandoned properties within a twenty-mile radius of Lisburn? He has to be holding her somewhere secure enough that he knows he can leave her there for a day or two without anyone stumbling over her. I could use Google satellite—"

Asha took a deep breath. "That's a great idea. Why don't you go down to Sergeant Jacob's office? Do you have your laptop in there?"

Nic nodded and patted the bag at her side. "And my iPad."

"Good. She can log you into the Wi-Fi. Tell her I sent you."

Nic nodded. "Okay. Let me know if you turn anything up, would you?"

Aaron smiled. "You'll be the first to know. Now, scoot."

"Nic?" Asha said when she was halfway out of the door.

"Yes?" She kept her back turned.

"Start the search with a five-mile radius first, then work your way outwards."

Nic closed the door behind her and leaned back against it. No one was even looking for Hazel. Was this how it had been when she was missing? All the time she'd been tied up in that cottage, her wounds burning and the only sound Colm's laboured breathing and groans, she'd kept on telling herself that they'd find her. That they'd be searching everywhere for her, and that, somehow, they'd work out what had happened. Any time soon, the torture would end, and they'd be released. It was the thing that had kept her going. Only at the very end, when her tormentor took up the boning knife and tested its edge, did it dawn on her that she wasn't getting out of there unless she got herself out.

Was that how Hazel was feeling right now?

No. Hazel didn't have the same reserves as Nic. Every day was a challenge for her: going out of the house alone; facing strangers, especially men. What had happened to Hazel three years ago had scarred her, but she'd survived it, with Nic and Ma at her side. She'd appeared in court, given her evidence, and the old man's family had hugged her and forgiven her — but they didn't have to listen to her screaming in the night.

Nic hadn't even noticed the burning behind her eyes until a tear trickled into the corner of her mouth, seeping between her lips with a salty persistence, forcing itself on her notice.

"Now, now. What's all this?" Lonnie's rich voice made Nic think of a warm fire on a cold day.

She opened her eyes, her vision blurred until she blinked. They were alone in the corridor. "Sorry, Sergeant. Just taking a wee moment there."

"Why don't you come down to my office. It's more private than anywhere else around here, and you can tell me what's got you so upset."

Nic took a deep, shuddering breath. "That's actually where I was heading. Asha sent me to ask you to help me log my iPad on to the Wi-Fi so I can search for possible places he might be holding Hazel."

Lonnie's eyes almost disappeared into her wrinkles. "That's one sensible young woman, that Asha. You come with me, and we'll see if we can't find out something to help your sister, huh?"

The office was warmer than it had been earlier, a heater in the corner blowing hot air into the small space. Normally, Nic would have felt claustrophobic in such an atmosphere, but now the warmth wrapped around her like a blanket, taking away the chill that her dark thoughts had left behind.

Sergeant Jacob lifted a new pile of files off the second office chair and plonked them on to another pile on top of a filing cabinet. The whole lot began to slide, and Nic made a lunge for it. She just managed to catch the edge with her fingertips and pushed it back until it felt a little more balanced.

Oblivious, Lonnie was dusting the chair off with her sleeve. "Here you go. Let's have that iPad, then you can do whatever you need."

Nic sat down, catching her balance by grabbing the edge of the desk as the chair rocked sideways. On closer inspection, she found it had a castor missing.

Lonnie tapped away at the iPad for a minute or two, then handed it back. "I've logged you on as a guest with limited access. You should be able to browse the internet okay."

Nic loaded Google Maps, changed the view to satellite and began scanning all the rural areas on the outskirts of Belfast. It took very little time before she realized how frustrating an exercise it was going to be. Not all areas had clear images online yet, and those that did were at least twenty-five per cent trees, and anything could be hiding under those. She tried looking for the cottage where she'd been held, but it wasn't even visible on the satellite view, hidden under a canopy of green.

That made her wonder how her abductor had found it in the first place, especially since it seemed he wasn't even from these parts. She frowned, opened a new tab and searched for one of the big property advertising websites. She put in the name of the lane she'd come out on after she escaped and hit search.

Nothing useful. A big house with stables for sale, a barn for development, which made her heart race until she opened the advert and found a photo of it: barely four walls, and no roof. It was also right on the side of a main road, in full view of passing traffic.

She widened her search, but found nothing, then she noticed that the site did rented properties as well. She clicked on rented and put in the same search terms. Nothing but agricultural land suitable for grazing. She was about to click away from that when some stubborn instinct made her scroll down. There wasn't much information about the next listing, except for acreage, but then a word caught her eye. *Field shelter*. She went back up to the photographs and clicked through them. There it was: a small, ruined barn that someone had stuck a tin roof on. No door, just a gaping hole where the front wall had partly fallen down. It wasn't her cottage, but it did give her an idea.

She'd been searching for buildings only and land with planning permission, but here was a building as part of a field. She went back to properties for sale, changed her search terms, and found it almost immediately. Twenty acres of rough grazing with woodland, and there was the cottage. If she'd found it like this, the killer could have too. And if he'd found one like this, he might have found others too.

She looked for the barn next, where they'd found Hazel's scarf. It came up under agricultural lettings. The advert was an old one, dating back a couple of years.

Nic sat back, and immediately regretted it as the chair lurched sideways. She banged her elbow against the desk. *Shit*. Lonnie looked up at her over a pair of half-moon glasses that balanced on the end of her nose, her eyes as bright.

"Found something?"

"I think I know how he found the places where he kept me and Colm, and the place where he set the trap. It might be a link to where he's holding Hazel."

"Good work. Keep looking."

Nic swallowed, suddenly nervous. Surely someone else would have done all this, wouldn't they? How could she, a physics student, find something the police had missed? But wouldn't Asha have told her if they'd made these connections? And she'd seen how busy the place was. Maybe someone like her, with time on her hands and the incentive of a missing sister, *could* actually help.

Lonnie was still watching her. "If I've learned one thing in all my years of policing, it's to follow your instincts. Trust your own judgement."

Nic clicked back to the search page. "He won't have chosen anywhere close to these properties, because it's too obvious. But he also needed to be able to get from wherever Hazel is to this shed to plant the blood and the scarf. Then he needs to have been able to get either to the airport or to the ferry in time to get to Leeds to abduct Meera."

A sharp breath from the other side of the desk made her look up.

"He's taken Meera Patel again?"

"Yes. I thought you'd have heard. That's why the inspector has gone for a walk, I guess. He probably wanted to phone his family in private."

Sergeant Jacob took her glasses off and rubbed her eyes. "That poor family. They didn't deserve that."

No, they didn't. All the more reason to find where he was keeping Hazel. Perhaps he'd bring Meera Patel to the same place.

Where could he be? Surely he'd have to be on the Lisburn side of Belfast, to the west and south? That would fit in with him being able to get to the empty shed to leave the scarf: it was about fifteen miles south of Belfast, but only about ten miles south of Lisburn.

She went back to the satellite photos. There was so much open country. She immediately discarded all the areas north of Lisburn as being too far on the wrong side of the city for him to reach the shed to leave the scarf and still make it to the ferry on time. It just wouldn't fit the proposed time frame. The likeliest area was to the west, or south-west. She started her search, identifying promising areas on the map and then searching for them on the property website.

Soon, she had covered two sides of A4 with lists of potential sites, and her vision was beginning to blur.

She looked up as the door opened and Asha's face peered round it. The corridor beyond was quiet compared to earlier on, eerily so. What time was it? "Any news?"

"Sort of. Jana's just sent up her preliminary report about the site in the shed from last night. The blood had an anticoagulant added to it, which widens our time frame a little. He could have been away from there a couple of hours before you arrived."

"Maybe you should go home and try to get a bit of rest," Lonnie suggested. "And I'm talking to both of you, here."

Asha gave a tired smile. "You're right. I hadn't realized how late it had got. Want a lift home, Nic?"

"Yes, please. But isn't it out of your way?"

"Depends where you're going. Lisburn or Stranmillis?"

It hadn't occurred to her that she could go back to the student house. Her laptop was at home in Lisburn, though, and her kidnapper had broken into her room in Belfast. Would she ever feel safe there again?

"If it helps, I live out towards Lisburn," Asha said.

"Then yes, please. I want to go home." And she really did. As soon as she said the words, a wave of homesickness washed over her, slightly tinged by guilt at the way she'd left her parents and Cian to face the day without her.

"Come on then." Asha glanced at Sergeant Jacob. "What about you, Sergeant? Don't you have a home to go to?"

"One of the few benefits of age is that the need for sleep reduces. I rarely leave here before midnight. Want to leave

131

that list with me, Nic? I can work my way through it for a couple of hours and see if I can narrow it down a bit."

Nic held it tight to her chest. She'd been going to continue working on it at home.

"I can take a photocopy, if you like?"

"That'd be great. Thank you."

Sergeant Jacob slid the single sheet into a scanner on her desk. It whirred and beeped. She repeated for the other side, then handed it back to Nic while the printer churned out copies. "There. Off you go, and don't spend the whole night working on it. You'll be more use to Hazel if you're rested and thinking straight."

CHAPTER 16

Nice idea, but sleep eluded Nic. By the time Asha had dropped her home, and she'd gone through the usual inquisition from Ma about where she'd been and who she'd been with, her eyes were almost closing of their own volition. Asha had given her a sympathetic smile, but abandoned her all the same.

The bed that had welcomed her into its soft folds the previous night was too soft now, claustrophobic in its clinging embrace. She threw off the thick quilt, letting the air get to her skin, then her scars began to itch.

She resisted the urge to scratch, but it kept her wide awake, the effort almost too much to bear. To distract herself, she ran over all the places she'd listed as possibilities for Hazel's prison. The main contenders were an old warehouse out on the Moira Road and an abandoned barn by the side of the motorway. She wondered if Lonnie would come to the same conclusions, and that brought her thoughts around to Inspector Ram.

He'd aged that day. What must it have been like, to have lost his daughter not once, but twice? Was that how Ma and Dad felt? Now he'd taken Hazel, she was beginning to get an inkling of what her family must have experienced when she'd gone missing. How Ram must be feeling. A tear trickled down her cheek.

At some point in the night she must have slept, because she woke to the vibration of the brick phone on her bedside table. Disoriented, it took her a moment to focus on the LED display of her old-fashioned clock radio. Three thirty. She patted the table, looking for the heavy little rectangle of plastic, but only succeeded in knocking it to the ground. *Fuck*.

She fumbled for the light switch and blinked, dazzled by the low-power bulb in her bedside lamp. The phone, of course, had bounced. She couldn't see it until she got all the way out of bed and dropped to her knees. It was right under the bed. By then, she was wide awake, but with a thumping headache and a dry mouth.

She slipped back under the covers, skin pebbled by the early morning chill in her room. It was a new text.

Too late for that. Last time U told the cops. Shame.

She sat up in bed, cheeks burning. No! *No!* She hadn't told them — they'd followed her. Her fingers groped for the buttons to send a reply, but her hand shook too much. She put the phone down and made herself take deep breaths until the panic subsided a little.

On the second attempt, she managed to type. *I didn't tell them. They followed me. No police now. I just want my sister back safe.*

She hit send, but continued to grip the phone like a lifeline until her fingers tingled with pins and needles. The screen went dark and remained that way. She checked the little battery symbol, worried it had run out of charge, but it showed almost full. That was the only good thing about these old phones, and lucky because she had no charger for it.

Sleep was a lost cause by now, so Nic slid her feet into the slippers by her bed and threw her dressing gown on before going down to the kitchen for a glass of water. The phone stayed clutched in her hand.

As she filled a glass from the tap, her eyes rested unseeing on the window. The glass overflowed, spilling icy water over her fingers. She blinked, and snapped to attention. There was something outside, in the dark garden. Something white standing over by the fence.

The glass slipped through her fingers and she only just caught it before it shattered on the stainless-steel draining board. There was water everywhere, but she was already running, fumbling with the door into the sunroom, across the cold tiles and out of the French doors. There, she stopped dead. It was the size and shape of a person, of Hazel, but it was a shop mannequin, naked, with its hands secured behind it with zip-ties.

Her breath came back as a sob. Suddenly she realized she was outside the house, wearing nothing but a thin dressing gown, and Colm's murderer had been here in the last few hours. Might still be here, watching her. She backed up through the door, and locked it again, but she couldn't keep her eyes off the figure, with its grotesque wig and painted smile.

Nothing moved outside. She backed away from the glass door, almost expecting it to explode. All the fine hairs on her arms were raised and the cold of the tiles was stealing warmth from her through the soles of her slippers.

What should she do? Her gut instinct was to phone Asha, but maybe that's what he expected her to do. Maybe this was another test and he was watching her from out there in the garden. Her eyes went to the hedge where she'd thought she'd seen Colm yesterday. Nothing, and now the sky was beginning to pale towards dawn.

Nic mentally shook herself and went back into the kitchen to clear up. By the time she'd wiped up the spilled water, the sun was almost up. She looked out at the shape in the garden. She couldn't leave it there for Ma to find, but where could she put it? And should she move it or leave it for the police?

Her tired brain struggled with the conflict. The police might find a clue on the mannequin — fingerprints or DNA, or something — but her attacker had been so careful every time, it seemed unlikely he'd trip up now. Alternatively, if she showed him that she had stepped away from the police, would he come for her and release Hazel?

Common sense said she should phone Asha and let the police take over, but her gut told her to play the game out. She'd made the first move, he'd responded by telling her the deal was off, but that was on the phone he must know the police had seen and were probably monitoring. Then he'd left this, a message aimed directly at Nic.

She made up her mind. The kitchen clock told her it was approaching half past four. Plenty of time before anyone would be up and about. She padded back to her room and got dressed in dark jeans and a hoodie. She carried her trainers and backpack in one hand and the mobile in the other. Once she was in the sunroom again, she made a show of putting the brick phone down on the table in full view and putting on her backpack, before she unlocked the door and went outside.

The mannequin was even more disturbing in the unforgiving light of early morning. The wig was pale ginger, cut in a short bob to mimic Hazel's style, but what she hadn't seen the first time was a network of lines drawn on the arms and back. She rubbed at one with an experimental finger and it left a greasy smear. Yes, lipstick. Neither she nor Hazel wore lipstick, so he must have bought it somewhere. Maybe it could be traced.

She pushed the thought aside. Her path was chosen, and there was no going back now, only forwards.

The figure was surprisingly light to lift, but unwieldy to carry. She hauled it down the path beside the garage and out into the silent cul-de-sac, praying there'd be no one about at this hour. Where to hide it? It had to be somewhere the police wouldn't think to look. The longer she could keep it hidden, the more of a head start she'd have. And if he was watching, he'd see her trying her best to hide the evidence, and know she was serious about no police.

The city was almost silent, unusual in itself as the buzz of traffic was an almost continuous background noise wherever you stood in Lisburn.

She thought she knew just the hiding place. It was close to the Antrim Road, where she was most at risk of being spotted, but it was still so early there was no sign of any traffic. A derelict Victorian house stood back from the road, steel mesh fence across the gateway to prevent the local kids from using it as a drinking den. Everyone knew there was a gap in the hedge where a determined person could force their way through.

She hauled the mannequin through after her, taking the wig off first so it didn't get caught on the thorns. The house was no good — too many teenagers probably lying doped to the eyeballs in there — but there was a garage around the back, and it had an inspection pit in the floor, well hidden. The only reason Nic knew about it was because the old couple who used to own this house had been friends of her granny's, and she'd visited here as a child. There was a trick to lifting the heavy covering, and she knew it.

It wasn't easy to manage the trapdoor with one hand and force the figure through with the other, and she was sweating profusely by the time she'd lowered it back down again. She bent down with hands on her knees to catch her breath, then started to move all the junk back on top of it. When she'd finished, she brushed her hands off against each other as though she was brushing off the mannequin and all it stood for.

Nic felt lighter as she squeezed back through the hedge, checking it was clear both ways before setting off up the Antrim Road, heading north, until she came to the petrol station at the far edge of town. It was almost full daylight by now, and there were cars on the road. She looked up the timetable at the bus stop. The first bus was due just before seven. According to her watch it wasn't even half past five yet. *Shit.* She pulled her hood up, shrugged the backpack to a more comfortable position, and set off walking.

Something about the crisp spring air filling her lungs, and the regular beat of her trainers against the tarmac, helped her concentrate. She went over the events since that night in Limelight, trying to see each stage from her opponent's perspective.

There were several things that didn't add up.

First, why did he take *two* people from the club, and not just either her or Colm? The likeliest scenario was that he'd intended just one, probably her, since her drink had been spiked with GHB. What if Colm had seen her being abducted and tried to help her? Would the kidnapper have knocked him out, and then been forced to bring Colm along too, since he'd probably seen his face?

She wished she could ask Yussuf if the body they'd found had shown any sign of being knocked out.

And that was the second point. She was certain that the body in the morgue wasn't the Colm she'd been getting to know. And what if she *had* seen him peering over the hedge? Was she beginning to lose her mind? She shelved that thought for now, not yet ready to deal with where it might lead her.

Third, why had he broken into her room in Belfast? If he could gain access to her house that easily, and if he was so dead set on abducting her a second time, why didn't he break in when she was there, maybe asleep in bed, and take her that way?

Her busy thoughts had taken her the whole way to the Knockmore Road. The first of the buildings on her short-list wasn't far out of town, out towards Ballinderry, so she decided to keep walking. Less likely to be remembered as a pedestrian than as a passenger on a bus, where she'd have to speak to the driver as she bought her ticket. Besides, it was still nearly half an hour before the first bus would pass her, and she needed to get as far as she could.

By the time the first bus rumbled by, belching diesel fumes, she'd reached the Ballinderry Road junction and was wishing she'd taken the time to eat something before she left home as her empty belly growled. She'd walked past a supermarket back there on the Knockmore Road, but it wasn't worth the risk of being seen. She stuck her chin up and kept moving out into the countryside.

The first building on her list was a barn with a corrugated roof in the middle of a field. On Google, it had looked isolated, but it was handy enough to let the kidnapper get to either the airport or the ferry, and to the shed where he'd left Hazel's scarf.

She missed it at first, but she soon realized she'd walked too far and retraced her steps. A slimy wooden gate, half collapsed and covered in ivy, was the only way into the field. Nic eyed it dubiously. He couldn't have got in this way without leaving some sign, but perhaps he'd approached from another direction. She'd come this far. She had to investigate.

The gate creaked as she climbed it, and it left green smears on her jeans. She dropped down into long grass and nettles, keeping her hands high to avoid being stung. There was no sign anyone had been this way, but she pushed through anyway until she reached the edge of the field. The grass here was long too. Nothing grazing here yet, but the ground was rough under foot as though cattle or horses had been here last summer.

The barn was more overgrown than the gate when she got to it. The door was just a gaping black hole in the side, and the roof had half collapsed since the Google image had been taken. One glance was enough for Nic to cross it off her list. She sighed. It had taken her hours to get here on foot, and this was the closest on her shortlist.

What had seemed feasible earlier this morning, in her own home, was beginning to look like a fool's errand now.

She made her way back to the road, checking to make sure there was no one to see her emerging from the undergrowth. The only witness was a young fox, which emerged from the hedge on the opposite side of the road and froze, staring at her as Nic froze and stared back. The rank scent of wild animal drifted across on the breeze, perhaps the last thing a small prey animal would be aware of as jaws closed over it, but the fox was no threat to Nic.

The next site was four miles away. Nic had left her iPhone at home, on her bedside table, in case it could be tracked. Now she regretted it, because she wasn't sure she remembered the route from here to the empty warehouse near the prison at Maghaberry. In fact, the more she thought about it, the less likely the warehouse seemed. It was too close to the prison, so surely the approaches would be under surveillance from cameras. Not ideal for someone who wanted to keep his presence hidden. Still, it was the closest one to her and all the others would require her to get a bus or hitch a lift.

Traffic was increasing now. A family passed her, a shiny German car filled with children in school uniform. A boy of about ten years old stuck his tongue out at her as the silver monster purred by, sending up a spray of gravel that stung her legs. She clenched her fists, and fought down the tears that threatened. Why was she even here, in the middle of nowhere? Why hadn't she just called Asha as soon as she saw the mannequin?

Another car approached, a big, old crew cab truck, of the type that farmers often used. It was battered and scraped, so dirty it was hard to be certain what colour the paint might be. She might not have given it a second look, but the truck slowed as it passed her, and she had the impression that the driver was staring at her.

The hairs on her arms all stood up as her skin goose-pimpled. She tried to read the rear number plate through the road dirt that obscured it. *PEZ* was all she could decipher, but the numbers that followed were totally obscured by mud. The truck disappeared around a bend and she plodded on.

The village of Maghaberry came into view, with its speed limit sign dented where someone had loosed off a shotgun from close range. A wee shop stood on the left-hand side of the road, and by some miracle it was open. Nic hesitated, looking longingly at the brightly coloured advertisements for the latest special offers in biscuits and fizzy drinks.

Her belly growled at her. She crossed over with firm steps. What were the chances of someone recognizing her this far out of town? Virtually zero. She tugged her hood closer around her face and pushed the door open. The smell of hot food carried to her on a breath of warm air from the back of the little shop. They did hot food!

The shop door closed behind her with a final clang of the bell. Nic jumped and almost left there and then. This was a trap. She'd walked herself into a dead end with only one way out, and now she found it impossible to walk away from the door.

Over to her right, the lad on the till tapped at his phone, grinning to himself. He had his back to her, and hadn't turned even when the doorbell jangled. He wasn't even vaguely interested in her.

Gathering her courage, she made her way to the display unit that held sausage rolls, ham-and-cheese crowns, sausages, and a pastry plait with a hot dog sausage in it. So much choice. A pile of foil-lined bags and a pair of tongs sat on the hot unit.

Nic dug a hand into her jeans pocket and shuffled the change in there. She had about five or six pounds, enough to buy a couple of items and a bottle of water. She used the tongs to load a sausage roll and a ham-and-cheese crown.

The teenager was still on his phone, and there was no one else but her in the shop. She pushed the bags of food and a bottle of water towards him. He glanced inside the bags, and tapped away on the till, without so much as a look at her face.

"£4.80."

She handed over the correct change and scooped up her purchases without speaking. He was already immersed in Facebook again, and didn't seem to notice as she left the shop. Once back outside, she took a deep breath. Her shoulders relaxed.

She couldn't bring herself to eat her food there, in full view of anyone who might pass, but the lane she needed to take wasn't that far out of the village, so she stuck the food bags in the pouch in the front of her hoodie, where it would stay warm, and tucked the water in the backpack. Knowing she had food and a drink lightened her steps, and in no time, she was off the main road and down a quiet lane. In the distance, traffic hummed along the main airport road, but here was peace and quiet.

Nic found a concrete fire hydrant marker to sit on, and opened up the first of her packages. Flavour burst out of the ham-and-cheese crown, filling her senses. She tried to make herself eat slowly. Not slowly enough. She licked the last few bits of flaky pastry off her fingers and thumb, then used a damp finger to dab at the ones that had fallen on her clothes, making sure she didn't miss any.

Once she'd satisfied the worst of her hunger, she went back to her steady pace, sipping at the water bottle as she walked. The hot food hadn't just filled an empty belly, but had lifted her spirits, too.

The warehouse was about half a mile ahead, and she was covering the ground swiftly, but the sound of a slamming car door brought her up short. The hedge here was tall and thick, and the sound had come from the other side of it. There weren't any houses or other buildings around. That had been one thing in favour of the warehouse as a potential hiding place.

She moved on quietly, grateful for the soft-soled trainers that made no sound on the grass verge. There was a steel gate up ahead. She moved up to it and peered around the gatepost cautiously. At first, it just looked like another field, but when she leaned forward a little more, she could see there was a faint double track, as of car tyres, across the grass towards some trees about a hundred yards away. Nothing else.

She bit her bottom lip, puzzled. Why would anyone drive across a field here? On closer examination, the gate had a shiny, new steel padlock on it, but the lock sat open. Inviting.

An engine roared to life and Nic pressed herself back into the hedge, out of sight. The engine grew louder, an irregular rumble as the vehicle bounced across the uneven surface of the field. For some reason, the approaching vehicle filled Nic with panic. Her skin broke out in sweat and her heart raced as though she'd just been running. The only hiding place she could think of was the last gateway she'd passed, a good couple of hundred yards back the way she'd come.

She ran as though the hounds of hell were after her, backpack bouncing on her shoulders. The lane here was straight for about half a mile, so there wasn't even a bend to hide her. There was the gate, another steel one, but no padlock this time, and the engine had settled to a low hum as the vehicle stopped at the other gate. Nic didn't dare look back, but ran on, throwing herself at the catch on the gate.

It was stiff, the bolt rusty, refusing to move however hard she hauled on it, throwing her full weight at it. The further gate let out a metallic squeal as someone opened it, and she was still in full view.

The car door slammed again, as the driver got back in to move the thing out on to the lane. Nic half leaped, half climbed over the gate and collapsed on the other side in thick grass. She scooted backwards on heels and hands until she was wedged against the base of the hedge, her backpack protecting her from the thorns that poked into her arms.

She straightened her legs, hoping the long grass would conceal her pale jeans and trainers. The engine was humming again as the driver got out to close the gate after him.

Probably some innocent farmer, checking his stock, she thought, but she couldn't convince herself. Her instincts were screaming at her to stay hidden. There was danger nearby: she felt it in the prickle of her skin, in the icy chill that made her hairs rise up and the nausea that roiled her stomach, threatening to make her spew up the food she'd eaten so recently.

The door slammed again, and the vehicle moved off. She closed her eyes tight, as though if she couldn't see, she wouldn't be seen either. Like an ostrich, she thought. Only after the engine had died away and the sense of danger faded did she curse herself as a coward. At the very least, she should have tried to sneak a look at the car and driver. What if it had been Hazel's kidnapper? She could surely have seen without being seen?

But the thought of even trying brought back the nausea.

CHAPTER 17

The sound of the engine faded into the distance, changing gear and accelerating away. Nic shivered, still afraid to move.

Irrational, she told herself, but it didn't help. Eventually, the trembling subsided and her breathing rate returned to normal. She took a sip from her water bottle, and remembered the sausage roll in the front pouch of her hoodie. It was probably squashed after her wild scramble over the gate, but at least it was food.

She fished out the sorry-looking package. Most of the pastry had flaked away, and the sausage meat was flattened where it had been caught between her and the steel bars, but there was still some warmth in it, and that was just what she needed right now. She wolfed it down.

The food gave her back some of her strength and she got carefully to her feet, keeping close to the hedge. The bolt on the gate opened easily from this side, now she was no longer in a panic. It was the sort that rotated to lock the bar in place, and all she needed to do was twist it to free the mechanism. She'd been too blinded by fear to notice the first time.

The tarmacked lane was quiet. No birds sang from the hedgerow. Nothing fluttered from branch to branch. Nic walked the short distance back to the other gate with all her senses on full alert, listening for an engine. She'd left her gate unbolted to make it easy in case she had to run again, but the further she got from it, the more afraid she became.

Wise up, she told herself. *The only danger here is the one in your head.* But the shiny, new padlock and chain on the gate still set her skin pebbling as she touched the cold metal. No opening this one: she'd just have to climb the gate.

Hinge end, she remembered. *Puts less strain on the gate.* Where had she picked up that little bit of country lore? She climbed the gate easily enough and dropped down on to the crushed grass where big, fat tyres had just rolled it flat a few minutes before. If she walked on its tracks, there'd be no sign of her passing.

The trail led over the low hill and down to a copse of trees in a little hidden hollow in the field. The trees would be dense enough to hide a good-sized vehicle, especially if it was already dirty, she thought, remembering the truck that had passed her earlier. The tracks wound around the back of the trees, and she followed them into the shade.

That's where she found it. Another cottage she'd never have spotted on the satellite images, because it was completely overgrown by a mixture of conifers and sycamore trees, ivy and brambles creeping up the walls and across the roof, to break up its outline, so even this close it wasn't obvious.

Nic forced herself closer. It was too similar to the place he'd held her. Even the dank moss softening her footfalls was familiar, and the smell of damp leaf mould and wild garlic. Still, she'd come this far. She had to know now. Had to.

Another padlock secured the wooden door. The clinging brambles grew too thick and high at the back to allow her access that way. She could probably batter down the door — it looked old and rotten enough — but then he'd know for sure that someone had been there. If Hazel wasn't being kept here, it might mean she'd lost her chance. But Hazel *could* be here. She had to find a way to look inside.

A single window stared out at her like a sightless eye, but the brambles were thick under it too. A fallen branch suggested one way in, and she freed it with difficulty from the dying grass and nettles that held it pinned to the ground, getting her hands stung for her pains.

She used the branch as a stick to shove the brambles back out of the way, and gingerly pushed herself into the gap between them and the damp stone wall until she could see in through the window. It took her a few seconds to see through the dust and dirt on the glass into the dark interior, but gradually her eyes adjusted to the dark and shapes formed from the shadows. An old-fashioned bed without a mattress, its springs partially dislodged and poking up in rusted peaks. A dresser with a crocheted doily covering the stained top. Then she saw the ring in the wall, and the little pile of plaster dust below it where someone had recently drilled to secure it.

A ring to secure someone using zip-ties. She whirled backwards in a dizzying swoop to the terrible pins and needles in her hands where the ties had cut off her circulation. It had been awful that day, when she'd woken from the drugged stupor and found herself naked and cold, her arms wrenched behind her back. Then he had come and the cutting had started, and she'd realized how slight her discomforts had been before.

She backed away, forgetting the brambles and paying the price as thorns embedded themselves in her thighs, through the thick denim of her jeans. The pain helped to steady her, to bring her back to the present. The scene in the cottage was blazed on the back of her eyes in every detail. There was no blood, not yet, so it still hadn't happened, and she could still stop it from happening.

She forced herself to take another long look. Only one ring that she could see, but there could be another on the front wall, where she'd not be able to see it. No cabinet? She craned her neck, and saw it. He hadn't fixed it to the wall yet. It was lying on the ground near the corner of the room, locked shut, but she knew what it contained.

Her instincts had been right. That had been Colm's murderer she'd heard. Now she needed to get safely away from here, to warn Asha and bring the full might of the law down on him.

But how? She'd left her mobile phone at home. Both phones. She had no way of contacting the police, or anyone else for that matter. *Fool of a girl, with your grand gestures to make a point.* As if her adversary cared.

A sound sent cold shards of terror lancing through her. It was an engine, approaching along the main road.

Nic pulled herself free of the tangled undergrowth. Despite the thick ground cover, there was no hiding place she could see where she wouldn't be obvious to a searching eye. And if she tried to force her way around the back of the building, she'd leave a trail as obvious as neon lights.

Frozen in indecision, she would have been caught like a rabbit in the headlights if it had been Hazel's kidnapper, but it wasn't. The engine note rose and growled past, fading into the distance. It was a wake-up call, though. If she didn't get out of there fast, she'd be a sitting duck.

A quick glance around showed her that she'd left no sign of her presence, except a damp patch of overturned leaves where she'd wrenched up the branch. She flung the branch away into the trees and stamped down the disturbed patch, scattering a few leaves over it. Even with close scrutiny, it would just look as though an animal had been scratching around there for seeds and nuts.

She followed her own steps back to the gate, horribly exposed as she crossed the open field and climbed the gate. All the way, she was wracking her brain to think how she could contact the police. She was the only one who knew where he was planning to take Hazel, and probably Meera too. She needed to get the information out.

The car he'd used had driven back the way Nic had walked, so presumably that was the way he would return. She turned in the opposite direction and hurried on down the lane, all thought of turning back towards the village forgotten. There must be somewhere down here, a farm or cottage, that would have a phone?

All the time, she strained her ears for the sound of an engine, and her shoulder blades itched as if eyes bored into her back, but every time she turned to look, the lane stretched as empty as ever behind her.

Nic tried to bring to mind the map of this area, but all she could remember was the abandoned warehouse and the prison. She couldn't remember seeing any farms or houses out here at all, and sure enough, the place was deserted. The lane had narrowed, and the centre of the road was starting to green, as though grass was trying to grow up where car tyres didn't touch it.

In the distance, the constant hum of cars on the main road sounded temptingly close, but to reach it, she'd have had to retrace her steps, and that meant running the risk of coming face to face with her tormentor.

The sun climbed high in the sky, and still Nic was alone on the road. No cars had come near enough to make her take cover, although she made a mental note of every gateway and potential hole in the hedges as she passed them. The constant hypervigilance began to take its toll. Her strength ebbed as she sucked the last drop of moisture from her water bottle, wishing she'd bought two while she was at it.

The sound of fast-moving cars was becoming louder. She wondered if there was another main road somewhere ahead of her, one she'd forgotten. She'd taken a couple of turns off the original lane by now, enough to confuse her sense of direction. Only the position of the sun, roughly south-east, gave her any idea which way she was heading.

Her legs were getting heavier with every stride, thighs burning and feet aching from the walking. She glanced at her watch. Nearly one in the afternoon. That meant she'd been walking, almost without rest, for more than eight hours now. Two greasy pastries and a small bottle of water weren't enough to sustain her.

Nic wanted to just sit down on the grass verge and put her head in her hands for a good cry, but she wouldn't let herself. One foot in front of the other. *Just keep going.* She shivered. That's what she'd repeated to herself on the night when she escaped from her tormentor. She had no illusions about what would happen to her if he caught her now, so close to his hideout.

Just as on that terrible night, she staggered out on to a main road and was spun around by the wind from a passing lorry. Once again, like a repetitive nightmare, air brakes squealed and gravel peppered her skin. She sank down, knees shaking, and pushed herself to the edge of the road. Thistles in the long grass prickled her hands, but she was safe. It was the Moira Road: she recognized the petrol station up ahead to her left. She must have gone under or over the railway without even noticing in her exhaustion.

One last push. There'd be a phone at the petrol station.

Then her instincts clamoured for attention again. There was a truck in the forecourt of the petrol station. It looked a lot like the one she'd seen hours ago near Maghaberry, the one whose driver had stared at her as she walked away from Lisburn. It was just a coincidence, she told herself. The driver must be getting something to eat, because the truck wasn't parked at the pumps but over to one side. Maybe she should just wait till he left, in case he remembered seeing her earlier. Nic pushed herself back on to her feet and creeped to the opposite hedge, taking cover in its thick, straggly growth. She watched, waiting for the driver to reappear.

There was nothing to suggest this was the same vehicle she'd heard at the ruined cottage in the field, but still she couldn't make herself leave her fragile shelter until the truck had moved off.

The driver straightened up from behind the truck, but he was too far away for her to see his face. He must have been putting air in his tyres. She imagined she could hear the door slam and then the engine roar as the battered crew cab truck pulled out into the traffic, heading the opposite direction from her, back towards Lisburn. She caught a glimpse of the dirty rear number plate as it took off: *PEZ*.

Only when it was completely out of sight on the long, straight road did she risk breaking cover. She dodged traffic and hobbled the short distance to the garage on feet that felt like raw meat inside her trainers. The short rest had only hammered home all her aches and pains.

"Do you have a phone I can use?" she asked the kindly woman on the tills. "It's an emergency."

The woman's eyes narrowed as they raked up and down Nic's body. She must look a fright, with bits of thistle and hedgerow material in her hair and dirt staining her clothes.

"Yes, love. Back here." She pointed to a door marked private. "Dylan! Take the till for a minute, will you?"

She punched a code to open the door and held it open for Nic to pass through into a small, dark office with a desk, an ancient computer and a couple of filing cabinets. On the desk was a phone that would surely be worth something to a collector of retro artefacts.

"Just dial nine for an outside line, love. I'm afraid I have to stay here though. Boss wouldn't be happy if I left a stranger alone in his office."

"That's fine," Nic mumbled, dropping her backpack to the floor and stretching her tired shoulders. "I'm phoning the police about a crime."

The woman's face hardened, then crumpled. "Oh, love. I knew I recognized you. You're that girl off of the news, aren't you? I saw the scars, and I thought, 'That's her, Gertie.' Anything I can do to help?"

Nic shook her head, glad of the kindness in Gertie's voice. "Maybe just make sure no one knows I'm here, until the police arrive?"

Gertie nodded enthusiastically. "That I can do. Don't you worry. I'll guard that door like a . . . like a guard."

That made Nic smile. "Thank you."

A dining chair sat behind the desk. Its wooden seat was hard and cold against Nic's thighs. She tapped her fingers on the worn Formica desk top, undecided. She'd prefer to phone Asha directly, but she didn't know her number — it

150

was stored on her iPhone, the iPhone she'd deliberately left behind her in Lisburn. What was that number they were always on about on the radio? The police non-emergency number. 911. No, that was America. 101, that was it.

She picked up the heavy receiver, hindered a little by the coiled wire that had become fankled and refused to untwist. Then she spun the dial around for each number, waiting impatiently for the circular display to return to its place each time.

A polite, but slightly bored-sounding female voice answered after the second ring.

"Police 101. How can I help you?"

"I'd like to speak to Detective Sergeant Asha Harvey, please, or Detective Inspector Ram, who's based at the Lisburn Road Police Station."

"What is the nature of your enquiry?" the voice asked.

"I'm Nicola Gordon, and I need to tell Sergeant Harvey something very important about an ongoing enquiry." Nic had thought long and hard about admitting to who she was, but on balance she reckoned the name might get her put through where an anonymous caller would just be fobbed off.

There was a moment of consternation at the other end of the call. Other voices chipping in in the background. "Could you repeat that name, please?"

Nic rubbed her aching temple with her free hand. "Yes, sure. Detective Sergeant Harvey or Inspector Ram."

"Please could you repeat *your* name, Miss—?" No humour, nor even a trace of human feeling.

"Nicola Gordon," she enunciated clearly. "*The* Nicola Gordon, whose sister is missing," she added. This was taking too long.

There was silence at the other end, the silence of a mute button pressed rather than that of a hand over the receiver. Nic imagined a wave of excitement passing through the station. She'd known, when she left the note for Ma, that her escapade would cause chaos.

Then a new voice came on the line. Male, confident, clearly expecting to be obeyed. "Stay right where you are, young lady, and we will have a patrol car with you shortly. Do you have any idea of the worry you've caused?"

They must have traced her call from the phone number almost immediately. Nic was impressed despite herself, but this man's arrogance made the skin of her face tighten in anger. "You're wasting time. Put me through to Sergeant Harvey or Inspector Ram now, please."

"As soon as the patrol car gets there—"

Outside the small office, brakes squealed and car doors slammed. Gertie slipped out, her eyes flint hard.

Always get their name, Dad had once advised her. If someone in customer service or whatever is giving you hassle, get their name, their position and ask to speak to their manager. Always freaks 'em out.

"Who am I speaking to? I'd like your name and rank, please." Her voice shook a little, but she hoped he wouldn't notice over the crackly phone line. "And then you can put me through to a senior officer."

Voices were raised outside, Gertie's shrill Ballymena shout cutting through the flimsy walls. "You can't go in there! That's private."

A male voice rumbled in reply, and Nic froze. He couldn't have come back already. Had he seen her after all, hiding in the hedge as he drove off? The phone fell from her numb fingers and clattered on to the desk. On the other end of the line, the annoying male voice made a loud complaint.

Nic stood, her eyes flashing around the room, looking for a weapon. Not now, not when she knew where he was taking Hazel. What had seemed like a fair exchange in the dark of night, her life for Hazel's, was revealed in the cold light of day as a stupid plan. Immature, and born of desperation. Why would he release Hazel when he could hold both of them?

There was a long wooden pole with a metal hook on the end, the sort that might be used to pull a blind down. She hefted it in her hand. The iron tip made it heavy, and it was long enough to get a fair swing in. The door lock buzzed

— someone must have keyed in the code. Had Gertie been overpowered, forced to let him in? The door burst open and Asha stepped into the room.

Nic's heart gave a leap in her chest. She ran and closed the distance, flinging her arms around Asha's waist. After a slight hesitation, the detective sergeant enclosed her in a hug, and Nic couldn't tell whose tears were soaking her hoodie. They stood there like that, trembling with relief, until Aaron cleared his throat.

"Hate to break this up, you two, but one of you needs to explain to the boss what's going on."

"Aaron!" Nic pulled out of the hug. "How did you get here so fast?"

"Friends of yours?" Gertie asked, still sounding a little out of puff.

"Yes," Nic said. "Thanks for looking out for me, Gertie."

Gertie smiled. "Well, all's good then. I'll leave you to your 'debriefing'." She winked and went back to the front of the store, leaving the three of them alone in the small office.

"How did you get here so quickly?" Nic asked, saying the first thing that came into her head to cover the emotions she thought must be written plainly on her face.

Aaron did the talking. "Your picture's been on every news bulletin all day. No one was certain if you'd gone under your own steam or if he'd abducted you again." He bent down and lifted the weighted pole she'd dropped when she saw Asha. "What were you planning to do with this? Joust with the killer?"

Asha punched him gently on the arm. "Don't. It was a good idea, and by the look on Nic's face when we blattered through that door, he'd have had a fight on his hands." Her face settled into its customary serious expression. "We were worried about you, Nic. *I* was worried."

"But I left a note. Didn't Ma tell you?"

"Yes, but she said it was so unlike you to be that irresponsible that she thought you must have been under duress."

153

Nic felt as if she'd been punched in the gut. Of all people, she'd expected Ma to understand.

"A lad called in," Asha said in a hoarse voice. "Worked in a shop where you bought food."

Nic shook her head, confused. "He didn't even look up when I was in there."

Asha smiled. "Maybe not that you saw, but he noticed you, all right. He phoned 101 not long after you'd left, but by the time we got out there, you'd disappeared again. We've been cruising the lanes hunting for you ever since."

"Then when we picked up the call to send a patrol car to this location, Asha burned rubber." Aaron grinned. "And here we are. Your friendly dragon out there didn't want to let us in, but a warrant card can be quite persuasive."

Nic eyed Asha's tailored silk shirt and Aaron's polo and jeans over scruffy trainers. "I can't understand how she wouldn't spot you as police officers straight away."

"It's a mystery." Asha smiled. "Now, what was that important information you needed to tell me or the inspector?"

CHAPTER 18

While Nic filled Asha in on the important parts of her story, downplaying the crippling fear, Aaron disappeared out to the car to radio for reinforcements. Asha wrote down all the details she could get Nic to recall, then used her tablet to retrace Nic's steps as well as they could from the shop in Maghaberry to the abandoned cottage.

"I reckon it must be somewhere close to here," Nic said, pointing to a spot on the satellite view. "But there are so many fields with copses of trees around this area I can't be sure. I hadn't gone too far along this lane before I found the gate, and that was a couple of hours ago, at least. It's bound to be closer to Maghaberry than to this place."

Asha pressed her finger to the screen to call up coordinates, which she scribbled on her notepad.

Aaron came in. "They're on their way. Any success pinpointing the place?"

"Yes. Send them this." Asha tore the page out of her notebook and handed it to him. "Tell them we'll meet them there."

To Nic's relief, Aaron refused to go close to the cottage until they had some backup. They didn't have long to wait until a dark-coloured van pulled up behind the Golf. "Cavalry's here," he said, looking in the mirror. "Let's' go."

The gate was exactly as she'd left it, with the shiny padlock closed. One of the armed squad was out of the van in a moment with huge wire cutters. The long arms made short work of the chain and he ran the gate open so the van could race through, cutting across the flattened grass.

"We wait here," Asha said uncompromisingly. "We'd only get in their way, and they know their job without us telling them what to do."

The waiting was terrible. Nic's fingers tapped a drumbeat on her thigh until she consciously stilled them.

"Can you hear anything?" Asha asked.

Aaron put the front windows down a couple of inches. Somewhere high in the sky, a bird sang a trilling melody, light and carefree, but there was no other sound, not even the van's engine.

One of the squad appeared at the front of the car, and Nic jumped. He'd materialized from nowhere without a noise. He put his face down to the passenger window.

"Place has been cleaned. We're waiting for CSI, then you can go in and have a look around. Someone's definitely been here, though." He glanced at Nic in the back seat. "I'll let you draw your own conclusions, ma'am."

"Thank you," Asha said.

CSI, Nic thought. That'd mean Jana again. She hadn't had the chance to thank the woman for her kindness the other night at the shed, so she was glad of the opportunity. But when CSI did turn up, it was Marley, the grumpy man who'd been with Jana the first time they met.

"I hope this is important," he said to Aaron as he walked past the car window with his box of tricks. "You've dragged me away from *D&D*, and I was Dungeon Master too."

He stomped off into the field, leaving two out of three of the car's occupants looking poleaxed. Nic bit her lip to stop herself from smiling. "*Dungeons and Dragons*," she explained.

Both the detectives turned around in their seats and stared at her.

"Was that supposed to clarify things?" Asha asked at the same time as Aaron said, "Dungeons. Of course. Why doesn't that surprise me?"

Marley was gone for ages. Nic spent so long staring at the hedgerow that she could have painted every twig and branch from memory. An old bird's nest sat tilted at an impossible angle, and primroses bloomed in the long grass of the bank beneath the hedge, their innocent pale petals a contrast with the frustration that was building inside her. What was taking so long?

Eventually, the same armed officer reappeared. "All clear, ma'am. You can come over now."

Nic erupted from the back seat, only to stop short. Her thigh muscles cramped up at the sudden movement and she had to grab the car door for balance. Her feet felt as though they'd swollen to twice their normal size inside her trainers too.

"You okay?" Asha asked.

"I'll be fine. Just seized up from sitting still too long." The cramp eased as she walked stiffly behind Aaron up the track. Nic was ultra-aware of Asha's presence, her warmth.

By now, after all the traffic across the field, a wide swathe of grass was flattened down, making it clear which way they needed to go. Even the undergrowth around the cottage was well trampled.

Marley, packing away his gear, gave them a sour look. "Same as usual. Not a hint of a fingerprint or DNA left behind, as far as I can tell. This guy's a real pain."

Nic followed Asha inside. The place where she'd seen the ring in the wall was in the tiny room to the left of the front door. There was nothing there now but bare wall, not even the pile of plaster dust. She pointed to the place, afraid to speak in case her voice broke.

Aaron kneeled down and peered at the wall from close up.

"Yeah," Marley said. "There'd been something in the wall there, maybe a screw. It's been filled, but the filler was still soft so I recorded it, then dug it out and took a cast of the hole. There's another one over there." He indicated the wall under the window.

Nic found her voice. "Was there a box here?" She walked over to the corner, where she'd seen the cabinet. "It was lying against the wall as though he planned to come back and hang it on the wall, like it was . . ." She tailed off.

"It's okay, Nic," Asha said. "Want to come outside?"

The fresh air helped, even though it was still under the trees. "Sorry, Asha. Just had a bit of a moment in there. I'm okay now."

"I understand."

She took a deep breath. "So, where do we go from here? Why did he clear out? I was certain he was just getting this place set up ready to bring Hazel here, and maybe Meera too, if she—"

"If she's still alive," Asha finished for her. "Inspector Ram has been taken off the case, but I doubt if that'll keep him away. I'm pretty sure his colleagues in Leeds will feed him information whenever he asks for it." She shrugged. "Can't say I blame him."

"But why would the kidnapper abandon this place? How could he know we'd found it?"

"Are you sure he didn't see you?"

"I suppose I can't be certain, but if he'd seen me, wouldn't he have just picked me up? Especially if he had this place all ready-made."

"Who knows? Maybe his instincts are as strong as yours." Asha touched her hand. "Didn't you say you were terrified as soon as you heard his engine? Something must have warned you. Something familiar. Think, Nic."

She shook her head, frustrated. "I don't know. I've been doing nothing but think about it, about why I sensed danger so strongly, and I can't work out why."

"Could you have heard that truck engine before some- where?" Asha coaxed. "Maybe when he held you and Colm?"

A spark of inspiration flared — and faded out again. Nic's shoulders sagged. "No. There was no sound apart from wildlife, and the awful scraping of that door every time he opened it."

"Well, at least you're still safe. We should be thankful."

I am, Nic thought, *but what about Hazel and Meera?*

"Back to the drawing board, huh?" Aaron said. "Let's go to the station and touch base with Inspector Ram, shall we? Unless he's flown back to Leeds."

They came out of the woods into the late afternoon sunshine. There were more cars at the gate, and a small crowd of men and women, some with long-lens cameras and a TV camera. Nic stopped dead.

"Oh shit. Aaron, get rid of them, please," Asha said, pulling Nic back into the shadows. A wave of excitement stirred the group at the gate and they shifted around, jostling for position as shutters whirred and clicked. A uniformed officer at the gate protested feebly, and was ignored.

Aaron cracked his knuckles and gave a grim smile. "My pleasure." He strode over to the press. Nic was too far away to hear what he said, but the tone of his voice was firm and uncompromising. The press argued, someone shoved a microphone in his face and a short scuffle ensued.

"What's he saying?"

"He's probably promising them a press conference later. If it's with me, I'll kill him myself."

The reporters dispersed reluctantly and with backward glances while Aaron stood watching, arms folded uncompromisingly in front of him. At last, the gate was clear and they walked over to join him.

"What did you say to get them to go away so tamely?" Asha asked. "If you've committed me to a press conference, your days are numbered. Just saying."

Aaron put a hurt expression on his face. "I can't believe you'd think I'd do that to you. Aren't you my partner? My friend?"

"You did, didn't you?"

He looked shifty. "Not exactly. I told them you would give them a quotable statement later."

"A quotable statement. How does that differ from a press conference, exactly?"

"I thought you'd be happy," he said, and winked at Nic. "Hard to please, our Ash."

Only as she climbed back into the car did Nic remember the mannequin in her back garden. Her heart thumped painfully. She'd well and truly blown her chances of convincing Hazel's kidnapper she was free of the police. It was bound to be on the news that she'd been picked up, and that another of his hideouts had been found.

"Guys—"

Aaron had just started the engine, but at the tone of her voice, he took one look at her in the mirror and switched it off again.

Asha turned around in her seat. "What aren't you telling us?"

Nic swallowed. "There was a reason I left this morning."

"I thought there must be," Asha said, so quietly Nic wasn't certain she'd heard correctly.

Nic took a deep breath. "He'd left something for me, in the garden." She went on to describe the mannequin, and the way she'd disposed of it. "I don't know what I was thinking. Sorry."

The truth was that in the wee small hours of the morning, grieving for Hazel and her family, the thought of giving herself up to her tormentor in exchange for her sister had seemed like a good idea, but now she'd remembered the bowel-watering fear she felt when the man was nearby, she knew how insane her plan had been. There was only one way to get Hazel back, and that was to work with Asha and the police.

Asha was on the radio, giving directions where to find the mannequin. Nic wondered if it would be Jana, or Marley, or someone she hadn't met yet who'd be doing the work on the plastic model. Not that she expected there to be any fingerprints to find. He was always so careful, and besides, she'd probably destroyed any evidence as she lugged the damned thing along the road earlier.

When she'd finished, she turned and tossed a phone back to Nic. "Phone your mum. There's a family liaison officer with them, but she'll need to hear your voice."

It was Nic's own iPhone. Its familiar weight in her hand gave her the strength she needed to make the call.

"Ma? It's me. I'm okay."

Her mother's sobs sent a stab of guilt through her, but there was joy amid the tears. She had to speak to Dad and even Cian, and by the time she'd finished, the car was turning on to the motorway, speeding towards Belfast.

The constant hum of the engine lulled Nic, and the heat, rather than making her claustrophobic as it had last time, brought security and warmth. She let her head loll against the cool window glass and closed her eyes.

She woke, disoriented, when the engine stopped. Her neck was stiff, she had pins and needles in her left arm and there was drool running down her chin. She sat up and wiped it with her sleeve, hoping no one had noticed. They were back inside the secure compound of the Lisburn Road Police Station, surrounded by marked and unmarked police cars.

Asha turned around. "Hi there, sleepyhead. Sure you're up to this? Maybe we should have driven you home?"

"No, I'm fine." And she was. The sleep had refreshed her mind and relaxed her body. She stretched as much as the limited space in the back seat allowed. "Did they find the mannequin?"

"Exactly where you said it would be, but no prints apart from yours, and no other evidence. The lipstick was a cheap one, available in every supermarket and cut-price retail outlet."

Nic nodded, unsurprised. She hoped she hadn't put the investigation in jeopardy with her rash actions.

CHAPTER 19

Seeing Nic in the lane had been a shock. When he'd left the present for her in her garden, he'd thought she'd surely tell the police and then they'd keep her locked up safe with her family. But instead she'd hidden it and gone out walking the streets. It was reckless, unpredictable. He hated misjudging people.

He continued on his way, teeth grinding in annoyance. The sooner he put a stop to that bitch the better. He accelerated, putting more distance between him and the trudging figure in his rear-view mirror, but his mind stayed back there with Nic. She wasn't behaving as she should. She'd barely been let out of the hospital, and she was away to the cottage with the police, poking around. At least that meant she'd have seen his message. Always better to see the threat first-hand.

And so he'd tried to scare her by breaking into her room, but she'd kept her head then too. Taking the sister might have been a mistake. She was so boring.

The field gate came into view. No one around, not down this obscure lane. It wasn't on the way to anywhere, and the only vehicles to use it seemed to be tractors, which wouldn't be near the silage fields for at least another month yet. He'd be away by then.

He let himself in and locked the gate behind him, noticing how the grass had sprung up since the last time he'd visited here. He parked under the shade of the trees and closed the door quietly. No point in taking chances. He hoisted the tool bag over his shoulder and unlocked the new padlock on the door. This place had been a lucky find. Not on any estate agent's details, he'd stumbled across it by chance, in an old and peeling handwritten advert on a wall. The field and the cottage were for rent, but there'd obviously been no interest. He'd researched the owner, only to discover that the land had belonged to an elderly woman who had since died. The land was subject to probate, so no one would be bothering with it for a while at least. Perfect.

The cordless drill made little noise, and he screwed the hook in tight, testing it with his weight before repeating the process on the other wall. It probably wouldn't matter if these two women saw each other, but he might as well keep to his routine. That way the police would know for certain it was the same MO.

When he went to drill the holes for the cabinet, he discovered the drill bit he needed was missing. Must have fallen out into the back of the truck. But when he checked, it wasn't there. *Shit.* He'd have to go and get another from his stores. Never mind. The girls weren't going anywhere for a while and he had plenty of time now.

On the way out, he set up his usual traps, a fine piece of thread across the doorway, and another across the gap in the trees any intruder would have to pass through. He locked the gate behind him and set the nose of the truck towards the motorway.

* * *

Someone had been here. The ends of his thread dangled, invisible unless you were looking for them, but snapped through. He'd set the trap at around four feet from the ground, so unless a big animal like a deer had been through,

163

this was human interference. His eyes scanned the ground around, wary, but there were no animal tracks. Hooves left deep impressions in the soft ground, but there was nothing here except . . .

A partial footprint. A trainer with virtually no grip on the sole, and small. He set his own foot beside the mark for comparison, and his size tens dwarfed it. Maybe a five or six? Female, then.

He realized he was grinding his teeth and made himself relax. There was no way it could be her. How on earth could she have found this place? He closed his eyes and breathed in, scenting the air. Leaf mould, freshly disturbed; moss; his own scent; the tang of diesel from the van; and something else. Something that set off a train of memories.

He'd carried her out to the van with her arm over his shoulder, as though she was helpless with drink. Her head lolled, the long ponytail falling forwards. The scent of her shampoo had filled his nostrils, clean and fresh and reminding him of strawberries and vanilla ice cream.

That was what he was smelling.

His eyes snapped open. She *had* been here. By whatever twist of fate or ill luck, she'd found this place. He stalked silently over to the cottage and checked the door. That thread was intact, so she hadn't managed to get inside. He studied the undergrowth under the window. A broken frond glared white against the dark greens, evidence that someone (*her*) had managed to force their way through to look inside.

A reluctant smile formed on his face. Perhaps she was a worthy victim, this one. No sitting around and waiting for him to make the next move, she was a huntress. This kill would be all the more joyous, and surely the pleasure would last longer this time.

He slipped on his rubber gloves and unlocked the door. Time for a change of plan. The other two would have to stay where they were for the time being, and take their chances in the cold and damp. He'd have to check out one of the other places on his shortlist before he could safely move them.

He didn't spend as much time covering his tracks as usual, because he was fairly sure the police would be here soon. He unscrewed the rings and put them with the cabinet in the back of the van, then slapped a bit of ready-made Polyfilla in the holes.

A last check around, but no sign of anything. He worked carefully out of habit, caution being a part of his nature. Once he had everything cleared up, he removed the broken ends of thread and any sign that they'd ever been there — no point in giving his tricks away — and locked everything up as he went. Back to his hideout.

The rough engine and vibrating steering wheel prevented him from relaxing as he coaxed the old vehicle to keep a straight line on the country roads. It kept veering to the left. That nearside front tyre must be deflating again. Maybe he should put some air in it, because repairing it wasn't an option just yet. He didn't want to be seen and recognized anywhere around here.

There was a petrol station, wasn't there? A couple of miles along the Moira Road towards Lisburn. Far enough from the cottage and remote enough to be an unlikely place for the cops to check. If he remembered right, it was a run-down place with little likelihood of CCTV too. Perfect.

He swung a left, fighting with the wheel to avoid the ditch on the corner. The sooner the better. That bloody air hose had better be working.

It was, and it was the sort that you put money in, not tokens, so he didn't need to go into the shop.

When he gunned the engine this time, the van stayed straight. He pointed the bonnet towards the motorway roundabout and leaned back, driving on instinct alone while he channelled his mind to solve the problem of a new base.

CHAPTER 20

"I do not care what the commissioner says. There is no one, *no one* who knows more about how this killer thinks and acts than me. To take me off the case would be the height of stupidity, and it would endanger lives."

Asha had a crease of worry between her brows. They were standing outside Ram's office in the corridor. Asha had been about to knock, when the sound of raised voices stopped her, with her hand still raised. *We shouldn't be listening to this*, Nic thought, but she didn't move away. She hoped the inspector would win his argument, because she agreed with him. He was her best chance of getting Hazel back in one piece.

He must be on the telephone, because there was silence for a period, then Ram started up again.

"Well I suggest you contact your opposite number in Leeds, and ask how much it impeded my work the last time my daughter was abducted. I think you will find that I was able to continue functioning perfectly well."

"What do you think?" Nic whispered.

Asha smiled. "He's the best man for this job, and he can stay detached enough to do it well," she replied, equally quietly. "And imagine what he'd feel like to be locked out of the investigation with his daughter still missing."

"Awful," Nic agreed.

"I forgot to give you this." Asha fished in her pocket and came out with the brick. "I thought you should probably have it back in case he tried to contact you again."

Nic pulled a face, and took it as though it might bite. The brick's screen remained blank as always. Her face must have showed her mixed emotions.

"Nothing since he rejected your offer to swap yourself for Hazel?"

"Nothing. I don't know what he's going to do now." And that was the problem. She'd tried second-guessing him, and it had got her nowhere. Worse than nowhere, because now she had no idea where he might be holding Hazel. And if he'd seen her near his hideout, as seemed likely now, he might decide to take it out on her sister.

No. She turned her thoughts away. That way madness lay.

Ram's office had been quiet for a few minutes now. Asha knocked on the door.

"Come."

The last time Nic had seen him, Ram had been a broken man, but something had changed. The suit was still just as crumpled, and the bags under his eyes were even heavier, but there was an urgency to his movements as he stood up and came part way to meet them.

The dark shadows around his eyes had deepened. "You've heard the news, then?"

"I heard they're trying to take you off the case, sir," Asha said, as she closed the door behind her and Nic. "Even knowing the service as I do, that strikes me as the most stupid and short-sighted action they could possibly take."

"It's the press, you see." He pushed a newspaper over the desk towards them, the local rag. The headline blared out in bold print: *Slasher Makes A Fool of Ram, Again.*

Below was a photo of Ram with his shirt unbuttoned and tie askew, running his hand through his thinning hair. He looked old and lost, and even more dishevelled than usual.

"That's ridiculous!" Nic blurted out. "You're the only one who has worked this case from both ends, and the one with the biggest motivation for catching this guy. Apart from me," she added.

"Be that as it may, the greater powers have decided that I'm too emotionally involved and they have removed me from the case." He locked eyes with Asha. "However, the one bit of good news is that you have been promoted. Temporarily."

Nic felt Asha's shock in the sudden intake of breath. "Sir?"

"Acting Detective Inspector Harvey. Congratulations."

"Sir, I—"

"Just find that bastard, Asha. Take him out of circulation before he can harm anyone else," Ram said in a fierce voice.

"Yes, sir." She glanced around, as if checking for eavesdroppers. "But are you staying here in Belfast? They're not sending you away, are they?"

"No, I'm allowed to stay here, provided I clear my desk and keep away from the case. I've been granted leave of absence on compassionate grounds." He managed not to sound as bitter as Nic thought he would be under the circumstances.

"Where will you be staying, sir?"

"They're putting me up in the Fitzwilliam, no less. Guilt money, I think."

"Well, keep your mobile on you, sir. There might be times I need to engage an independent consultant to help with my investigations."

Nic bit her lip. Trust Asha to find a way. "Does this mean Asha is in charge of the investigation now?"

"Yes. I can't think of anyone I would trust more to bring my daughter and your sister home safe, but if it does go wrong, Asha, know that I won't blame you. You have an unenviable task ahead of you."

In the heavy silence that followed, the brick phone's ringtone sounded like the knell of doom. Nic looked down at it as it lay in her hand, vibrating and flashing for an incoming call.

"What'll I do?" she asked in a whisper.

Ram nodded to Asha, deferring to her.

"You'll have to answer. Hold it away from your ear so we can hear."

Nic pressed the accept button and held it near enough to speak into it. "Hello?"

There was silence for a long heartbeat, some scuffling and a noise Nic couldn't identify, a sort of slapping sound, then Hazel's voice came out of the tinny speaker, as clear as if she was in the next room.

"Nic? Are you there?"

Nic forgot all about letting Asha and Ram hear. She clutched the phone to her ear. "Yes, I'm here. Are you okay? Has he hurt you?" The unsaid word, *yet*, hung in the air between them.

"No. I'm fine, just cold. So cold and—"

A hand must have snatched the phone from her and blocked the speaker because all Nic heard was muffled voices and crackling, then Hazel came back on.

"I'm not to tell you anything about where we are, but we're fine. He says to tell you he's considered your offer, and he might accept. Nic, what have you done?" The last words were wrenched out of her in a sob that shattered Nic's composure into a thousand pieces.

"Hazel! Hazel, speak to me."

The line clicked and went silent. Nic's knuckles ached from gripping the phone. She made herself place it carefully down on the desk. "She's gone."

"What did she say?" Asha asked at the same time as Ram said, "Meera. Did she mention Meera?"

"She didn't mention Meera, but she said *we're* fine. We. It sounds as though he has them both together and he hasn't harmed either of them."

Asha lifted the phone from Ram's desk. He got up to make room for her, and she sank down into his chair without seeming to notice that she'd usurped his place. "Get me Bishop," she snapped into the receiver, tapping her fingers on the desk while she waited.

Ram moved quietly over to the wall as though he was trying to avoid notice.

"Bishop. Tell me you got that." Her face relaxed. "Good man. Send it over now, please, and send a copy to Forensics to see if they can pull anything from it to tell us where he might be keeping them. Thanks."

"You're still recording calls to that phone!" Nic said, startled.

"Mmm. He didn't let her speak long enough to get any real sort of trace, but we do have a general direction. They're working on it now."

As she spoke, Asha was tapping away at the keyboard on Ram's computer. Nic moved around the desk to read over her shoulder. She was logging into some sort of database that had the PSNI logo on its main page. She scrolled through a few pages, then found the file she wanted, and double-clicked it.

A sound bar opened up, and the speakers crackled to life. Nic jumped as she heard her own voice, sounding ridiculously young and uncertain, say, "Hello?"

Together, they listened to the rest of the conversation. Asha kept replaying the beginning, where that strange slapping sound had mystified Nic.

"What is that?" Nic asked. "It sounds familiar, but I'm not sure where I've heard it before."

"I'm hoping Bishop will be able to pin it down for us. He has the equipment to separate the sounds out and isolate them."

The phone rang and Asha picked it up. Before she even spoke, Nic remembered where she'd heard that sound before. It was on a boat, when they'd been on a family sailing holiday. Dad had switched the engine off and they'd hove to for lunch. Nic had gone down below to the heads and heard waves slapping the side of the hull as the little yacht bobbed in the water.

"Waves," she said. "They're on a boat!"

Asha looked up at her. "That's what Bishop says, too. They're trying to get a narrower idea, you know? River, canal, lake, sea. It'll take a while, but it gives us something to work with while we're waiting. Do you want to go back to Sergeant Jacob and do a bit more searching, Nic? You did a good job of finding his last hideaway."

And I'll be safe there, Nic thought. *Out from under everyone's feet.*

Ram followed Nic to the door. "I'll leave you to it." He held Asha's look for a moment. "You know where I'll be, and I'll have my mobile on me at all times. Good hunting."

Nic followed him down the corridor until they reached Sergeant Jacob's door. He stopped there and turned, taking Nic's hand in his warm, dry one. His mouth twisted with some emotion. "Asha will get them back for us. I feel it in my bones."

Nic's mouth was too dry to answer. He turned and walked away, shoulders slumped, like a man defeated.

Lonnie seemed unsurprised to see Nic. She winked at her and gestured to the spare chair, which was once again covered with stacks of files. Nic lifted them carefully and deposited them on top of the most stable pile she could find.

"I had a feeling you'd be back, looking for more. You left your iPad here last time, in your rush to be gone."

Nic tapped in her passcode and went straight to the browser to google boats for sale near Belfast.

Several pages popped straight up, and she smiled to herself as she went into the first one, but her enthusiasm waned when she saw how many boats were listed. Everything from jet skis and speedboats to a wooden fishing boat that was in Norway, of all places. So much for "near Belfast".

Refining the search wasn't that easy, either. It was asking her what sort of boat, but she had no idea. Not a jet ski, certainly, but other than that it could be almost any type of boat. Nic closed her eyes and tried to recall the sound. There'd been a hollow thump when the water hit the hull. Wood?

On a whim, she did an advanced search for wooden-hulled boats in Ireland, but there were still scores of them, all over the country. None of them looked as though they might be sitting, abandoned, on the water. Most were on trailers or in yards. Some were floating, but the photos showed them with happy families aboard, or with weather-beaten men in oilskins beating to windward, or whatever.

"No luck yet?" Lonnie asked.

"Too much luck. I'm trying to find a boat listed somewhere that is on the sea, or maybe a lake or river, that's isolated enough to be private but close enough to Belfast and the ferries and airports for him to be able to reach it quite quickly."

"What about a lough?"

"There are loads for sale in Strangford Lough, and Belfast Lough. Some in Lough Foyle and Larne Lough too, but nothing promising."

"Have you looked for boats on Lough Neagh?"

"What, that puddle of brown water down the motorway? Are there boats on it?"

Sergeant Jacob laughed. "Yes, there are boats on it! There are massive sand barges ploughing up and down, a healthy fishing fleet." She stopped and frowned. "Eeling fleet? They catch Lough Neagh eels and export them all over the world. And there are pleasure boats too."

Nic closed her mouth, which had dropped open. "I thought it was just a giant drain for all the rivers to pour into."

"You'd be surprised. My son takes me down there every weekend after Sunday service and we eat at the café at Oxford Island and watch the boats sailing by. It's very popular. You should go sometime."

"I think I will. Is it the sort of place where someone could keep a couple of people tied up in a boat without anyone noticing?"

Lonnie thought about it. "Yes, I'd say so. There's a marina there with dozens of boats. At this time of year, I'd say it'd be pretty quiet."

172

Nic called up Google Maps again, and searched for Oxford Island. It was a nature reserve, apparently, but as she zoomed out a little, a marina came into view, with its parallel rows of jetties. There were the little ellipses of boats from above, maybe a hundred or so, and more in an enclosed yard over to the right of the image.

"I've heard there are several places on the lough where people keep boats," the sergeant said, "but I think the one near Oxford Island is the biggest."

"Kinnego Marina," Nic read aloud.

"Yes, that's the one. I believe there's a café there too."

"Thanks, Sergeant. If there's a café there, it's probably too busy for our man, but I'll see if there are any other likely hideouts." As she spoke, she zoomed back out and began a scan of the lough, looking for quiet wee places where a boat might lie undisturbed. She barely registered Lonnie asking her if she'd like a cup of tea, and didn't reply.

As she worked her way northwards up the eastern shore, Nic realized there were dozens of little inlets and bays with boats tied up. It would take days to search all of them, and most were isolated enough that someone could keep prisoners hidden without anyone being any the wiser.

There had to be a way to narrow it down. What if she took into account the driving time from each of the places to the airport and then to the main ferry terminals?

She went back to Kinnego Marina and right-clicked to get directions, writing the times and distances down on an A4 pad she found on Sergeant Jacob's desk. Before long, it became clear that most of the promising places were down tiny, winding lanes that would take far too long to navigate.

From Kinnego Marina, it was roughly forty-five minutes to either of the two main airports, and not much more to the big ferry terminal in Belfast. Out of curiosity, she checked the travel time and route to the cottage she'd found. Thirteen minutes.

Surely he wouldn't keep Hazel and Meera at a tourist place like a marina, would he? But then he'd snatched Nic and Colm from Limelight, right under the noses of their friends, so who knew what he'd dare.

She made a shortlist of other hiding places he might have used that weren't too far from main roads, but her mind kept drifting back to Kinnego Marina again and again.

Lonnie came back in and put a chipped mug next to her elbow, brimming with dark, treacly tea. "Didn't know if you took sugar, so I put two spoons in just in case."

"Thank you, Sergeant Jacob," Nic said. "I wonder if Asha would take me out to Lough Neagh. I think you could be on to something, because there are loads of quiet little inlets where he could have a boat tied up."

"I doubt if she'll want to risk you going out there, but she might send someone else to look. DC Birch, maybe. Have you told her what you've found yet?"

Nic shook her head. "No. Did Officer Bishop get back to her? He was going to take the sounds apart in that phone call and see what else he could make of it."

"You'd have to ask Acting Detective Inspector Harvey that one." She chuckled. "Officer Bishop. He'd like that. Ken Bishop is a civilian technician we subcontract for jobs like this."

Nic took a sip of the hot tea, scalding her tongue. It was bitter, despite all the sickly-sweet sugar, and tasted as if it had been brewing for weeks. She could feel her teeth staining, even after such a tiny taste.

"That good? Strong tea's good for you, you know. Puts hairs on your chest," Lonnie chuckled.

"I think it's put hairs on my tongue." She put the mug down carefully, only noticing as she did that there was an old lipstick stain on the rim. Nic didn't wear lipstick. Her stomach churned. "I'll go and find out if there's any more news about the recording. Back in a minute."

CHAPTER 21

He'd been lucky to get this hideout. The old man he'd propped up the bar with in Belfast had been so drunk he'd struggle to remember who he'd been talking to, never mind that he'd lost his keys.

"It's a bargain, son," he'd slurred. "A thirty-foot wooden sailing barge. They just don't make 'em like that anymore. All she needs is a bit of TLC and you'll have a beauty."

He'd pretended to be interested, but at the time he hadn't quite worked out what he could do with it. They'd been tucked away in a corner of a busy place with a live band playing something noisy and wordless at one end and a giant TV showing a football match at the other. No one paid any attention to the two men, and he could barely hear what the old drunk was saying anyway.

When the man got up to leave, he'd got up at the same time, needing a leak. He came back out of the gents' loo to find a group gathered around a huddled shape on the floor. The old sot had passed out. He was probably the only one who noticed the bunch of keys under the barstool. They must have fallen from the man's hand as he collapsed, but the cork ball float attached to them marked them as boat keys, and the pieces dropped into place in his mind.

He bent to swipe them, muttered a few words of concern, and stepped carefully past the pile of rags to get to the front door. For some reason he looked back before he left. The old man stared at him with sightless eyes, sending a chill across his skin, but then someone leaned down and closed them with a gentle hand.

That gave him pause for thought. If the old bugger had cocked his clogs, there was an even better opportunity. The last thing any relatives would be interested in was a wreck of a boat that would be worth nothing in the current market. It'd be weeks or even months before anyone came to check the thing, but until then it was all his.

He locked the steel gate behind him and padded silently along the slimy wooden jetty, out to the far end, where the wooden hulk was tied to the hammerhead. Tucked away out here, no one would be walking past the boat. Most of the pleasure craft that lived here had been lifted out of the water for the winter, and it'd be late May before many of them were relaunched for the summer season. The scattering of boats left on this jetty were dark with mould and sloshing with rainwater. It didn't look as if anyone came down here much.

The boat was probably sitting on the soft mud at the bottom of the lough. She didn't even dip as he stepped aboard, placing his feet carefully to avoid the rotten places in the deck. He unlocked the hatch and ducked inside after a casual glance around. Not a soul to be seen. The café wasn't even open yet, so no day trippers here.

With the hatch closed again, the cabin was dark, the sound of his movements muffled. He drew in the smells: stagnant water, overlaid with the sharp tang of urine and a heavy, cloying smell where one of the girls had fouled herself. No blood, not yet. This place wasn't suitable for cutting. He tied the scarf over the lower part of his face and pulled his knitted hat low, until just his eyes showed, before he turned to stoop through into the forepeak cabin.

The Indian woman had woken up. She moved feebly, her limbs slow and heavy, and a groan came from behind the gag. Her eyes were fixed on him, filled with pure hatred. He smiled underneath the mask, looking forward to finishing this one's lessons in humility. What joy. He'd break her spirit, and her father's, at the same time.

The younger girl lay where he'd left her, staring at the peeling paint on the bulkhead a foot in front of her. She didn't even flinch as he bent down and gripped her chin between finger and thumb, turning her face towards him. His first instinct had been right: this one would be useless, except as bait to draw the sister out. He let her go, and her head flopped back to where it had been. She was the one who'd soiled herself too. He turned away, disgusted.

He closed the door to the cabin, trying to shut some of the smell away, and made his way aft to the galley. The big silver coffee machine took up the entire counter space, a fat white elephant here, where there was no electricity and he had to carry any water he needed. He had to make do with the cafetière and a kettle on the gas ring.

CHAPTER 22

Nic was surprised to find it was dark outside the window in the corridor. How did this keep happening? Since she'd escaped from the killer, she'd been racing through each day. It was nearly six in the evening, and she'd had very little sleep the night before. Why wasn't she more exhausted? Maybe the adrenaline was keeping her going, the thought of Hazel, tied up helpless and naked in a cold, damp boat.

She marched down the corridor, eyes down as she wracked her brain to think how she could find her sister, so she wasn't looking where she was going. She smacked hard into Aaron as he rounded the corner, going equally fast. Nic rebounded a step, slightly winded, and he put a hand on her arm, steadying her.

"Whoah! What's the rush?"

She smiled up at him, reluctantly. "Pot. Kettle. Black."

"Yeah, well," he grinned. "I'm on a mission from our acting detective inspector, who seems to have sloughed off her sense of humour with the altitude she's climbed."

"Oh? Where's she sending you?"

He glanced over his shoulder before replying, and Nic noticed, for the first time, fine lines of worry around his eyes. "Apparently there's a boat down near Downpatrick, moored in the River Quoile. Bishop thinks the sounds in the background of Hazel's phone call fit with the size and shape of it, so I'm off to have a look."

"In the dark? On your own? Besides . . ." She tried to bring up an image of the map in her head, with routes to the ferry and airports from Downpatrick. "Wouldn't it be a bit remote for him to have travelled to Leeds and got back in the time frame?"

"Three quarters of an hour to George Best Belfast City Airport," he said, but she could hear the reservation in his voice.

"How far to the ferry, or to the international airport?"

"Ferry's just under an hour, Aldergrove a bit more than an hour."

"If he's brought Meera back here, and Hazel did say *we* quite clearly, then he must have used the ferry, unless it was his own boat he used?"

Aaron ticked the objections off on his fingers. "He'd have to be a good sailor. A small boat, single-handed, would take the best part of a full day to make that crossing. He'd have to have left a car somewhere to pick up. Probably a van or truck, so he could hide Meera out of sight on the journey back from Leeds."

"You're right. In that case, surely it has to be the ferry, and that means Belfast to Scotland, because the Liverpool one also takes all day or all night to make the crossing."

"Ye-es," he said, slowly. "But Asha wants me to go and look at this boat on the Quoile anyway, even if it's just to eliminate it."

"Bring me with you," Nic said breathlessly. "I have some other ideas about places he might be keeping her, and maybe we could check those if the Quoile doesn't pan out?"

"We'd have to clear it with the boss." His mouth twisted in doubt. "She's not in the most approachable of moods."

"I can text her from the car once we're on our way?" Nic suggested. "Ma always says it's better to ask forgiveness than permission."

Aaron shook his head, but he was smiling again, and Nic knew she'd won. "I know which parent you take after, Nic. Your mum is a terrible influence. Okay. You can come, but you do realize Asha will kill us both, don't you?"

Nic bit her lip. She didn't want to get Aaron into trouble, but her instincts were screaming at her to find Hazel. The more time that passed, the more chance he'd harm her. She gave a sharp nod, avoiding his eyes.

"Come on, then, before she spots us. Car's this way."

They jogged down the stairs, meeting no one, until Aaron beeped the remote to unlock the Golf. A uniformed officer was just getting out of a marked patrol car and he glanced across at them. Nic recognized the man from yesterday, the one who'd been in the rec room, exchanging racist chat with the man in the corridor.

She ducked into the car, but she was pretty sure he'd recognized her from the raised eyebrow and a smile she didn't quite like.

Aaron tapped coordinates into the satnav on his windscreen. "Belt up. It's a reasonable drive. Rules are that the driver gets to pick the music, but I'll make an exception for you." He nodded towards the glove box.

Nic opened it, curious about the sort of music he'd have. There were a handful of CDs in there, varying from Frank Sinatra to Aurelio Voltaire. She sorted through them, looking for something she'd be prepared to listen to, but the only one she recognized was a Celtic punk band, the Dropkick Murphys. She ejected the current CD (Westlife, no box for it) and put in the Murphys.

It was a good sound system, she'd give it that. The guitar and drums blasted out, followed by the forty-a-day gravelly voice of the lead singer.

We had guns and drums and drums and guns.
Hurroo, hurroo.

Aaron glanced at her curiously. "Interesting pick."

"Interesting collection," she countered.

"You found the only one that isn't mine. That one's Asha's CD."

Heat rose in Nic's cheeks and she was grateful for the flickering orange street lights as they threaded the side streets off the Lisburn Road on their way south via the Malone Road.

The roads were still busy, but traffic was moving, on the whole. As they passed the House of Sport roundabout, Nic cast a longing look down the turning that would take her home to Lisburn, but Aaron took the first exit past Shaws Bridge. She sighed. Ma would be worried, but she'd be fiercely determined to hide it.

"I should give Ma another call. Tell her I'm still okay," she said.

"Go ahead." Aaron paused the CD.

Ma answered on the fourth ring, as they'd been instructed to by the tech boys who'd tapped the line, in case it was Hazel's kidnapper phoning them. Asha would no doubt be informed about her call, so she'd have to be careful what she said in case she got Aaron into trouble.

"Hi, Ma. It's just me."

Ma let out a breath. "I thought you'd be coming straight home. Where are you? I've been worried sick."

"Sorry, Ma. I've been at the station with Asha and Aaron, going through some necessary paperwork. I didn't mean to worry you, just time sort of got away from me." How much did Ma know about where Nic had been earlier today? Did she know about the abandoned hideout? "Anyway, I'm fine. Just knackered. Any news?"

"You tell me," Ma said drily. "You're the one with a finger on the police pulse."

Nic didn't know what to say. Knowing Ma, she could be referring to the case, or to an imagined relationship. She didn't even know if Ma might mean Asha or Aaron, and she realized she didn't know herself, either.

"Nothing new, Ma. I think they're looking at a few places where they think he might be holding Hazel, but they

181

have to be careful in case they alert him, I guess." She realized she was getting into dodgy territory here. "I'd better go, if I want a lift back to the house. I'm staying in Belfast tonight. Bye, Ma."

And she rang off, cheeks burning with worry that she'd said too much, and at the same time too little. Ma had always been able to spot a lie from any of her three children, even on the phone.

Aaron restarted the CD without comment, and the familiar Irish music, sung in such an angry way, helped to wash away some of her guilt. Some.

By the time she was in a fit state to notice where they were, the little car was passing the garage they'd stopped at the other day, where they'd seen the grey van. It seemed like weeks ago, not just a few days. So much had changed since then. Hazel had been free, for one thing. The kidnapper seemed to know this area surprisingly well, and he'd chosen hideouts in this direction twice now. Perhaps Asha was right about the boat on the Quoile.

Once they were through the bottleneck at the Carryduff roundabout, the roads became clearer and Aaron accelerated. No street lighting now, and the music fitted with the way the headlights lit up skeletal trees and reflected off the wet road surface. Nic settled down in the seat and closed her eyes against the beginning of a headache. The regular swish-squeak of the windscreen wipers didn't help the headache, but she must have slept at some point, because when Aaron switched the engine off, she jerked awake with a cry.

"It's okay. We're here, or at least as close as we can get by car. I'll have to walk from here, but I'll leave the key in, in case you need to put the heater on. It's still pretty cold in the evenings and I don't know how long—"

"I'm coming," Nic said, firmly. "There's no way you're abandoning me alone in the car in the dark, and a second pair of eyes and ears might be useful."

"I really shouldn't . . ."

"I promise not to get in the way. I'll walk three paces behind you if you want, like the Duke of Edinburgh does with the Queen."

He gave a short laugh. "I must be insane. No lights, then, and put your phone on silent before you get out of the car. Oh, and don't let the door slam. Close it gently."

She put both phones on silent. She didn't remember putting the brick in her pocket, but she must have done it automatically.

Together, they creeped along a narrow gravel track that wound between bushes, heavy from the rain. Their feet made little sound, but every light crunch set the hairs on the back of her neck on end. As they went on, the smell of wet grass became overlaid by damp seaweed and salt water. Nic remembered from her earlier search that this area was riddled with a network of small tidal inlets, all of which opened out into Strangford Lough.

A stray memory surfaced from her days in school. They'd been learning about Saint Patrick and her teacher had told the class that the saint had landed in Downpatrick by accident. He'd been intending to sail around Malin Head to come ashore in Lough Swilly, but the massive tides in the mouth of Strangford Lough had sucked in the boat on which he was a passenger, and he'd decided to make the best of a bad job, called it the will of God, and built a church where he happened to come ashore. She wondered if it was true or not.

Aaron was nothing but a patch of deeper shadow, but his hand was still warm when it touched hers. He stepped up to her and brought his lips to her ear. "The boat is just ahead. I think I can hear water slapping against the hull from here. Will you stay put until I've had a look? It's easier for one to move quietly than two, and it means you can still run for help if it goes tits up. Here's the car keys."

He pressed them into her hand and closed her fingers over them.

"Okay," she breathed.

He melted away soundlessly, leaving her in the velvet darkness. The night was far from silent, now she was still enough to listen. Somewhere in the distance, a car engine droned along. Closer, there were occasional rustlings in the undergrowth. Probably mice, she told herself, but some of them sounded bigger than that, and this close to the river there'd probably be rats. She shivered and wrapped her arms around herself, wishing she'd brought a coat.

Something creaked, rope against a deck. Aaron must be climbing aboard. Was he mad?

A moment later, the night was lit by a high-powered beam that cast long shadows across the grass and bracken. Water sloshed against the bank and Aaron cursed in a high-pitched voice she barely recognized.

"Who's there?" a voice demanded. "I've warned you before! This time I'm calling the police."

Nic let out the breath that had frozen in her chest. This wasn't the voice of the killer, although she couldn't have said how she knew. Too old, perhaps.

"I *am* the police, sir," Aaron said breathlessly. "If you let go of my arm, I can show you my warrant card."

There was a short scuffle and the sound of panting breath. Feet slid across a deck and then there was a dull thud and a cry.

"Aaron! Are you all right?" She couldn't stop herself calling out.

"Who's there?" The torch beam swung her way, blinding her. She raised her forearm to save her eyes, but it dropped down almost immediately, playing down her body. "A lassie, by God. What the hell are you doing here with this bastard?"

"He *is* a police officer! He's Detective Constable Aaron Birch."

There was a pause and some more creaking, then a groan. "Let me up, will you?"

Nic moved closer, trying to see what was going on. Where was the moon when you needed it? A boat loomed up from the darkness, sheer sides standing a good three or four feet above the edge of the bank. The torch was pointed at Aaron's face, and he was down on the deck, with a wiry old man half-sitting on his shoulders while he searched Aaron's pockets.

"It's in my back pocket," Aaron grunted.

The stranger's hands reached under Aaron's jacket and felt around. Nic couldn't take her eyes off his face, searching for a resemblance to the one engraved on her memory, where it had hung over her, just the eyes showing above the mask, but there was nothing familiar about the bushy, grey eyebrows or the unruly thatch of hair that looked like a Brillo pad.

"It's all right, Aaron. It's definitely not him."

Aaron tried to turn towards her. There was a dark stain on his forehead where a thin stream of blood had trickled down to pool across his brows.

"Aaron! You're hurt."

"I'm fine," he lied through gritted teeth. "But I'd be better if this guy would get off me."

The old man had found the warrant card and was examining it carefully in the light of the torch. He grunted and slid it back into the wallet before releasing Aaron and standing back, surprisingly supple for someone as old as he looked to be. "Okay, I believe you now, but what the hell were you doing prowling around my boat in the middle of the night?"

Nic glanced at her wristwatch. "It's just after seven in the evening."

The torch came back to her face and she blinked, but didn't cover her eyes this time.

"I know you from somewhere." He scowled down at her, then clicked his fingers. "You're the woman from the news. Saw your picture in the paper. I see the scars now."

Nic swallowed down the panic. She'd almost managed to convince herself they didn't show anymore, but now the old fear was back in full. "Yes, that's who I am. Have you heard that he's abducted my sister? I'm sorry if we scared you, but we're just trying to get her back." Her voice broke at the end of the sentence, and his face relaxed from its fierce expression into sympathy.

"No, lassie? Not your sister? I don't buy the newspapers, ye ken, but sometimes I catch a headline or two when someone else is reading one." He held out a hand to help Aaron up.

The young detective needed it. He reeled a little, grabbing the guard rail of the boat for balance before he straightened up.

"That's a strong left hook you have there," he muttered.

"Aye, well. If ye live alone like me, ye need to learn to look after yourself. Can I get you a wee dram to help put the misunderstandings behind us?"

Aaron took an unsteady step and Nic reached up to give him her hand.

"Thank you, sir, but I'm on duty, and clearly this isn't the boat we're after. We'd better be on our way."

"Did you say you'd been having trouble?" Nic asked. "Vandals?"

"Aye. Tried to burn the boat with me in it, but I'm a light sleeper. Local thugs from yon town there. Thought that was what you were up to, creeping around in the dark." He nodded to Aaron, probably the closest they'd get to an apology.

"I can call it in, if you like," Aaron offered. "Local boys can come down tomorrow and take a statement from you. Might help with the insurance, if nothing else, if they do manage to cause any damage."

"Dinnae bother, laddie. I'll be away with the tide tonight anyways. Off back to Troon on the morrow. Thanks, though." He held out a horny hand. "Name's Compton. Danny Compton. Boat's called the *Matilda Dee* and we're usually based on the west coast at Troon if you need to contact me again."

Nic had a sudden thought. "Aaron, do you have a copy of that recording on you? The one of Hazel?"

He patted his pockets and came out with his mobile. "I have it on here, but the sound quality isn't the best." He

186

seemed to be following Nic's train of thought. "Would you mind listening to a short recording, Mr Compton? It's what sent us hunting for a boat moored in an isolated backwater."

"Go ahead."

Aaron hit play, and Nic heard her own voice, then Hazel's. Her heart lurched all over again.

"That's terrible quality, laddie. Why don't ye both come below and we'll see if we can't get a better sound out of that thing?"

Nic and Aaron exchanged looks. He reached down and helped her up the long step on to the side deck — her legs were considerably shorter than his. They followed Compton down into a cosy cabin lit by a paraffin lamp and lined in soft, golden wood. Crimson velvet cushions lay on the bunks, adding to the old-fashioned charm of the interior.

Then Nic's eyes caught a gleam of reflected light on black plastic. A stacked Kenwood sound system from the '90s stood on a shelf behind the main bunk, a blue light blinking in an understated way to show that it had power to it.

At her expression, Compton's eyes crinkled in a smile that changed his whole face.

"Don't get to use it often, because I'm always trying to save the domestic battery, but I'll be running the engine in an hour or two, so we can probably afford to be profligate with the electricity." Even his voice had softened as he talked about the music player, losing the hard Glasgow edge it had earlier. "Give me your phone, laddie."

Aaron handed it over, a little reluctantly, and Compton connected it up via a USB cable he had tucked away behind the seat back.

He gave a short laugh. "Close yer mouths, you two. This stuff is my day job. I'm a sound engineer for BBC Scotland."

Sure enough, this time when he played the message, it came out crystal clear from huge speakers mounted on the bulkhead. Nic closed her eyes as she listened to her sister's voice again. With this degree of clarity, the stress and fear came through unmistakeably.

"There. That's the sound," Aaron said after the slapping came across.

Compton went back and replayed that section again and again, then he took a deep breath and let it out as a gusty sigh. "Well, it's not a river, and it's not the sea. Those aren't natural waves, either. D'you hear that sound in the background?" He played it again, but Nic couldn't hear anything new.

She shook her head helplessly.

"That's an engine. I think it's a personal water craft." They must both have looked confused. "A jet ski," he explained. "It must have passed by before he phoned you, so it's away in the distance, but the wash from its wake is just hitting the hull of the boat they're in, so it must be a wide body of water, like a lake to take that long to get there."

Nic's mouth was dry. She licked her lips. "Like Lough Neagh?"

He smiled at her. "Yes, exactly like Lough Neagh. And you're after a wooden boat, I'm certain. Probably quite big, perhaps twenty-five to thirty feet in length."

Aaron shook his hand. "Thank you, sir. That's been incredibly helpful."

Compton shook his head. "Anything I can do to help get the wee lassie back for you, I will. I don't have a mobile phone when I'm sailing, but I'm always listening on channel 16 when I'm on the water, so you can get the coastguard to give me a shout on the VHF if you need me."

CHAPTER 23

"Okay, you can say it," Aaron muttered as they buckled up their seat belts, back in the warmth of the car.

Nic bit her lip. "I hate to say 'I told you so', but—"

He gave a sigh. "Feel better, getting that off your chest?"

"No, not better." It was hard to resent the time they'd wasted by going first to the Quoile, because Danny Compton had been so useful with his sound system and his knowledge, but she couldn't help feeling as though there was an alarm clock ticking somewhere in the depths of the little car as Aaron reversed it to turn and go back the way they'd come. In her imagination, the clock was an old-fashioned one, like she'd had on her bedside table as a child, and wires ran from it to a device like a miniature guillotine that hung suspended over Hazel's neck.

The digital clock on the dashboard showed just after eight o'clock as Aaron turned on to the roundabout at the edge of Downpatrick. The traffic had cleared now, and Aaron was able to open up, letting the Golf show her speed.

The road unrolled before them in the light of his head-lights, and neither of them mentioned the idea of music.

"I really ought to call in and report," he said, as they drove through the village of Annacloy at only a little above the speed limit of forty miles an hour, but he didn't sound convinced.

"If you do, how likely is it that you'll be called back to the station?"

"Likely. Asha will probably want to hear what Compton said before she'll even consider letting me go to the lough."

As though mentioning her name had brought them to her attention, Nic's phone vibrated in her pocket. She lifted it out and stared at the screen. Asha's name glowed in harsh letters. Nic looked helplessly at Aaron. "Will I answer it?"

He shrugged. "I really don't know. It's up to you."

The phone vibrated silently. Then it stopped, and the screen went dark. She unlocked it and saw a missed call, then a few moments later, the voicemail icon appeared at the top of the screen.

She dialled her voicemail and put the phone to her ear. Asha's message was short.

"Nic, get your arse back here now. I mean it!"

"She says we have to go back. Now."

"Has she worked out you're with me?"

"I don't know. She didn't say. Just said I had to get back there straight away. She didn't mention you."

Then Aaron's phone lit up in its cradle on the dash. Asha again. He took a deep breath and tapped the hands-free answer button. Before he had a chance to speak, Asha was already talking. "Aaron? Where the hell are you? Why haven't you reported in? Nic's disappeared. If I find out you've had anything to do with this, I'll go through the pair of you for a shortcut."

He grimaced as he listened, then put a finger to his lips, telling Nic to keep quiet. "Sorry, ma'am. I was literally just about to call. I'm back on the road again now, heading in. The boat at the Quoile was a non-starter. Old codger living on his own, and he let me in without any problem. Place is clean."

"Oh." She sounded a little mollified by his open tone. "Well, we have an update from Bishop about that wave sound.

He thinks the boat's probably on the sea, or at least a big body of water."

"What about Lough Neagh? That's a big body of water, isn't it?"

Nic held her breath while she waited for Asha's reply.

"A big, shallow puddle. No, the tech boys think it's probably the sea. I've sent a couple of uniforms to the marinas around Belfast, Bangor and Carrick, but if you're still near Downpatrick, you could maybe do the places on the west bank of Strangford Lough. I'll text you a list, with contact numbers for keyholders. Apparently, there are scores of boats on moorings there, and that's a big body of water, all right. Then there's the marinas down the east coast. Ardglass, Kilkeel, Carlingford Lough. I might need to send another uniform there, as they're all a bit far for our man to be able to get to the airport or the ferry."

"Unless he managed to get on to the Newry freight ferry? He drove a van that looks like a commercial vehicle, didn't he? Good for hiding an unconscious body in too."

"Good thought, Aaron. I'll put someone on it. You just stick to Strangford for now. That's much more likely, I'd say."

"Yes, ma'am."

There was a suspicious silence, then she came back with a lighter tone. "What's with all the 'yes, ma'am' business all of a sudden? Is this your way of telling me I've been throwing my weight around?"

"No comment," he said, and Nic could see the bitter smile playing across his lips.

She felt a surge of guilt. She'd persuaded him into helping her, into going directly against orders, and it was Aaron, not her, who'd take the punishment if this came to nothing. What if she was wrong about Lough Neagh?

Then she remembered Compton. He'd come to the same conclusion as her, but by using scientific deductions rather than by going with his gut. It reassured her.

Aaron ended the call, and now his face had fallen into deep thoughtfulness.

"What are you planning to do?" she asked tentatively.

"Listen to my instincts. Isn't that what you said you always do? By the time Asha realizes I haven't gone to Strangford, we'll be at Lough Neagh and hopefully we'll find something worth calling in backup for."

Hopefully. Hopefully both their instincts were right, and hopefully they could find where he was keeping Hazel and Meera, and hopefully they could call in a team to rescue the two captives before the killer hurt them. So many unknowns.

Once he was on the motorway, Aaron really accelerated. The miles still went by far too slowly for Nic. She hitched herself around in the car seat, fiddling with her seat belt and glancing at the satnav to see how far they still had to go. He fumbled in the space between the seats and came up with a bar of chocolate, which he offered to her. She shook her head. The thought of eating something so sweet made her stomach churn.

"Break me off a piece, will you?"

She did. He refused a second piece, so she wrapped the rest up and put it back where he'd found it.

"When we get there, I'm going to park well away from the marina and walk down. Same as last time, but I hope without the left hook." He rubbed his temple and winced. "That one's on Asha. She's the one who sent me there."

Aaron parked up under overhanging branches on the side of the approach road to the marina. There were a couple of other cars already there. They were covered in raindrops, so they'd probably been there a while.

"Fishermen," Aaron muttered as they walked past, feet silent on the close-cropped grass verge. There was a gate across the access lane, a padlock heavy on the latch, but Aaron led them around the side of it, where a human-sized gap had been left. The place was unnaturally quiet with not so much as a rustle in the undergrowth to suggest life being lived around them.

"The marina's that way." Aaron pointed to the left, where a white building gleamed under spotlights. If they walked much further, they'd be lit up like a Christmas tree, and anyone watching for strangers would be alerted before they got nearby.

"If we keep to the edge of the trees, we can maybe stay out of the light until we get to the far end of the car park," Nic suggested in a whisper.

"Good call. We certainly don't look like fishermen, do we? Unless . . ." He stepped into the woods and rustled around, making what seemed to Nic like far too much noise. The bare branches high above him swished and scraped with whatever he was doing, and she was about to hiss at him to be quiet when he reappeared, panting slightly. He had a long, thin branch in each hand and was busily stripping them of their side-twigs with a pocketknife. He handed one to Nic. "Fishing rod, from a distance."

She smiled and took it while he trimmed the second pole. "Good thinking. It might get us a bit closer, anyway."

Then they drifted silently along the edge of the trees. Like ghosts, Nic thought. They were so quiet that they startled a fox. Aaron was in the lead with Nic close behind when the animal, not much bigger than a domestic cat, appeared between them from the trees. It froze, staring at Nic with wide eyes, and she froze too. The hairs on the back of her neck rose of their own accord: this predator might be small, but there was an air of menace about it that spoke to something deep inside her.

Aaron must have sensed there was something wrong, because he stopped and looked back. The magic was broken and the fox disappeared as silently as it had appeared. Nic let out a breath and started forward again.

Aaron stayed a few steps ahead of her until they reached the far end. He stopped and she came up to him to listen.

"Same as last time. You stay here with your phone handy. I'll go and have a look-see. If you hear or see anything suspicious, first get yourself under cover, then phone Asha and tell her where we are."

Nic nodded. She knew in her heart that this was the right place. Blood called to blood: Hazel was nearby. Nic knew Aaron was the best person to find her. He'd shown how resourceful he could be.

"Good luck." The warmth in his voice sent a tremor through her.

He'd already disappeared into the shadows. She strained to hear or see what he was doing, but all she heard was a faint chink of metal, and that was so quiet she wondered if she'd imagined it.

The silence stretched out. Darkness deepened as the floodlights at the marina switched off, presumably on a timer, leaving just two low-level security lights shining from the corners of the building. Nic began to see shapes in the darkness, areas of shifting grey and black that made her draw her breath in and back up into the soft arms of the conifers behind her.

Fog. It was mist, drifting in from the water. Nic's shoulders lowered as the tension left them, then, just behind her, a twig snapped with a sound like a pistol shot.

She spun, heart hammering.

Pain flared out from the back of her head. She tried to bring her hand up to feel for damage, but her arm wouldn't obey her. And where were her legs?

The ground rushed up towards her. She hit the ground face down, damp grass and mud filling her mouth. The last thing she saw before darkness took her was a pair of worn trainers with dried bloodstains in the fabric.

CHAPTER 24

They thought they were so clever, following him here. How had they found him? What detail had he missed?

The two figures slipped around the gate, paused to confer with their heads close together, then darted to the left, along the treeline where the grassy mounds of the empty caravan site hid them from the probing floodlights of the marina. In a second, they were gone, shadows into darkness. He sat up in the little Peugeot Partner van he'd "borrowed" from outside the builders' merchants.

He slipped out of the driver's seat, pushing the door to gently so it didn't bang, and set off after the woman and the copper. It was the same one she'd been with in the garage at Carryduff, the one who'd tried to get a glimpse of his face when he was reversing the van away. Arrogant prick, with his cocky walk and his designer chinos.

They were standing on the edge of the path that wound through the trees up towards the discovery centre, and the young copper was whispering in her ear, leaning in close, too close.

Rage sent electric shocks down his arms, making his fingers twitch. He steadied his breathing, focused the anger, let it build. He should have known from the first day that she'd be fickle. No loyalty, after all he'd tried to give her. But she'd pay. They all paid in the end, for the sideways looks, and the whispers they thought he wouldn't hear. Maybe didn't care if he heard.

The copper had gone, off towards the jetty. She was alone now. In the darkness. He was moving before he'd thought out what he would do. Twenty feet. Fifteen. Ten. Three strides.

Crack!

Fucking hell. She spun around at the sound, face white under the faint moonlight that filtered through clouds, but he'd already moved past the dead branch. His clenched fist came up in a swing that had his weight behind it, driven by all the anger and frustration of everything that had gone wrong since this woman came into his life.

She dropped like a stone, eyes still open but staring, unseeing. Had he hit her too hard? No! That's what happened when he let his anger rule his actions. He stepped closer, and her eyes followed his movement, focusing on his feet. He let out a breath. Still alive.

Her eyes closed and her shoulders sagged. He checked her pulse: strong and steady. He left her where she lay. She'd be going nowhere for a while, long enough for what he needed to do, he hoped.

When he reached the gate, the padlock appeared to be closed, but on closer inspection, the bolt had been left open. *Clever boy, leaving yourself an escape route.* He must have picked the lock.

The gate opened silently — he'd made sure of that before he brought his captives here — and he pushed it gently back to where he'd found it, secure as far as the casual observer would see.

The grooved boards of the jetty were slimy, so he had to walk carefully. One slip would be enough to warn the young copper. He'd already made one mistake tonight, he wasn't about to make another. Was it chance that had brought them to the right jetty straight away, or had they somehow worked out which boat he was using?

Chance, it seemed. He froze as a shadow straightened up from one of the finger pontoons. The copper had been bent down, peering into the interior of a wooden sailing boat that was moored there. He must be no sailor, if he thought that little cockleshell would be big enough to hide two fully grown women.

The arrogant git didn't even glance back down the jetty, but walked on, peering from side to side in the dim, distant light from the buildings. The rest of the boats between his position and the end of the jetty were all open boats, or too small, but there was one more the copper might be interested in. It was an elderly fishing boat that hadn't been anywhere in years, by the look of her. She had peeling red paint on her hull, and a gaping hole where her diesel engine should be. Stagnant water sloshed so deep in her bilges that she'd probably sink the next time there was a heavy rainstorm, but if the lad went down that pontoon, it might be the best chance he'd have of stopping him before he got too close.

There was a cabin of sorts in the front of the boat, accessed through the wheelhouse. The lad might well think it worth investigating. That would be perfect.

He held his position, keeping low so his silhouette wouldn't stand out should the copper glance his way. He needn't have worried. The fishing boat tipped, sending little waves that rocked the other boats on either side of her and set halliards jangling. Under cover of the noise, he closed the distance between them. He remembered there was a boat hook lying on the side deck of the red-hulled boat. As he moved silently along the narrow pontoon, his fingers closed around the roughened wood of the heavy pole. It scraped as he lifted it, just the tiniest sound, but it brought the copper upright, already spinning and raising his fists. His reactions were faster than the woman's.

Too slow to save him, though. The heavy metal end made a noise like the shell of a hard-boiled egg might if you were to crack it in the side of a granite work surface, and the policeman dropped into the filthy water at the bottom of the boat.

He leaped nimbly into the fishing boat and grabbed the policeman by the lapels of his thick woollen jacket, trying to lift him out of the water, but he was heavier than he looked, and gangly with it. Long arms and legs flopped like dead fish, making it hard to balance the unconscious body.

Eventually, he got the man hoisted over his shoulder, staggering to keep his balance. The boat rocked and plunged, coming up short against her mooring lines with a jerk. He lowered the body to the gunwales, checked for a pulse, and then tipped the feet up so the policeman slid head first into the dark water of the lough. His pulse had been faint and irregular, and he was out cold. At this time of year, it'd be moot whether the cold water would kill him with hypothermia or by drowning, but either way, this one wouldn't be causing any more trouble, for sure. The body floated, the air trapped inside the clothes, settling in the water as the wash from the waves pushed it further out.

There hadn't been any fat on that lad. He should sink fairly quickly, and it'd be days before he resurfaced as the gases of decomposition made him buoyant. By then, he'd be clean away, and it'd be too late.

He scrambled back on to the pontoon, dusting off his jeans and sweatshirt, although he'd probably find himself covered in green slime when he got into the light. When he reached the main jetty, he paused, considering. He should really check on the two captives tied up in the boat, but there was no guarantee the other one he wanted would stay unconscious for much longer, so she should be his priority. He set off along the jetty with confident steps.

CHAPTER 25

Nic choked on mud. She was drowning in it. Her arms flailed, uncoordinated, and too weak to lift her, but she could turn her head, lift her face out of the dirt. The sudden movement brought a surge of vomit that filled her throat with burning acid. Panic lent strength to her arms, and she pushed herself up to her knees, spitting and coughing.

Where was she? *Who* was she? Something nagged at her, trying to break through the mists that pulled her thoughts to and fro, preventing them from settling on any one subject. There'd been someone else here, someone important. Who?

The thoughts wouldn't come into focus, but a sense of urgency drove her to her feet, clutching at low branches as supports. As she pulled herself upright, the branch she held snapped with a dull crack, and that brought back a memory. A twig had snapped, close behind her, and then she'd . . . what . . . ? Fallen?

Her free hand went to the back of her head and she winced as her fingers found a lump the size of a hen's egg. He'd hit her, and that's why she'd fallen. Trainers. He'd been wearing bloodstained trainers that she'd recognized.

It all came back to her then in a flood of sensations. The sound of her blood drip-dripping; the warm aroma of coffee brewing; Colm's groans; and the deep, ever-present pain of the wounds that drained her strength and will with every minute she remained tied up.

She knew she had to get out of there, to safety. She couldn't let him find her here again, and he would be back for her, of that she was sure. Why hadn't he taken her while she was unconscious? There must be a reason, but her aching head wouldn't let her think of it.

She staggered from tree to tree, staying off the path. The ground dropped away under her feet and she tumbled into a ditch, twisting her ankle as she landed. The pain was distant, belonging to someone else, and nothing for her to worry about.

She tried to climb the bank, but the stones were slippery with mud, and she just slid back down again. Panting with the effort, she stopped. If she went back up, she'd be easier to see. The bottom of the ditch was thick with rotten leaves and mud, but not much worse than the ground above. Maybe she'd just stay down here and see how far it took her.

Left or right? She had no idea where she was. *Eenie, meenie, minie, mo, catch a squirrel by the toe. If he wriggles, let him go. Eenie, meenie, minie, mo.* That was the PC version, Ma had said. Used to use a nasty, racist word when *she* was a child. Her thoughts were rambling, but she turned in the direction the rhyme took her and stumbled forwards, still driven by that vague sense of urgency.

A splash somewhere not far away brought her to a halt, ears straining for another sound, but there was only the swish of waves against a muddy bank and the clunk of boats. Boats?

The marina. She'd talked Aaron into coming here with her. She must be very close to the lough to be able to hear the water that clearly, much closer than the place where she'd been knocked out.

And that answered the other question that had been nudging at her. The reason he hadn't dragged her off immediately was that he had to deal with Aaron first. He'd incapacitated her and then gone off to put Aaron out of action too.

The splash. She retched again, but there was no food left inside her to come up. If that was Aaron's body that made the splash, then she'd been directly responsible for his death. And it meant the killer would be on his way back to finish his work with Nic. On the thought, she heard a faint clink of metal. The gate. He was already off the jetty and looking for her. What would he do when he found she'd gone?

Her instinct was to cower down in the ditch and hope he went away, but what remained of her senses told her it was the wrong thing to do. What time was it? She scraped the mud off her watch, but was too afraid to light the face up to read, in case it caught his eye, so she had no idea. It'd be morning before anyone else appeared at this time of year, and in the meantime, he'd have the whole night to search for her.

She hadn't been in any state to think about hiding her trail either. He could already be close behind her. A sudden vision of him flashed through her mind, churning through the woods with his head down like a bloodhound, following the broken branches and crushed grass straight to her hiding place.

The clouds were back, covering the moon and stars, so she wouldn't see him until he was on top of her, and she couldn't hope he'd step on another twig to give her warning. For all the good it had done her last time, she thought, touching the lump again.

Even the slightest pressure sent lights flashing behind her eyes. He could have fractured her skull with that blow, but there was nothing she could do about it until she got herself to safety.

Aaron. Nic bit her bottom lip in indecision. But she had to know what had happened to him. He'd have done the same for her.

She was just about to pull herself up from her hiding place when the undergrowth rustled, not close, but not very far away, either. She lowered herself back down, holding her breath.

Footsteps sounded, and panting. Then a voice rang out. "Here, Jake. Come."

The scuffling sounded louder, and something scrambled out of the ditch not twenty feet from her. It was a dog, shining pale even in the darkness.

"Come on, Jake. Where are you?"

The dog whined. It must know she was hiding there, and be torn between obeying its master and going to say hello to the filthy figure in the ditch. Nic willed it to go away, and it did, with a swish of its tail.

"Good dog. Where were you?"

Thank God for dog walkers, out in the middle of the night. Who walked their dog in the pitch black in the middle of nowhere? Never mind. Nic owed him, whoever he was. He was chatting to the dog now as the pair of them moved away down an unseen path. Nic used the noise they made to cover her own rustlings as she used a branch to pull herself up out of the ditch and on to the level ground at the end of the car park.

She knew where she was now. She'd managed to travel quite a long way and was down the side of the jetties where a long spit of land jutted out into the lough, a breakwater to protect the boats from wind and waves. The boats on the north side of the last jetty had their backs to her, so she was looking at them end on instead of from the side.

She was about to turn back towards the gate when something caught her eye in the water. It was a dark shape, half floating, and it had just moved.

A bird, she told herself, but it was a big bird. A very big— Aaron?

She slipped down the sloping bank to the water's edge, but the object was too far away. Now she was closer, she couldn't be sure if it had moved, or if it was just an effect of the water. It looked like floating debris, or a big clump of weed.

Then a ripple radiated out from it, and she gasped as a white face turned towards her. It was Aaron, and he was badly hurt. She'd never forgive herself if—

She waded into the water. It was cold, so cold she sucked her breath in, sending shards of pain radiating from the lump at the back of her head, but there was no time to worry about that now. The water got deep really quickly, and in seconds she was out of her depth, floundering towards him, making far too much noise. She'd just have to hope the dog walker had sent the killer running off in the other direction.

Her outstretched hand touched a piece of clothing. She gripped it, but her numb fingers slid off, and she only managed to push him further away. Her clothes dragged her down, clinging and swirling around her, and there were weeds on the bottom too. They snatched at her legs, trying to tie her to the muddy floor of the lough.

Nothing for it. She let herself sink, bending her knees, until her feet buried themselves in the thick mud, then she pushed off with all her strength.

It was enough. She came up right beside Aaron, and took a fistful of his thick jacket, turning him over on to his back so his face was out of the water. Was she too late? Too dark to see, with the boats and the jetty shadowing them from the marina lights.

She didn't know how she got them both back to the bank, but the sucking mud enveloping her lower legs was one of the best things she'd ever felt. She dragged at Aaron's clothes, but he was so heavy. Too heavy by far to lift him out as a dead weight.

At school, they'd had to take lifesaving classes as part of their Duke of Edinburgh training, and Nic had reluctantly learned how to resuscitate a victim of drowning. Now, she wished she'd paid more attention. At seventeen, it hadn't seemed possible that the life of someone she cared for might depend on her ability to carry out such a basic operation.

CPR. Circulation, pulse, respiration? Was that it? Wasn't circulation and pulse the same thing? She put her fingertips to his neck, trying to find a pulse, but his skin was cold and slippery, and she couldn't remember where she was supposed to feel.

Wrist. That might be easier. She felt along his arm and came up with a hand, but it was hard to support his head above the water at the same time as holding his wrist so she could feel for his pulse. She was about to give up and move on to his breathing when she felt something under his skin. It was only the faintest fluttering, barely there, but it was better than nothing.

"Come on, Aaron," she whispered, teeth chattering. "Stay with me." The hand she held moved, sliding out of her grip, and he nearly went under. It took all her strength to keep his heavy body at the surface. She put the back of her hand up to his mouth. A soft breath stirred the fine hairs.

She was grinning, teeth clattering together, but it was too soon to celebrate yet. He was out cold, and there was still a killer somewhere nearby, hunting them.

Maybe if she could walk them both along the edge of the breakwater, she'd find some sort of beach where she could drag Aaron into shallow water and do something to bring him round. Now she had him, she felt even more lost than when she'd been on her own. It wasn't just herself she was responsible for now, but Aaron too.

Movement nearby froze her before she'd taken the first step. Someone was walking the length of the jetty. Despite their soft, careful steps, their feet made a hollow sound on the wooden planks and occasional creaks where one had worked its way loose. If she hadn't been so close, she'd never have heard him, but if she could hear him, then he'd be able to hear any sound she made too.

Nic switched from willing Aaron to respond to willing him to stay quiet. He was cold and limp in her arms, but who knew when he'd stir again?

The figure reached the end of the jetty and there was a soft thump as he jumped down into a boat there. Waves slapped the hulls of the moored boats, and several of the smaller ones rocked a little. Wood scraped against wood. A hatch being opened? How close had Aaron got before he was discovered? Was Hazel really so close to her?

Belatedly, Nic remembered Aaron's final command: to phone Asha if there was the slightest hint of trouble. Events had overtaken her, and now the phone would be useless, submerged as it was in murky lough water.

Still, she had to try.

The iPhone was in her left-hand jeans pocket, easily reached, but it was totally dead. No surprises there. It wasn't easy to reach into the other pocket for the brick, and she almost lost her grip on Aaron, but eventually her icy fingers managed to pull it out. With no hope at all, she pressed the button, and to her amazement the screen lit up.

She didn't have Asha's number saved on this phone. She'd have to call 999 and hope she could convince someone to treat her seriously. Who was going to believe her if she told the truth?

She swapped hands and unlocked the phone with clumsy fingers. Her hand shook as she held it to her ear, listening for the connection to be completed. It rang, and she sent a silent prayer up to whatever spirit of the lough might be listening. But it continued to ring, and ring. This shouldn't happen with a 999 call, should it? An operator would surely pick up straight away, even if they were flat-out busy.

Then it clicked and a familiar voice came on the line.

"Nic. We've been worried sick. Where are you?"

"Asha," she gasped. "Lough Neagh. Kinnego Marina. Aaron's hurt. Help—" Then she went silent. Someone had jumped back on to the jetty. Her heart kicked painfully in her chest. So close, he'd hear anything else she said. He must have heard something from inside the boat, but he maybe wasn't certain what, or he'd have been down the jetty as fast as he could move.

"Nic?" Asha's voice sounded tinny with the phone held away from her ear.

Would he hear that? She held the phone against her chest, muffling the sound until she saw him step back down into the cockpit again, then she whispered into the mouthpiece, praying she could be heard.

"He's here."

CHAPTER 26

"Keep the connection open, Nic," Asha ordered her. "You don't need to speak, but we can listen in."

Aaron stirred in her arms and groaned. It wasn't loud, but she was sure it could be heard across the water on a still night like this.

"Shhh, I'm here," she whispered. "Help's on the way."

He turned his face towards her, but his eyes reflected silver in the moonlight, the pupils wide and staring. There was no awareness there, and Nic shivered, not just from the cold that was sapping her strength, but at the blankness of his expression. He'd already taken a blow to the head earlier in the evening, and now who knew what injuries the killer had inflicted on him?

She probed his head gently with her fingers. There was a lump that matched the one she had on the back of her head, but it was on the side of Aaron's, and there was a strange feel to the bone under her fingers, like burst bubble wrap. As she touched the area, he moaned, an animal sound that would definitely travel across the still water.

It did. A hatch clattered open and the killer appeared on the jetty again, staring straight at them where they hid under the overhang of a bushy tree. Nic put her hand over Aaron's mouth, ready to silence him if he moaned again, but he was silent. His eyes had closed, and he was too still by far, but she could only thank providence right now. Worry could come later.

If the killer had a flashlight, they'd be done for. He wouldn't be able to miss them this close, but she had to pray he'd be too wary to give away his position. So far, her luck had held.

And then, between one laboured breath and the next, it didn't.

Aaron's body convulsed, limbs thrashing. A gurgling scream erupted from his mouth. One arm made contact with the side of her head, stunning her, and she let go. In seconds, he was drifting away, still thrashing, and sinking under water. He must be fitting from the head injury.

Running feet pounded the jetty. The killer was on his way around, but for the moment, he'd seen only Aaron, not her. She was no further than twenty yards from the jetty, and the boat at the end. He'd have to navigate the gate, then run along to the breakwater and down the narrow spit of land in the dark to reach the place where Aaron still thrashed like a drowning man. Which he was.

She didn't give herself time to think, but shoved the phone down her jumper, into her bra, and struck out towards Aaron, grabbing him by the collar of his coat, and swam sidestroke towards the boat as it rocked gently on the waves from Aaron's thrashing. There was no sign of the killer. He'd be at the far end of the jetty by now, out of sight and earshot as he wrestled with the lock on the gate.

Her hand hit the side of the boat with a dull clunk and she made her way around it towards the stern. There'd be a boarding ladder, had to be. Aaron had gone still and quiet again, but she had neither time nor energy to spare to check him. He'd have to take his chances.

There. There was a ladder, but it was tied up, way out of her reach. Her heart sank and she spun in the water, looking for something she might use to reach up to the rope. Her eyes caught the dull gleam of metal in the starlight as the clouds cleared for a moment. A safety ladder on to the jetty!

She swam across to it, and hooked Aaron's arm over one of the rungs so he hung there like a puppet with its string severed, head lolling, but out of the water. At least he wouldn't drown in that position, if he hadn't already.

Nic flung herself at the slimy metal ladder, but she'd been in the cold water a long time, and her legs wouldn't take her weight. She had to use her arms to hoist herself up, shoulders popping with the effort, until she landed on the wooden jetty like a haddock chucked on to the deck of a trawler, gasping.

No time. She crawled on hands and knees, willing her legs to work, until she reached the side of the boat. Luckily it was a similar height to the jetty, so she could roll herself off the edge and land in the cockpit, a foot or two below. It knocked the breath out of her, but she kept moving towards the open hatch, a black rectangle in the silvery moonlight.

She slithered through it, grabbing at the steps to slow her fall, but only succeeded in wrenching her shoulder even more. She hit the bottom boards with a wet thump and a gasp. There was a paraffin lamp, turned right down so it cast barely any light, but with her eyes already adjusted to the dark, it was enough.

Two pairs of eyes stared at her over filthy gags. One pair was terrified, the other filled with tears. Nic gasped. "Hazel!"

Both of them were naked, and now her brain registered the stink where they'd both fouled themselves where they lay. Their hair was matted, and the Indian woman, Meera, had a bruise darkening her left eye, but there was no sign of wounds on either of them. Nic pulled herself to her feet on trembling legs and staggered the couple of paces to her sister. She pulled the gag free, then looked for a knife.

There was a galley, of sorts, with a primus stove and that silver, gleaming coffee machine she'd glimpsed before. She flung drawers open, searching, until she found a broken pair of scissors that'd have to do.

The zip-ties that held Hazel's wrists together didn't give in easily, but finally her hands fell apart and she let out a long sigh that was part relief, part pain as the circulation returned.

Then Nic turned her efforts to Meera. She freed her wrists first, then worked the gag loose. As it slipped down, Meera's eyes widened, the pupils huge. She threw herself sideways, knocking Nic off balance. Nic's shoulder caught a glancing blow off the edge of the seat frame that sent tingling pain down her arm. Hazel screamed.

By the time Nic had righted herself, the killer was on her, pinning her face down into the semi-liquid faeces swimming around down there. He tried to push her face into it, and she pushed back, the terror of drowning in liquid shit giving her the strength to resist.

Then his weight fell across her shoulders, bearing her down, and she was choking.

She pushed with all her strength, but he was a dead weight. Nic tried to hold her breath, but he was compressing her lungs and the desire to breathe was almost irresistible. Then the weight lightened and disappeared. Someone pulled on her arm, twisting her around.

She fought back, slapping blindly, eyes burning with the filth that ran down her face and into her open mouth.

"Stop, Nic! It's me. You're safe," Hazel said, her voice hoarse.

She stopped fighting and used her sleeve to wipe her eyes and mouth, spitting out the worst of the contents, but she didn't think that taste would ever go away.

A figure lay face down on the floor of the cabin. Meera tottered over to the paraffin lamp, which by some miracle was still upright, and turned the wick up. The cabin flooded with warm yellow light, showing the state of both captives. Hazel's hair hung lank either side of her face, her skin grey with fear and fatigue. A large frying pan dangled from her fingers. When she saw Nic looking at it, she let it slide free and it landed on the back of the man who lay prone on the floor.

He was more lightly built than Nic had expected him to be. She remembered a podgy belly and stooped shoulders, but this man was slim, younger. Were there two of them?

Almost afraid of what she'd find, she bent to turn him over, but as soon as she touched his shoulder, he let out a yell and twisted in her grasp, scrambling on all fours back towards the stairs to the cockpit. All three of them leaped back in shock, but Meera recovered first. She hurled herself at his legs in a rugby tackle.

They came down in a tangle of limbs: lithe brown legs and stained jeans entwined. Meera was thrown backwards as he surged up again, flinging himself at the stairs and out as Hazel and Nic, both far too late, tried to grab him. They collided. Rebounded. Nic tripped over Meera and landed on her back on the long bunk.

The hatch slammed above them, followed by a lighter plink as he slid a locking mechanism into place. Nic ran over and tried to force the wooden doors open, but couldn't make them move more than a centimetre. The boat dipped and rolled as he jumped ashore, and the sound of his running feet faded into the distance. At least he hadn't stopped to notice Aaron on the ladder. If Aaron was still there, Nic thought wearily. She thumped the hatch in frustration.

"It's locked," Meera said. "He locks it every time he leaves us."

"There must be another way out of here," Nic said. She slipped and slid the other way, towards the bows of the boat. There was a wooden door that opened with a kick, revealing a cramped second cabin with a V-shaped bed piled high with canvas bags. It was too dark to see much else.

Hazel appeared at her shoulder with the lamp, casting smoky shadows ahead of it, but it showed a solid, square wooden hatch in the roof of the cabin, and this one had a latch on the inside. Nic started tossing the bags aside to make room so she could climb on to the bed.

The latch was stiff, thick with rust. "Is there anything I can use as a hammer?"

Meera reached forward from the main cabin with a tin that said *coffee* on it. Nic hefted it to check the weight. A bit light, but it'd have to do.

The latch yielded eventually, but Hazel and then Meera had to take turns before the rusted spring finally snapped and allowed the bolt to draw back. Together, shoulder to shoulder in the confined space, they pushed upwards. It lifted with the creak of swollen wood and slammed back against the deck, allowing fresh air to rush in.

Nic drank it down, like water to a parched throat. Above her upturned face, the moon now shone in a clear sky and a myriad stars gleamed, the Milky Way spread out like a motorway through the heavens.

She dropped back to let the other two through first. Hazel needed help to climb through the narrow opening, but eventually, after kicking Nic in the teeth with one swinging foot and apologizing over and over, she was outside. Nic looked around for Meera. She had emptied out one of the canvas bags and was poking through the contents.

She seemed to sense Nic watching her, because she looked up defensively. "There are some clothes in here, but they're pretty gross, all mouldy."

"If you find any to fit yourself and Hazel, throw them up. It's freezing outside. I could do with a dry set too. I'm soaked."

Meera threw up a knitted jumper and a pair of jeans, then another pair of jeans and a sweatshirt. "Try these."

Nic threw one set to Hazel and held the other gingerly at arm's length. "I stink even worse than the clothes. Maybe I should try to wash a bit first?"

Meera gave a sharp laugh, bordering on hysterical. "We all stink, love. Unless you'd rather freeze, put 'em on."

Nic dragged herself through the hatch and stripped off her wet clothes, forcing nearly numb legs and arms into the dry clothes. The woollen jumper scratched her healing wounds, but it was nothing compared to what she'd been through, so she shut it away. Meera appeared in the opening, wearing fleece trackpants and a checked shirt that hung off her shoulders.

"Now what?" Meera asked, her flat vowels reminding Nic of Ram.

Ram. Asha. "Aaron!"

Nic jumped clumsily off the bow of the boat, somehow managing to navigate the wires that fenced the edge of the deck. Her feet slipped on landing, but she caught herself and used her momentum to swing over to the metal handrails that showed her where the steps were. How could she have forgotten him?

For a moment, she thought he'd fallen in and drowned, then he lifted his face up to her, eyes wide.

"Nic," he slurred. "Knew you'd come."

"Help me!" she cried as she grabbed the arm she'd hooked around the rail. His body weight hung off it, making it next to impossible to lift him clear from above. There was nothing for it: she'd have to get back in the water.

Hazel reached past her and took a hold of his sleeve, and Meera grabbed the back of his collar. Maybe together they could lift him clear.

"One, two, three, lift," Nic said, gasping with effort on the last word. He came up about a foot, then Hazel lost her grip and his weight dragged him back down again.

"Meera, would you go below and see if there's any more warm clothes? Then bring them here. I'm going back in to push from below. I think it's the only way we'll get him out of here."

Meera smiled, her teeth white in the dark, and disappeared back towards the boat. Nic stripped down to her underwear and sat on the edge of the jetty, waiting for Meera to come back. She wasn't long.

The water felt even icier the second time. As she allowed herself to slip over the edge, it embraced her as a lover, silk against her bare skin. The wood of the jetty glistened with millions of tiny diamonds. No wonder they were so cold. An unseasonable frost had struck.

Aaron's skin was like a dead fish: unhealthy white and not an iota of warmth to Nic's touch. But he'd been alive and talking just a moment ago.

"When I push him up, pull for all you're worth," she said, teeth chattering. Hazel took a better handful of material from his sleeve. Meera bent down and took a fistful of cloth too, her mouth a tight line.

Nic felt for the bottom step with her foot, then gripped the side rail for balance and braced herself. "Ready!"

She ducked under the water, almost gasping at the cold shock, and got her shoulder beneath Aaron's hip. Her other foot found the step, and she jackknifed up, using all the strength she could summon to launch Aaron into the air. He barely moved at first, then the momentum built as the two above took some of the strain. His arm came loose from where she'd hooked it and his body lurched backwards for a moment, overbalancing, then the others caught him and he continued up.

Nic's face surfaced and she filled her lungs with air, still pushing, water streaming into her eyes and mouth. Aaron moaned, but the others had his upper body on the deck now, and only his legs trailed in the lough. Nic shifted one hand to his knee and shoved again, then the other hand.

"Got him!" Hazel gasped. "Get out, Nic, before you freeze."

Meera had to help her up the slippery steps, dragging her the last few feet until she collapsed next to Aaron, water streaming off both of them and pooling in silver lakes on the ice-encrusted planks before it drained down the gaps and back into the lough.

A shudder wracked her body, but Aaron lay still where he'd landed, no sign of life. Nic crawled over to him and shook his shoulder. No point in being careful in case of a spinal injury now — he'd been dragged about so much, any damage would already have been done — but he'd die for sure if they left him here, with no heat in his body.

Nic started to massage his arms and legs, wishing she'd listened more attentively in those first aid classes, but Meera pushed her aside.

"Get some clothes on or we'll have two dead bodies instead of one. I'll deal with him."

"S'not dead," Nic tried to say, but by now her teeth were chattering so much it was probably unintelligible. She reached for the pile of clothes she'd dropped, and Hazel helped her get her rubbery arms into the sleeves, and her legs into the trousers. Extra layers were only useful if you already had some heat in you, and she didn't.

She went back and kneeled by Aaron's side. Meera was running experienced hands across his skull and neck, a frown on her face.

"I think he has a fractured skull," Nic said in a small voice. "I felt it earlier when we were in the water."

"He does," Meera said. "It's enough to kill him without the hypothermia. We need to get him to a hospital, fast."

The brick. Nic felt in her bra, where she'd left it, but it wasn't there. It must have fallen out, but where? If it had fallen into the lough, there'd be no chance of finding it, but maybe it had come out during the struggle in the boat?

She was scrambling to her feet when the sound of a roaring engine shattered the night and headlights swept across the car park. For a moment, they lit up a shadowy figure, shambling along near the treeline, then the figure disappeared into the woods. A van followed the first car. It slid to a halt and the back doors opened. Men spilled out, splitting up and running towards the trees.

Nic willed them to come to her, but they'd never hear her shout over the sound of their own voices. She realized she was speaking though. She was repeating the same thing, over and over. "Asha. Asha. Asha."

As if in answer to her prayer, a slim figure broke away from the crowd of men and started running towards the gate to the jetty. It must have been open, because she barely hesitated, feet drumming a tattoo on the hollow planks. More people followed her, and now a blue flashing light joined the other vehicles: an ambulance. Nic breathed a sigh of relief. Help for Aaron.

"Nic! Are you all right?" Asha was right there, holding her, eyes searching hers. "You're frozen!"

"Never mind me," Nic stammered. "Aaron needs help. He's badly injured."

Asha let her go and dropped to her knees by her colleague's still body. A sob shook her. "No!"

"Stand aside, ma'am," a deep voice said. It was one of the paramedics in a dark jumpsuit. How he'd got there so fast, and carrying a heavy bag, Nic didn't know, but she was limp with relief.

"He has a fractured skull, and he's been in icy water for a long time too," Meera said in a matter-of-fact voice. "He has a pulse, but it's faint, and he's deeply hypothermic. I don't know how much water he's inhaled, either."

The paramedic started working over Aaron's body, Meera talking to him in a low voice. How did she stay so calm? *Because she doesn't know him,* Nic answered herself. *He didn't risk his career to follow one of her hunches.*

Asha drew her away. Someone wrapped a tinfoil blanket around her and started prodding at her, but she pulled away. "Hazel?"

"I'm here," her sister said. She was seated on the side deck of the boat, wrapped in another blanket and with her own paramedic fussing over her. "Is he going to be okay?"

"I don't know," she breathed. "Asha, I'm sorry. So sorry. If it wasn't for me——"

"If it wasn't for you, he'd have moved these two and we might never have found them." But Asha's voice was tight and thick with worry.

"Have you told Inspector Ram?" Nic asked. "He needs to know that Meera is safe."

"Shit," Asha said. "I'll phone him now."

"Let me," Meera said, straightening up painfully. "If you'll lend me your phone?"

Asha handed it over. "I have his number saved, if you don't know it by heart."

Meera took the phone, turning away to speak. "Papa? It's me. I'm safe."

A voice erupted from the tiny speaker in a rush, speaking a language Nic didn't know. Asha and Nic backed away to give her space, and went to join Hazel where she still sat, her bum now resting on the edge of the cabin roof and feet on the deck. Nic sank down next to her and put an arm around her sister's shoulders.

"I'm so glad you're okay."

"Yes," Hazel said in a flat voice. "I'm fine."

A cold shard pierced Nic's heart at that tone. She'd heard it before, in the days following the armed robbery, and again after the court case. In the months that followed, Hazel had gone quiet, avoiding all the things she'd enjoyed, and turning inwards.

CHAPTER 27

As soon as Meera finished, Nic phoned their mother. Ma wasn't coherent, but Dad came on after a moment, and although his voice sounded choked up, as if he had a bad head cold, she managed to get the message across that both she and Hazel were safe. They didn't need to know how close it had been, or about Aaron. Time enough for that later.

Voices spoke over one another. Radios crackled. More blue lights arrived on the scene, and Aaron was carefully lifted on to a hard plastic stretcher. An officer came over to where Nic and Hazel sat, with Asha hovering above them.

"I need to move you all to the far end of the car park, please. We're expecting a helicopter shortly to airlift the casualty to a specialist team at the Royal."

Nic rose to her feet and helped Hazel up. Her sister didn't meet her eye, but stumbled along with the others until their feet crunched on the hard surface of the car park. Nic's bare feet were numb, but every so often she felt the pressure as she stood on a stone and wondered what state the soles of her feet would be in when the feeling came back. They reached the far end of the car park, where the police cars and ambulances were being shuffled out of the way until they were parked in random order, with their backs to the steel mesh fence that surrounded the buildings. Barely in time. Rotor blades beat the air in the distance and everyone strained their necks to look up.

Lights appeared in the sky, a counterpoint to the still-flashing blue lights of the emergency services, and the din rose to a crescendo as a red helicopter hovered above them. The downdraught set up a whirlwind that lifted Nic's saturated hair and whipped her face with it. She snatched at it and tried to tuck it inside her collar, but her hands were clumsy and the hair was as lively as Medusa's snakes. Hazel turned and buried her face in Nic's shoulder, and Nic abandoned any attempt to tame her hair in order to wrap her arms around her sister.

They both trembled with cold, but as Hazel clung to her, Nic's shoulders shook with sobs. She held her even tighter, kissing the top of her head.

The helicopter settled down, its rotors still turning, and green-uniformed paramedics lifted the stretcher that held Aaron, running with it to the craft. A doctor hopped out and came around to examine Aaron, then climbed in alongside him as the stretcher was fed inside. In no time at all, it was airborne again, and the winds died down, leaving Nic deafened and feeling as though she'd survived a violent storm.

Asha reappeared, talking on her mobile. She waved to one of the other paramedics, and pointed to Hazel and Nic. He trotted over to them with his bag.

"Would you two come with me, please? We need to take you to the hospital for a check-up."

They followed him to one of the ambulances and he turned to help Hazel up the steps, but she wouldn't let go of Nic.

"Come on, love. It's warmer in here, and you'll be together."

"It's all right, Hazel. I'm not letting you go. See? I'm coming in with you."

With coaxing and persuasion, they got her up the steps and into the back of the vehicle, with its bright white lights and sterile smell.

"Here, strap in, will you?"

Nic helped her fasten her seat belt, then settled into the other seat and fastened her own as best she could with one hand gripped tightly by her sister. "Where are we going?"

"Craigavon, I expect, unless they tell me different."

"Any chance you could take us to the Royal? It's where they took my friend, in the helicopter. I'm really worried about him."

The paramedic frowned, then his face lightened. "From what I heard, you're the only reason that guy still has a chance, so I guess he owes you. I'll see what I can do, but no promises."

Another face appeared at the rear door. "All set in there, Chris? We're ready to go when you are."

"Hang on, mate. Radio Dispatch and ask if they can task us to the Royal instead of Craigavon, would you?"

The other medic raised his eyebrows, but he nodded cheerfully. "I'll try, but you know how it is. Depends how busy they are."

He slammed the door shut and a moment later Nic heard the driver's door close. She smiled at the paramedic. "Thank you."

"Like I said, no promises, but we'll soon know. If he turns left at the roundabout, we're off to Belfast. If it's right, Craigavon."

Nic wondered how she'd know which way they'd turned. The ambulance windows were tinted dark and there were horizontal blinds as well, blocking the view even more. The vehicle bounced and squeaked across the car park, and she did feel the turn as they went left out on to the main road. In fact, the whole vehicle tilted and the contents of the cupboards slid noisily around. She met the paramedic's startled gaze.

He grinned at her, but then he licked his lips. "Ron's making a run for it before Dispatch can give us another call," he said, but his discomfort was obvious. Nic found herself digging fingernails into her palm and made herself relax her hand.

They did turn left at the roundabout, but it was with a squealing of rubber on tarmac. Nic wondered if the driver knew something she didn't, and the next thought was that he'd heard some news about Aaron's condition. He must be trying to get them there quickly.

Lights flashed past the side windows, too fast for Nic to have any chance to work out where they were, but it seemed far too soon when the ambulance slowed and veered to the left, indicator ticking. Chris, the paramedic, half stood to look out of the window, then he sat back down, mystified.

"Where are we?"

"Turning off at the Moira junction," he said in a tight voice. "Maybe we've been sent to the Lagan Valley instead." He turned back to the partition that separated them from the cab and knocked. "Ron? Where we heading, mate?"

There was no reply. Chris's smile was strained. "He'll have his music on, I expect. Getting deaf in his old age."

The ambulance lurched around the big roundabout. Now she knew where they were, Nic was beginning to get a really bad feeling. The Moira roundabout was only a stone's throw from Maghaberry and the field with the cottage in it.

Hazel sat hunched, turned sideways in her seat so she could keep hold of Nic's hand, but her breathing was steady and rhythmical. She could be asleep. She moved limply with the turns, like a rag doll.

Nic searched as well as she could without making it too obvious, looking for a handy weapon, but there was nothing. All the useful stuff must be locked away in cupboards in case a drunk got hold of something that could do damage.

Indecision was written across Chris's face. She wondered if he was reading her mind, or at least reading the situation and coming to similar conclusions to her. She tried to think of a way to communicate with him without alerting Hazel, then she spotted the biro that was clipped to the top of the chart he'd left on the empty stretcher. She reached over to it and took up the whole clipboard.

I think we might be in trouble. Not Ron? she wrote and passed it to him over Hazel's head.

He read it and wrote a reply. *Not sure.*

Anything we can use as a weapon?

His mouth was slack with shock. He shook his head violently.

Nic gritted her teeth and reached for the clipboard, but Chris was already writing furiously.

This is an ambulance. You're safe in here.

Huh! She snatched the clipboard. *I think the kidnapper is driving this ambulance. He needed to get off the motorway before they found Ron. He must have knocked Ron out. Or killed him.*

Chris shook his head, disbelieving. He didn't want to believe, but then he hadn't had the experience that Nic had of her tormentor's ability to use an opportunity.

Please! She wrote, running out of space on the side of the assessment sheet. She cast her eyes to Hazel who still swayed with the movement of the ambulance. That sick feeling of doom she'd felt while she hid in the hedge as the killer drove by was growing again, threatening to paralyze her. She had to be strong this time, for Hazel as much as for herself.

The ambulance made a sharp right turn and bounced as the back wheels rose up over some bump, perhaps the grass verge. If she'd needed confirmation, this was it.

Even Chris seemed unsure. He unclipped his seat belt, far too slowly, then began to rise, reaching up towards one of the overhead lockers. Nic hoped there'd be something in there they could use to defend themselves. Maybe scissors or a scalpel? But the young paramedic was off balance as he stretched his arm, and the ambulance did a sudden swerve over rough ground, bouncing so much Nic feared it would tip over completely. Chris was flung across the narrow space and into the metal rail along the side of the stretcher.

The wheels hit the ground, and the whole vehicle groaned with the strain as the back end swung from side to side. Could the driver see them, here in the back? Did he know what they were up to? That swerve had been all too timely. Chris tried to grab something to steady himself, but the ambulance swerved the other way, and he fell again, hitting his head on the arm of Hazel's seat.

Hazel jerked her head up, either waking or just becoming aware that something wasn't right. She turned startled eyes to Nic, who gripped her hand even harder as the vehicle bounced and bumped across rough grass, engine roaring and wheels spinning for traction.

"Nic! Is it him?"

Nic nodded, seeing her own sick realization mirrored in her sister's eyes. "Yes, but he's got to stop this thing some time, and then we can tackle him. Sit tight."

Chris was pulling himself back into the seat and trying to fasten his seat belt with shaking hands. Blood ran in a steady stream down the side of his face.

"Believe me now?" she said, having to shout to be heard over the engine.

His lips were blue, his skin pale grey. "What'll we do?"

"He has to stop some time. We'll only have seconds to find something to defend ourselves with, and he might have a knife. Or more than one."

Chris reached into his pocket and brought out a mobile, then twisted his face in disgust. "No signal. There's nothing much in here, except scissors, and they're only small ones. Even a scalpel blade would be no match for a knife. Unless you want to use the defibrillator?"

"There are three of us," Hazel said, surprising Nic with the ferocity in her voice. "Surely we can overpower him if we work together? We managed it on the boat, and we were cold and naked then!"

Nic caught a glimpse of her own reflection in the dark window and was shocked by the death's head appearance of her face. It would hardly inspire confidence. "That's the spirit," she said, for something to say.

Heart hammering, Nic waited for the engine to slow, but it didn't. Why wasn't he stopping? Where were they that they were still bouncing across grass? She tried to bring to mind the satellite view of the area near the prison. There'd been fields and farms, but not many. And the quarry. Shit!

Her mouth was too dry to speak. She knew what he was doing now. He was going to drive them all off the edge of the quarry. He'd searched this area for hiding places at least as thoroughly as she had, and there's no way he'd have missed the quarry.

She met Chris's terrified eyes. "There's a quarry around here. We need to jump out! He's going to drive us all over the cliff."

He shook his head again, and she resisted the temptation to go over and shake him by the shoulders until she'd knocked sense into him.

"Hazel! We need to get out of here."

Hazel looked up at her with trusting eyes. "How?"

Nic unfastened her seat belt and dived for the rear door. She managed to grab the yellow handrail, but then the ambulance swerved violently, and she was thrown sideways before she could get a grip on the door release. A second engine roared nearby, but she could see nothing through the dark window.

On the second attempt, she managed to release the door and it swung open, almost dragging her with it. She wavered for balance, arms flailing, then someone caught her by the waist of the jeans she wore and hauled her backwards. She landed heavily on someone who let their breath out with an oomph. Hazel.

"Hold tight!" she shouted over the noise, which was much louder with the door open. Nic crawled back to the rear of the vehicle on hands and knees, hooking her arm around the stretcher legs to keep herself from being flung around. If it moved now, she'd be in so much trouble.

When she got to the open door, the ground rushed under her in a blur of speed, lit an eerie red by the ambulance's rear lights. Way too fast to jump. There had to be some way to slow it. She cast her eyes around the interior of the ambulance. There was the stretcher. What if they all climbed on that and let it run off the back? Would that absorb some of the impact and protect them?

Chris appeared at her shoulder, also on his hands and knees. She shouted her thoughts at him and he nodded. "We could lower the stretcher ramp so it wouldn't be such a long drop too."

Nic saw what he meant. There was a vertical door that folded down to become a horizontal ramp. If they rolled the stretcher on to that and lowered themselves before taking the brakes off, it would be a much better landing. But the seconds were ticking away. How far were they from the quarry?

Then the ambulance swerved again, throwing her into the paramedic. There was a frantic moment where they each tried to grab anything solid to keep themselves from falling out, then it dawned on Nic that every time it swerved, the ambulance lost a bit of speed.

Another swerve, and a whine as the driver slammed through the gears, pushing the engine to the maximum. Nic pulled herself to her feet and tried to look out of the window. There was a police Land Rover zigzagging in front of them. She could just catch glimpses of it as it appeared briefly on her side of the ambulance. And the technique was working. The ambulance driver was finding it impossible to keep going at the same speed with all the avoidance tactics. Nic wondered for a moment why he didn't just ram the thing, if his plan was to drive them all off the edge of the quarry anyway, but then he probably intended to bail out before they reached the edge, and leave the three of them to fall to their deaths.

"Get ready to jump!" Nic shouted. Chris's jaw was set, his eyes tense. But Hazel smiled up at her.

"Love you, Nic," she said.

Tears pricked at the back of Nic's eyes, burning. "Love you too, Nutcase." She hadn't called her sister by the nickname in years. "Come on. Let's do this together, shall we?"

Hazel would be weakened from her captivity, short though it was, so Nic planned to hold her to her chest as she jumped, shielding her with her own body to protect her as they hit the ground. Hazel might have read her thoughts, because in one smooth movement, she unclipped her seat belt, pushed between Nic and Chris, and dived out of the back door, just as the ambulance did another sharp swerve. Nic was thrown out after her sister, and her last sight was the paramedic's startled face, backlit by the bright lights in the ambulance, then she hit her head on something. Pain seared through her skull, and the world faded through red to black.

CHAPTER 28

Fucking hell! Where did that bloody Land Rover come from? He swung the wheel violently, hearing the clatter from the back as something went flying. *Bloody suicidal maniac.*

He'd researched this route before, when he was looking for an alternative place to take his captives, once he'd got that bitch back again. There was a workman's hut in the abandoned quarry, all derelict and overgrown like the rest of the place. He doubted if anyone remembered it was even there. He'd even opened all the field gates from the road to give himself an easy route through to the road that led down into the quarry. He was glad of all the extra work now, as he bounced across the grass.

Another gateway loomed up in his headlights, and he gunned the engine, rocketing towards it, but then the Land Rover cut across the front of him again, almost ramming the ambulance. He spun the wheel, fighting for control as the top-heavy vehicle threatened to topple over. The gateway flashed past his window and thorns squealed across paint-work as he brushed the hedge before he was able to wrench the thing away and turn back into the field. The opposite direction to where he needed to go.

And this bitch of an ambulance didn't want to turn. There might be something wrong with the suspension, maybe after that last turn, because it was listing to one side and pulling to the left as well.

He glanced in the passenger-side mirror. The back door was swinging wide open. Had that last turn shaken it open? No, it'd be that bitch, interfering. He should have killed her and let the other one live while he had the chance. She was nothing but trouble.

But the thought was half-hearted. Killing the man had always been the plan. He was just a by-product, a catalyst to the world of terror and shock he liked to create in his survivors. That was most of the fun, letting them go, and then catching them again. They'd never be free of him.

He swerved again, viciously, hoping to cause an injury to one of his passengers, but then the Land Rover reappeared, herding him back towards the hedge. He changed down and slammed his foot on the accelerator, heading straight for the white vehicle. This time it was the copper who swerved, and the Land Rover did a nasty tilt, with air under the nearside wheels.

He grinned. It was even more top-heavy than the ambulance. If he could force the cops to do that again, the whole damned thing might go over. His brain began to formulate a plan. The edge of the quarry was the other side of that next field, if he could only get into it. How well did the copper know this area? Not as well as him, he reckoned. Chances were they wouldn't know about the drop-off that could loom out of the darkness, protected only by two thin strands of wire, overgrown with brambles and nettles.

He completed the wide sweep he needed to face the gate again, and gripped the wheel with both hands, jaw locked in determination. Let the bastards play around in front of him all they liked. Nothing was going to stop him going through that gate now.

There it was, coming in from the right again. He held his course. The gateposts were grey shadows at the end of the range of his main beam, and he corrected slightly to pass between them. The Land Rover dropped in front of him and hit the brakes, but he had control of himself now. He kept his foot flat to the floor. The rear of the police vehicle seemed to rush towards him, and the impact, when it came, was harder than he expected. His ribcage hit the steering wheel, knocking the breath out of him and sending flashing lights across his vision.

It must be affecting the Land Rover driver even more, though. The thing was still oscillating as the driver tried to regain control. Stubborn bastard, though. He wasn't moving over. They went through the gate with the front of the ambulance still nudging the back of the Land Rover, almost pushing it along.

The other vehicle broke free and shot off to the left, but then it was back, side-swiping the ambulance. The steering wheel bucked in his hands, and the squeal of grinding metal filled his ears as the bulletproof police vehicle rammed into the side of the ambulance.

He was off course, and he'd lost at least one headlight. Now he had no idea which way he should be going. He took his foot off the accelerator for a moment, to try to get his bearings, but without light he was totally disoriented.

And there was the bloody Land Rover again. He was thrown sideways, and lost control of the wheel. The ambulance veered right and started to topple. He fought the wheel, but he was being thrown around too much. Everything tilted sideways and next thing he was falling towards the passenger door. It seemed an awfully long way.

CHAPTER 29

The world was filled with noise and bright lights. Nic's head thumped with every beat of her heart. She had no awareness of where she was, or how she'd got there, but wetness had seeped through the rough jumper she wore. The chill against her skin had woken her. She was lying on her right side with her face pressed into something soft.

She tried moving, but pain shot through her back, and she couldn't feel her feet. Hot tears tracked down her face, pooling above her nose before overflowing. By the time they reached the cheek closest to the ground, they'd turned icy cold.

"Over here!" someone shouted and one of the bright lights detached itself from the cluster, bobbing towards her. She tried to call out, but there wasn't any air in her lungs either.

The ground shook slightly as feet ran towards her, sending more shockwaves of pain through her back. Suddenly, she didn't want anyone near her, moving her and probing her for injuries. She didn't want to know. She closed her eyes against the dazzle of a flashlight.

"She's alive!" The voice was familiar, but she couldn't place it. It barked out instructions to someone and the ground shook again as people scattered to obey.

A face loomed in front of the light, just a silhouette, but there was a flash of green and that symbol you see in medical centres: a staff with a snake coiling up it, surrounded by a circle of stylized leaves. Nic fixed her eyes on it, focusing on the detail to keep the panic at bay.

"Easy now. Don't try to move," said a steady voice. She latched on to it with relief. Here was someone who understood. He wasn't going to hurt her or move her. Hands touched her face, a fine-beam torch shone into each eye, and fingers closed around her wrist. She could feel that touch okay, but when he moved lower, she could feel nothing.

"I think we might need that helicopter back, Joe. Can you radio it in, please?"

A second voice answered from further away, but she couldn't hear what it said.

"My name's Ned," the first paramedic said. "And my mate there's Joe. You took a nasty fall, there, and banged yourself up a bit, but we're going to take you into the hospital, and they'll soon get you fixed up. Can you hear me okay? If you're unable to speak, just blink twice for 'yes'."

Nic opened her mouth to speak, but only a croak came out, and she didn't know if it sounded anything like "yes", so she blinked twice as well, just to be safe.

Nothing else mattered right now, except for Ned. He would keep her safe and stop anyone from hurting her anymore. Where had that thought come from? Had she been hurt before? That was Hazel, wasn't it, filled with fear ever since she'd come so close to death? Not her. She put the problem aside to deal with later.

"We need to move you on to a stretcher, Nic. That's your name, isn't it?"

She blinked twice. Talking was just too much effort. But she didn't want to be moved. The panic must have shown in her eyes, because a warm, dry hand gripped hers and squeezed gently. "It's all right, pet. I'm going to give you something for the pain first, and we'll be really careful. I promise."

231

He rolled up her sleeve, fastened something around her upper arm, and stuck a needle in the inside of her elbow, taping it in place. She could see everything out of the corner of her eye, without moving, and it was bringing back a feeling of déjà vu. A moment later, something cold and sweet flooded her veins, and she stopped caring.

The next part was a bit of a blur. Voices echoed and lights turned from points into long rainbows of colour. Someone put a mask over her face and cool air flooded her mouth and nose.

"On three. One . . . two . . . three." She was aware of being lifted, then lowered and Ned told her she was a star, a real hero. She wanted to thank him, but then her mind grass-hoppered to the fine detail of the irises of his eyes. They were such pretty eyes, all different colours, with a bottomless pit of darkness in the very centre that sucked her in and downwards.

Something hovered over her, like a giant dragonfly. She tried to swat it away, but her arms wouldn't move. Then it disappeared as Ned leaned over her, blotting it out with his body. Her hair whipped around like snakes. Maybe that was why Ned had a snake on his uniform. She tried to see it, to see if it was writhing now, but he was too close. He smelled of aftershave and stale cigarette smoke.

Then there was a lurch that sent pain lancing through her again, and she screamed.

* * *

A machine beeped nearby. She'd been hearing it for ages, but now she'd noticed the sound, it began to irritate her. She'd been here before, but they'd let her go, hadn't they? Why was she back again? She tried to sit up to look around, but nothing happened. Her muscles didn't belong to her anymore.

"It's all right," Hazel said. "You're going to be fine, the doctor says. You just need time."

Nic licked her lips. "What happened?"

"You saved us," a second voice said. There was something familiar about it, but Nic couldn't place it. Flat vowels, but a pleasant lilt as well.

"Meera's here too," Hazel said, and then Nic remembered a little.

"Meera. Is Inspector Ram here?"

"He came," Ma said, from the other side of her bed. "The doctor wouldn't let him in, though. Too many visitors, she said. Dad's here, and Cian."

"Hi, Nic," Cian said. "We were worried sick about you." Then someone hushed him and he said, "What? I only said—"

Pathetic. Why was she crying again? She wanted to wipe away the tears, but she still couldn't move. A hand came into view, wielding a soft tissue. The Celtic-style ring on the third finger identified it as Ma's hand, but it was so frustrating not to be able to turn to see.

"What's wrong with me?"

No one seemed to want to answer. It was Hazel in the end who bit the bullet.

"You injured your neck, jumping out of the ambulance. They had to operate, but apparently it all went well, and the doctors think you're going to be fine. They had you heavily sedated for ages so you wouldn't move."

Panic creeped in through the edges of her armour. It sneaked in through her tear ducts, where she'd shown it her vulnerable areas. "But I still can't move."

"It's okay," Ma said. "You won't be able to just yet. The drugs are only beginning to wear off. Give it time." But there was concern in her voice. Not being able to see Ma's expressions helped Nic to focus on the way she spoke so heartily, yet clipped the ends of her words off short.

"Asha?"

"She's with Aaron," Hazel said. "He's getting out of hospital today, and she's driving him home."

Aaron. She'd forgotten him too. Again. "Is he going to be okay?"

"He'll have an attractive scar, and he's going to be a skin-head for a while until his hair grows back after they shaved it for the surgery, but yes, he'll be okay."

There was reserve in her sister's voice too. There was something people weren't telling her, but she was too afraid to push them for the answers.

"That's enough for now," a cool, professional voice said in a tone that brooked no argument. "Nic needs rest more than anything. You can come back and see her tomorrow, when she'll be feeling much stronger."

Feet shuffled on a hard floor and the air changed as a door swung open somewhere, letting in a background buzz of muted conversation. Then the door closed with a soft swish and only the bleeping machine remained. Or that was what Nic thought, until someone leaned over her and touched her arm with cool fingers, then tapped some buttons on another machine that gave a different type of beep.

"It's all right. I'm Carole Strong, one of the consultants looking after you." Her voice was as cool as her fingers, but it was relaxing to listen to and she sounded calm and in control. "You've had an operation on your neck, and you have a mild concussion, but the early signs are that everything is going well, and you should soon be back on your feet again."

A weight lifted from Nic's mind. The panic when she'd been unable to move ebbed, leaving a feeling of well-being behind.

"I'll leave you to sleep again for a while."

Nic took a deep breath, then another, her eyelids growing heavier. The doctor was right: she was tired. Sleep would heal her. That's what Ma always said. "Sleep is the best medicine." Cured everything from a head cold to a broken arm, apparently.

* * *

The next time she opened her eyes again, there was someone in the room with her, although Nic would have been

234

hard-pressed to say how she knew. She strained her ears, listening for the rustle of cloth or an indrawn breath, but there was only the steady beeping of the machine again.

Then rubber squeaked against the floor, as though someone wearing trainers had turned around too quickly. Nic forced her eyes open against the drugs that still filled her head with cotton wool. This time, she could turn her head ever so slightly, but a hard collar stopped her going too far. Still, she was in time to see a back disappearing through the door. It seemed familiar. Something about the shape, and the way he walked.

Never mind. It'd come back to her later.

* * *

This time, her mind was clearer, her body rested. Nic stretched her toes, luxuriating in the feel of crisp sheets against her bare skin. While she was sleeping, someone had tilted her bed so she was partially sitting up, which felt so much better. Less like a corpse and more like a patient who'd be getting out of hospital soon.

The machine still bleeped its regular rhythm, but it seemed like an old friend now, as reassuring as a mother's heartbeat is to a baby in the womb. She took a deep breath and glanced down, wiggling her toes. She was reassured to see them move under the white hospital blanket. Next to her bed, a brown table held a jug of water with ice cubes floating in it and a scratched plastic glass. Nic realized she was thirsty, and put a hand out to pull the table closer.

The plastic collar, padded under her chin, prevented her from looking down too close to her, so pouring the water was largely a matter of guesswork. She pushed the table away again and was pleased to see that she'd only spilled a few drops. It tasted wonderful, but after half a glass, her thirst was quenched and she put the glass back down.

The door swished open to allow a young nurse in. He grinned at her. "Hello, Sleeping Beauty. How are you?"

"Great. When can I go home?"

"You know I can never get over the ingratitude of patients," he teased. "Try as I might, they never want to stay a moment longer than they have to!" As he spoke, he tugged her sheets straight and plumped up her pillow with the gentle efficiency of long practice. "Doc says when you're able to walk without pain, you can go." He straightened up. "Now, can I get you anything? You slept through dinner. And lunch, come to that. Maybe I can rustle up some toast and jam for you?"

"Mm. Maybe." She didn't feel much like eating, but perhaps the smell of toast would kick-start her appetite.

"Your wish is my command. I'll see what I can find at this time of night." And he bustled out, letting the door swish closed behind him.

A few minutes later, it swished again, but no one came in. The door was too far behind her to see properly. "Who's there?" she called. "Ma? Hazel?"

No one answered, but she thought she could hear breathing over the sounds of the monitor. *That does it. Time to get up.* She folded the sheet and blanket back in a triangle and swung her feet out on the same side as the drip stand, which was unfortunately the opposite side to the door.

She locked her jaw in determination and slid off the side of the bed, holding on for balance in case her legs gave way. The door was still open, or at least, she hadn't heard it swish closed again.

Her legs held, barely. She turned around, still keeping a grip on the frame at the side of the bed, until she could see the door. It was open, and there was someone standing there, just staring at her, but he was in the shadows, because the hallway lights were out for some reason.

"Hello?" she called, annoyed to hear a wobble in her voice.

The figure leaned forward into the dimly lit room, and the breath caught in her throat. Familiar brown eyes regarded her with a hungry expression, too bright in a thin face, a

236

straggly beard partially hiding his mouth. He even wore the same clothes he'd worn the night they'd been taken.

Nic put out a hand towards him. "Colm! How?"

His lips curled and his eyes hardened to granite. She'd seen that expression before, over the top of a scarf that covered the lower half of his face, only then the eyes had been green. Pain flared in her chest, and her knees gave way, but she didn't feel the cold lino on her bare legs as she collapsed in a dead faint.

CHAPTER 30

"He was very clever," Asha said, her hands wrapped around a mug of tea. "How he escaped from that ambulance, I'll never know. I was there seconds after he crashed, but he'd already gone." She glanced at Nic where she sat on the edge of her bed with her arms around Hazel. "But we'll catch him. I promise you that."

At the other side of the room, Aaron lounged in jeans and a checked shirt, his face still pale from his brush with death. The hair was growing back in a fuzz all over his scalp, but Nic thought the short look suited him. It brought a hardness to features that had been almost too pretty. Or perhaps the hardness came from the experience he'd been through. Certainly, it was enough to age any man.

A cold chill breathed down Nic's neck. No one seemed to believe her that Colm had visited her here in the hospital. An effect of the morphine, the doctor had said, but there'd been a crease between her brows as if she didn't really believe her own explanation. But Nic knew what she'd seen.

"Have you reviewed the CCTV footage yet?" she asked.

"We had a uniform detailed to go through it, but that suspected car bomb in Shaftesbury Square diverted all the manpower we might have used. The hospital authorities have the same problem. Their staff are stretched too thin to have anyone to spare to look for your ghost."

Basically, no one could be bothered.

"It *was* Colm, you know," she said. "It was the eyes. I don't know how I didn't spot it when he held me in the cottage. He must have been wearing some sort of padding to thicken his waist, and that distracted me enough that I didn't recognize his eyes. And Inspector Ram must have been right about contact lenses."

Asha was watching her with sadness in the thin line of her mouth, but Aaron nodded. The action went on a little too long, as though he had lost some control over his neck muscles. "I think we sh-should listen to her," he said, tugging at Asha's sleeve. "After all, it was Nic who discovered where he was keeping Hazel and Meera." His speech was a little slurred, too. Her heart bled for him. If only she'd been quicker to drag him from the water, maybe he wouldn't have been so badly affected.

Asha looked down at him from her position on the arm of his chair. Her face softened.

"I'll get on to it. Maybe I can find someone to go through the footage. Sergeant Jacob's just finished a case."

Nic let her breath out in a sigh. Lonnie was just the person. She'd keep an open mind, and she didn't miss a trick.

Asha had her mobile out and was tapping in a number. "Yes. Hi, Sergeant. Will you do me a favour?"

Nic zoned out while Asha spoke, and drifted back to the previous night, when Colm had put his head through the door. There had been a flash of joy, followed by confusion, then dread as she put two and two together, but now no one would believe her. He was still out there, possibly masquerading as a friend, luring some other woman into his tangled web, and Nic was powerless to prevent him.

Hazel stirred, tilting her face up to look into Nic's eyes. "I believe you. He always wore the mask when he came to us, but he didn't have any padding around his middle. He was slim and moved like a young man." She spoke to Asha as she put her phone away. "I told you all that in my statement, and I expect Meera said the same."

"We can ask her," Aaron said. "She's around here somewhere with her father."

Asha frowned and opened her mouth to speak, but the door opened to let Ram in, clutching a phone in his hand. Nic had to smile at the change in him since the last time she saw him. He walked with a lighter step and there was a joy in his face that was miles from the hunger she was used to seeing there.

"We have him," he said. "I've just got the news. Caught him trying to board the Liverpool ferry."

The silence that greeted this announcement seemed to delight the inspector. He grinned and did a little foot shuffle that was almost a dance. Nic realized her mouth was hanging open and closed it with a snap.

"How do you know it's him?" Asha asked in a hoarse voice.

"Apart from the knives in a cabinet in the back of his van? And the scarf he used to cover his face?"

"I want to see him," Nic said, surprising herself, because the revulsion she'd felt when Ram mentioned the knife cabinet made her think she never wanted to see him again, but she needed to know if they had the right man.

"There will be an identity line-up," Ram reassured her. "We have some procedures we have to go through first, and I'm told he's screaming his innocence and demanding a solicitor."

Well, he would be, Nic told herself, but a little voice kept whispering that Colm was too clever to get himself caught at a ferry port. He'd managed to sneak to and fro under their noses several times already, so why had he suddenly become careless? And did that mean the police had withdrawn all the manpower they had searching for him?

"I need to see him now," she said. "Please?"

Asha exchanged a long look with Ram and Nic saw her give a miniscule headshake. She bit her lip. How could she persuade Asha? It was vital. Nic knew that with every fibre of her being.

Then Ram surprised her by coming down on her side. "I think we might manage to get some of the CCTV footage sent over here from the station. What's the harm in that, Asha?"

"Go on, Asha," Aaron coaxed. "I'll call B-Bishop with the request, then you can say you knew nothing about it."

Asha's face relaxed into the ghost of her old smile. "The answer's no." She held up her finger before anyone could interrupt. "But I'm leaving to go to the loo now and as the visitors' one on this corridor is probably closed for the fore-seeable because someone stuffed whole rolls of paper down it, I'll have to go the one upstairs. I might be a while."

Nic and Aaron shared a conspiratorial look.

"Okay, boss," Aaron said. "You might want to use the s-stairs. The lift felt a bit dodgy when I came down in it earlier."

Asha rolled her eyes and let herself out of the room. The door had barely closed behind her and Aaron was on the phone, sweet-talking Bishop into sending a clear shot of the man they'd arrested.

"Give me your iPad, Nic."

She dug it out from the locker by her bed, entered her passcode, and handed it over. He tapped away at it for a few minutes, frowning. His coordination still wasn't great, and his hand shook as he held the iPad.

"Here we go."

They all crowded around him, except for Ram, who picked up a copy of *Ulster Tatler* and appeared to be totally engrossed by photos of local Northern Irish celebrities he couldn't possibly know, coming from Leeds.

The footage was surprisingly clear, showing the main entrance of the station and the front desk, where a uniformed officer wrote laboriously in a large desk diary, his left hand holding the phone to his ear.

"There." Hazel touched her arm.

The door swung open and three people came in. Two uniformed officers flanked a young man who had his hands cuffed behind him. His head hung low, chin on chest, defeated. They each had a hand gripping his arm, and they were none too gentle: the suspect reeled and staggered as the bulky man on his right gave him a shove. The other officer snatched him back, yanking him upright. They knew they couldn't damage him, Nic thought, but they were pushing it to the limit.

She tightened her lips. Why wouldn't he look up? The build and height were right, and the straggly hair, but—

Then he did look up, right into the lens of the camera. Hazel gripped her arm and Nic clasped her sister's hand. The eyes that stared up at the camera, stilled as Aaron froze the image, were not the ones she'd seen day after day over the scarf. They weren't the ones she'd smiled at across a coffee cup, and they weren't the ones she'd stared into in the hospital the day before.

"It's not him," Hazel said in a dull voice. "He's still out there, Nic."

"He's still out there," Nic echoed. "I don't know how he did it, but that's not him. Close enough, but not him."

"Are you certain?" Asha emerged silently from the corridor. Nic wondered if she'd ever gone as far as the next floor or had just hovered in the shadows, watching.

Nic swallowed painfully. "We're both certain. Ask Meera, if you don't believe us."

Asha's mouth twisted. "It's not a case of belief," she said. "Of course I believe you, but how did he do it? I've got Forensics working on the knives, but preliminary reports confirm traces of human blood. It's even the same grey van he used before. They're sweeping it for traces as we speak." She rubbed her eyes with the heels of her hands, then ran her fingers through her hair as though she wanted to pull it out by the roots. "Come on," she said after a moment. "I'm getting you two, and the rest of your family, into protective custody. Inspector Ram—"

Ram was standing, the magazine in a crumpled heap at his feet. His face was grey beneath the brown skin, his eyes haunted.

Her eyes widened. "Inspector? Where's Meera?"

"She went to get me a coffee—"

A pain flared in Nic's chest and she realized she was hyperventilating. She tried to force her breathing to slow and deepen, but the muscles wouldn't obey her. Spots danced in front of her eyes until Aaron's arm came around her shoulder, a warm weight that steadied her.

"Come on," he said. "Let's get you sat back down."

"No. We need to find Meera."

"Okay."

She wondered if he'd have capitulated as easily before his injuries.

Asha was talking into her phone, issuing instructions. "I've told hospital security to get straight up there and not leave her side. I'm heading up there now." She shot out of the room, leaving the door to bang back against the wall in her wake.

"We've got to go too," Hazel said. "We have to stay together."

She was right. Inaction was impossible. Hazel helped her along with an arm around her waist, and Inspector Ram helped Aaron, who was still weak. He kept lurching to the left, and without Ram's steadying arm he'd have crashed into the wall several times.

Once inside the lift, they rose up through the floors in a silence Nic didn't care to break. It was so bloody slow, stopping at every floor, but neither she nor Aaron could have managed the stairs. As the doors opened on the café level, Asha rushed towards them.

"Meera?" Ram asked, tersely.

"She's not here. I've sent Security looking for her, but we did find this." She pointed to a pair of paper coffee cups, their contents pooling across the floor, as if the person carrying them had been about to press the call button for the lift.

"Bugger that for a lark. I've got to find her," Ram muttered. He let go of Aaron, who teetered, off balance, until Asha caught hold of his arm. By the time Nic drew breath, Ram was gone, running along the corridor.

Nic didn't waste her breath speaking, but set off in the opposite direction, dragging Hazel along with her. She heard Aaron's pitiful cry of "Wait for me!" but didn't slow down.

As they rounded a corner, they almost ran into two security guards who were helping a familiar plump figure up from the floor. Lonnie staggered to her feet and pushed them away. They stepped back as if glad to let go of her.

"He has Meera," she said in a voice that would have cut ice. "I tried to stop him, but he got away. I'm sorry." Blood was flowing from a cut across her temple, and one eye was swelling already.

Asha must have abandoned Aaron, because suddenly she was there with them. "Which way did he take her?"

Lonnie shook her head. "I'm sorry, ma'am. I didn't see."

They were at a junction of three corridors. He could have gone down any of them.

A cold pit yawned open in Nic's stomach. She tried to speak, but the words wouldn't come. Her feet carried her forwards, past the two security officers. She didn't pause to question why, but let her subconscious decide which way to turn at the end of the hall. It took her left, away from the café, into an area she hadn't been to before. Hazel stuck with her, a warm arm supporting her, trusting her judgement.

It was quiet here, without the chatter from the social areas behind her. The doors on either side had no windows and were close together as if they were storerooms rather than offices. The carpet was less worn too, as though this corridor was rarely trodden.

She found Meera huddled in a corner, her arms wrapped around her knees and face buried in the sleeve of her parka. Nic froze, fearing the worst. Then she saw the other woman's chest expand in a shuddering breath and she let go of Hazel and dropped to her knees beside her. She reached out, but stopped short before touching her.

"Meera? Are you okay?"

Meera shrugged away from her and whimpered.

Nic took a deep breath that made her chest ache. "He was here, wasn't he?"

A tear-stained face lifted up to her. The dark eyes, so like her father's, were bloodshot, wide and staring sightlessly over Nic's shoulder. "He said he's still going to come for us," she breathed. "All of us. He said we'd never be safe. Never."

Nic collapsed from her knees to a sitting position, her legs shaking. It was just the sort of thing he would say. She could visualize the cold glee in those hard eyes as he pushed his face close to hers and hissed the words.

Their hands touched and clutched, like drowning souls to a lifebelt, and Hazel joined them, wrapping her arms around them both. A shoe scuffed the carpet, and all three girls leaped apart, expecting an attack, but it was only Lonnie, looking worse for wear. She leaned against the wall and let herself slide down until she was sitting on the carpet alongside them. "He got away, then?"

Nic sighed. "So it would seem."

"I checked the hospital CCTV footage," Lonnie said. "You were right, Nic. He was here."

It should have been a relief, to hear that she hadn't imagined the encounter, but numbness was creeping over her now, a lethargy that made her want to close her eyes and sleep until she could no longer remember any of the events of the last few weeks.

Lonnie's voice came from a long way away. "But I didn't need to see the footage to believe you, girl. That's why I got Bishop to give me a micro tracker."

Nic opened her eyes and sat up. "A what?"

"A micro tracker. A tiny device that transmits a signal through GPS." She met Meera's questioning look. "You know when I tried to tackle him in the corridor just now, when he knocked me down and kicked me?" She put a hand to her ample stomach, just beneath where her ribs must be.

Meera almost smiled. "And you grabbed his foot and tried to pull him over?"

"Yes. I managed to get it attached to his shoe." She fished in her pocket, grunting as something twinged, and pulled out a small device, about the size of a mobile phone. "Wherever he hides this time, we can find him."

EPILOGUE

He awoke in darkness, but with the sense of movement somewhere nearby. His head felt heavy, filled with cotton wool, his thoughts sluggish. His mouth was desert-dry and swollen, filled with cloth that stretched his lips. Something was very wrong.

There it was again, that illusion of movement. A current of air caressed him, cooling the sweat on his skin. He tried to straighten up, to stretch muscles that didn't quite yet belong to him, and that's when the cuffs dug into his wrists. Disbelief made him slow to accept that he was bound, hands behind his back, shoulders forced into a painful position. That first movement set slow flames licking through his joints.

He tried to work moisture into his mouth behind the gag, but it was too tight, so he gave another impatient tug at his bonds. This must be a dream. A nightmare. If he tugged hard enough, maybe he could wake up and go back to his own familiar certainties.

Dawn found him slumped, exhausted, blood dripping from the plastic cuffs with a faint splat on to the concrete below. A pale rectangle creeped across the floor, highlighting shapeless lumps that might have been old animal droppings or even dead small animals, covered with a thick layer of dust.

He blinked gritty eyes, trying to squint into the shadows. There was something familiar about this place. Had he been here before? His perspective was slewed, seated on the floor as he was, but even if he hadn't been here, he'd surely seen a photo of the place, hadn't he?

As the light grew stronger, another shape emerged from the darkness. A shoe, no, a boot. Patent leather, gleaming oily in a ray of dusty sunlight, and with a high, narrow heel. He could see no further, because a wall hid his view, a wall covered with peeling wallpaper and crumbling plaster. Was the boot attached to a person?

A door slammed and footsteps sounded, muffled as if in an adjacent room. Something clinked, then hissed and a few moments later, the rich, dark aroma of brewing coffee reached him.

His breath caught in his throat. Even through the thickness of sedatives that must still be in his bloodstream, this seemed achingly familiar. He tugged again at the cuffs, but a hot spurt of blood brought him up short. Tears burned behind his eyes. There must be some mistake. This didn't happen to him. It couldn't.

A door creaked, grating against the floor as if it was coming off its hinges. He pressed his back into the cold, damp wall, pushing with his feet, then surged forward. Had that been a bit of give in the ring tying him to the wall? It had to be a ring, screwed into the wall. He could even see it in his imagination, that dull, galvanized steel and a little pile of brick dust beneath it on the floor. If it was loose, he could escape.

His eyes darted from side to side, trying to see where the attack would come from, but there was no one in his limited field of view. Who was there? Was this a copycat crime? If so, where were the knives?

He tugged and tugged again, ignoring the pain and the blood. Panic was twisting his insides, turning his bowels to liquid. This couldn't be happening!

And then he saw the boot move. It was drawn slowly, soundlessly back out of sight.

"Who's there?"

At least that's what he tried to say. It came out as a wordless moan around the gag. He strained to hear, but there was no sound. Who was that? Who was wearing the boot? It had looked like a woman's boot, fashionable, small feet. At least his brain was working again, albeit slowly.

He must have slept at some point. He couldn't imagine how it was possible, with his arms drawn tight behind him and the gag digging in, but one moment the pale patch from an unseen window was growing longer and brighter, the next it had faded into darkness again.

The smell of coffee still lingered in his nostrils, but there was no sound at all now, not even the dripping of his blood. Where could he be that was so quiet? And cold. He shivered. It reignited the pain in his shoulders and back. His bladder was filled to bursting, and the gag made him want to retch.

How long had he been here? Not more than a day and a night, surely?

In the gathering gloom, the scratching sound was loud as a gunshot. He held his breath, but the only sound was the pounding of his own pulse in his ears. His nostrils burned with cold fire as he hyperventilated in the icy air.

Something moved, there in the shadows. A rat, it had to be. Too small for a cat, too rapid and furtive in its movements. While his attention was on the shape in front of him, another must have sneaked up behind his back. A sharp stinging pain lanced through his thumb, the fat part where it joined the hand.

He shook it off, but with his bindings granting such limited movement, he knew it wouldn't have gone far. Now his breathing was out of control, rasping through his nose and around the edges of the gag. He was whimpering, begging, pleading, but there was no one to hear. Every nerve ending was on high alert, waiting for the next bite.

Time slowed. Hours passed, days even, yet the rectangle of light from the window barely moved, fading to invisibility as night creeped in so slowly. But not slowly enough, for once true night descended, he was sure the rats would find new courage.

And then, the door creaked again. He was saved!

Heels tapped across the floor of the next room and into this one. The same long, patent leather boots, with black leggings tucked into them and the bottom edge of a light, silk tunic in a bold pattern, bold enough to see even in the dim light. He strained to look up.

An Indian woman, her long, black hair pinned up into a bun. She wore a scarf that covered the lower half of her face, but there was no mistaking those glistening eyes. He'd seen them before, both in his dreams and in real life. Then, they'd stared up at him, brimming with unshed tears, pleading silently for mercy. Now, they glittered with an entirely different emotion: hunger.

THE END

ACKNOWLEDGEMENTS

I've had help and support from so many people that it's impossible to name them all, but special mentions must be made for Jo Zebedee, who took me under her wing when I was a fledgling writer, and Anne McMaster, poet, philosopher and best friend, who has put up with my crippling self-doubt and encouraged me to keep going even when I was certain my writing had no merit. Raquel McKee was by my side as I began writing the opening chapters of *Knife Edge* and she was involved again at the end, sensitivity-reading an early draft and helping me bring Sergeant Lonnie Jacob to life. Any shortfalls in my presentation of Sergeant Jacob are mine and not the result of Raquel's advice.

I began to develop the characters and plot for *Knife Edge* during a crime-writing workshop run by the wonderful *New York Times* bestselling author Brian McGilloway, in 2017. Three years later, I was lucky enough to attend another workshop by *Sunday Times* bestselling author Steve Cavanagh, at the River Mill Writers' Retreat. Steve read the opening of *Knife Edge*, which I'd done nothing with since finishing the first draft, and told me I needed to start submitting it. Without his encouragement, the novel would probably still be sitting neglected on my hard drive.

The Arts Council of Northern Ireland have been generous in their support, funding day care for a close family member so I can make time to write, as well as a weekend writing retreat at the River Mill. In these troubled times, River Mill is a true oasis, where the talented Paul Maddern soothes mind and spirit with his gentle calm (not to mention the exquisite cuisine!).

I am so grateful to the team at Joffe Books. From the day Emma Grundy Haigh emailed me to say she loved my story, everyone has been positive, supportive and responsive to every concern of a debut novelist. My editor, Sam Matthews, is a wonder. I nickname her Eagle Eyes for her attention to detail, but her editing has also been perceptive and sympathetic. She's been a pleasure to work with.

And of course, the book would never have happened at all if it hadn't been for the patience of my long-suffering family. My addiction to writing fiction began abruptly in 2014 and hasn't ceased since. Forgotten meals, unanswered texts, grumpiness when disturbed. I really don't know why they put up with me.

If you've got this far and have finished *Knife Edge*, you might like to look out for the next novel, *Small Bones*, which is coming soon.

Thank you for reading this book.

If you enjoyed it please leave feedback on Amazon or Goodreads, and if there is anything we missed or you have a question about, then please get in touch. We appreciate you choosing our book.

Founded in 2014 in Shoreditch, London, we at Joffe Books pride ourselves on our history of innovative publishing. We were thrilled to be shortlisted for Independent Publisher of the Year at the British Book Awards.

www.joffebooks.com

We're very grateful to eagle-eyed readers who take the time to contact us. Please send any errors you find to corrections@joffebooks.com. We'll get them fixed ASAP.